The Action

Francis King

THE ACTION

Hutchinson of London

Hutchinson & Co. (Publishers) Ltd
3 Fitzroy Square, London W1P 6JD

London Melbourne Sydney Auckland
Wellington Johannesburg and agencies
throughout the world

First published 1978
© Francis King 1978

Set in VIP Garamond by Input Typesetting Ltd

Printed in Great Britain by
The Anchor Press Ltd, and bound by
Wm Brendon & Son Ltd, both of
Tiptree, Essex

ISBN 0 09 134710 6

To Jeremy Trafford

Expect poison from the standing water.

BLAKE

1

'One of these days you're going to get yourself killed, you bloody cow!'

The police car, slewed halfway into the gutter, had been travelling at twice the speed of any other traffic in the street. Martha Kingsley, often described as a handsome woman even if she did have the body of a dachshund, had scuttled out in front of it in order to board a 49 bus snarled to a standstill in the middle of King's Road.

The short arms heaved and the short legs braced themselves. 'Oh,' she gasped. 'Oh. Thank. Goodness. Thought I'd. Have to wait for the next one.'

The young man beside whom she had plopped herself shifted and shrank. He had a bad cold and hoped malevolently that he would give it to her as she crowded over him. The bus jerked on, while the police car jerked backwards and forwards in an attempt to sever the ravelled threads of oncoming traffic.

'That's not how you expect a police officer to talk. Is it now?' the long-haired, ladylike conductor lisped as he swayed daintily down the aisle.

The young man beside Martha snorted with a rattle of catarrh in his blunt, inflamed nose. An elderly woman, dandling a Harrods shopping bag on her knees as though it were a baby, shook her head and sighed. Another elderly woman in a plaid tam-o'-shanter made a clicking noise of disapproval with tongue against protuberant teeth.

But Martha neither heard nor saw them, any more than she had either heard or seen the police car. She was still exalted from the meeting in the basement, concrete-floored and murky, one windowless room leading off into another, where Bronislaw Mozoomdar and the Sanctum Regnum of the Grand Orient had their headquarters.

Bronislaw claimed (and Martha did not doubt his claim) to be the son of a Polish countess and a Cingalese guru who had aban-

9

doned both wife and infant son in Hampstead Garden Suburb in order to return to a life of meditation and self-denial in his own country. Bronislaw's accent, however, was neither Polish nor Cingalese nor even Hampstead Garden Suburb but a nasal Cockney and his skin was neither pink nor black but the greenish-white of plants etiolated by a long exclusion from the sun. His wife and three small children spoke with the same accent and had the same appearance of plants kept pallid and nerveless in artificial light. 'He doesn't look well,' a woman had hissed as he had risen and left the room in order to open the door to a late-comer. 'Oh, he takes it out of himself all right,' her female companion had sighed. 'And what's to put it back?' What indeed? Martha had thought in an access of love and pity.

It was cold and damp down in the basement and the one bulb, dangling naked from the ceiling, seemed of a wattage inadequate to light the room. But the Master's presence, vehement and hectic, the cheekbones flushed and the eyes flashing, irradiated and warmed. His wife and children, glimpsed vaguely as pale, silent, motionless presences in the sitting-room through which the celebrants had been conducted, took no part in the meeting. It was only later that the period — how long? ten? twenty minutes? — of what the Master had called 'Ingrowth' (momentarily, Martha was ashamed to acknowledge to herself, she had thought of toenails) had concluded with the thin girl-wife, in the corduroy trousers and polo-necked sweater of clashing shades of red, handing round cups of stewed Indian tea, while one of the children clung to her waist as though in fear of drowning in the sea of adult strangers. Later the girl had also handed round the salver for the collection. (Martha had added a pound note to the two fifty-pence coins and the scattering of smaller silver and even copper already in it.)

What was it the Master had given them as their subject of meditation? She shifted heavily against the cold-ridden young man, impervious to the murderous gaze he darted at her, and summoned back the nasally pattering voice, raindrops to the lightning of the Master's gaze and the thunder of his gestures. THE FUTURE IS ALSO IN THE PAST, IT IS NOT WHOLLY CONTAINED IN THE PRESENT. Or could it have been — she tried it out, her lips moving in a slight hiss of escaping air — THE FUTURE IS ALSO IN THE PRESENT, IT IS NOT WHOLLY CONTAINED IN THE PAST? She could not be certain; and the lack of certainty made her shift again, as though her clothes were too tight for her. She tried out both phrases yet again and then gave up.

. . . Oh, but she had liked that bit about each of them being like a vessel, a crystal vessel. Empty yourselves, one and all of you, of the hatreds and resentments and mean and impure desires that are stagnant within. Pour them out. Pour them out now. Imagine that you are tipping the vessel forward, that this sludge within is leaving the crystal sides. (Martha at that moment had seen herself as a glittering cut-glass jug, held in hands that were hers and yet not hers. On the bus that same vision now came back to her.) Cleanse the sides of the vessel, let not a particle remain. (Martha's eyes were closed as the bus jolted to a standstill outside what had recently been Biba and was now Marks and Spencer. She was using a spiritual Brillo pad on those sides.) And now fill yourself, fill yourself with the universal odic force. Fill yourself to the brim. To the brim. Feel it rising within you, like some inexhaustible spring, cool and clear and pure . . .

'Excuse me, please.' The young man, standing up, banged her left knee with his right. *'Excuse me, please!'*

Oh, heavens! They were past the Earl's Court Road! Long past her stop!

'EXCUSE ME!'

'Just one moment. One moment! Let's have some manners! I'm getting off too.'

The short arms heaved, the short legs braced themselves.

It was only when she was on the pavement that she realized that she had never paid her fare. But, so far from feeling any guilt, the crystal vessel of her being was filling up with a pleasure wholly incommensurate with the triviality of the sum out of which she had inadvertently cheated the London Passenger Transport Board.

2

Nigel Kingsley, Martha's brother, sat surrounded by carrier-bags, with The Book in his hands. For many months now it had been, not the book, but The Book to him and Hazel. It felt far heavier and far colder now that it had been printed and bound than it had ever felt when it had been an untidy bundle either of typewritten sheets, dog-eared at the edges, or of ink-spattered page-proofs. In fact, it felt like a stone.

He propped the elbows of his aching arms on the coffee table in front of him, leaning forward to do so. He was carrying all the passionate desolation of her last seven years. If he dropped it, it would thud through the floor at his feet to crash on to the head of one of the three Persian students who were Hazel's basement tenants.

'So there it is.'

'There it is,' Hazel agreed.

Whereas he felt overweighted, she felt miraculously light. As a child she had been shown by a knowing older cousin how, if she placed an arm against a wall and then leant against it, it would, as soon as she had resumed an upright position, float up, up, up of its own accord. That was how she felt now, her feet at least six inches above the carpet.

'I like the jacket.'

'I'm not sure about it.'

The jacket showed a mother, her hair screening her face, bending over a child that gazed up at her, eyes bulging oddly beneath a bulging forehead, with an expression of total blankness.

'Why?'

'Too explicit. Sentimental.'

Nigel ran a thumb under the title as though to underscore it. *To Laugh, To Cry*. He sucked in his cheeks.

Hazel felt yet again the pathos of his unfulfilment. When they had been at Oxford together in the aftermath of the war, he had won all the Classical prizes. Since then, in the world, he had won

12

none. At Oxford, too, he had slept with a number of women, herself included. Now he slept alone in the narrow bedroom next door to Martha's spacious one.

'I don't know.' He put his head on one side. When sitting, he was handsome; but he, too, like his sister had the body of a dachshund so that, when he stood up, the inadequacies of the body nullified what surmounted it.

'That was the one thing I didn't want the book to be – sentimental.'

'Oh, it isn't, it isn't.' She had been relentless to everyone, most of all to the decaying vegetable (she had used that phrase herself) that had been her child and to her heroic, hopeless self. 'Not at all.' He shook his head vehemently, again sucking in his cheeks. 'What does it feel like – to have it all done at last?' He balanced the book in the palm of his right hand; again his arm ached with the weight of it.

'Wonderful.' She floated across the room to the window that looked down the narrow, sour London garden to a crooked lane winding, a rivulet to the sea, towards the thunder of High Street Kensington. 'It was an agony to live and an agony to write. Now it's all behind me.'

'And the success lies ahead.'

'Oh, I don't really care about that. If it comes, it comes – and I'll be glad of it. But if not . . .' She shrugged her shoulders.

'Oh, it'll come,' he said, in a tone more of foreboding than of reassurance. He was thinking not only of the price that she had paid in the past but of the price that her frankness might exact in the future.

'It's wonderful that you have so much faith in me. Dear Nigel.' He shifted uneasily. These days it embarrassed him if she ever demonstrated her affection to him. 'It's really your book as much as mine.'

'Mine?'

'Without you I'd probably never have started it. And without you I'd certainly never have finished it.'

'It's wonderful that you've at last overcome that writer's block.' Strangely, he no more wished to talk of his own share in the production of the novel than the father usually wishes to talk of

13

his own share in the production of an illegitimate baby.

'Yes, I really feel now that I can go on and on and on. I feel I've so much I want to write that I can't really believe that for all that period I felt I had nothing.'

He held out the novel. 'Inscribe it for me.'

She went to the walnut Queen Anne secretaire and scrabbled among papers for a pen. 'Where have I put it? Hell!'

'Use this.' He produced a biro, chewed at the end, from the breastpocket of his tweed jacket.

She shook her head. Her italic script, of which she was proud, would not show to advantage if she did not use her own pen with its wide, diagonal nib.

'There!'

'Oh!' He gasped. 'I love your handwriting. I wish I could write like that.'

His face had crimsoned. What had, in fact, overcome him was not the calligraphy but the actual words:

Dear Nigel

In gratitude and understanding

Hazel

'The cistern contains: the fountain overflows'

What did she mean by that 'understanding'? And what did she mean by that quotation? A number of possibilities, not all of them agreeable, jolted through his mind, but he did not dare to ask her.

'Now I'll treasure this even more.' He studied it again; and as he did so, head cocked to one side, she was once more transfixed by the pathos of his unfulfilment. 'Thank you.'

'I wonder what the reviewers will think of it.'

'You *know* what they'll think.'

But she only knew what they ought to think.

'Well . . .' He pushed the book into one of the carrier-bags, on top of the lettuce that he had had to trek to Notting Hill Gate to buy because Martha said that vegetables were cheaper there than in the High Street, and then rose to his feet. His trousers, pushed out at the waist by a small, rounded paunch, were too short for him and the sleeves of his tweed jacket were too long. 'I suppose I'd better be on my way ... Martha has this mania for eating early, as you know.'

'Give her my love.'

'She sent you hers,' he lied. Though conscious of his disloyalty, he could not resist turning at the door to tell her: 'The latest is someone called Bronislaw Mozoomdar.'

'Called *what?*'

He repeated the name, adding: 'The Sanctum Regnum of the Grand Orient.'

'Well, provided she's happy.' She laughed.

She watched him from the window as he trudged up the hill. She could almost feel the strings of his carrier-bags biting deep into her own palms; she could almost hear his breath snorting from her own nostrils.

In taking away the copy of the book, he seemed also to have taken away with him some part of her pleasure in it.

3

Nigel and Martha Kingsley lived farther up Campden Hill in a house larger and later and less attractive than Hazel's. Alone of all the houses in the street, it had curtains that were unlined, Martha having bought them, ready-made and an absolute bargain, at the closing-down sale of Pettits a few months before. It was these curtains, already drawn in the winter dusk and faintly luminous with the light behind them, that told Nigel that his sister was already home.

'Nigel?'

'Yes. Am I late?'

'You know you are. Where are those mackerel?'

'Here. In my shopping bag.'

'Well, let me have them. You went to the little man in the Portobello?'

'Yes.'

In frantic haste, Nigel threw The Book on to the top of the television set in the sitting-room and began to dig deep into the shopping bag. Martha, in the kitchen, called again:

'Nigel!'

'Yes.'

'What *are* you doing?'

'Getting out the mackerel.'

'Getting them out or catching them? Oh, for heaven's sake, bring the things in here.'

Martha examined each of his purchases in turn, even holding the mackerel up to her nose to sniff and sniff again. When an earwig wriggled out of the cauliflower, she darted him an accusing look, as though he had put it there.

'Did the television man call?'

'I don't know.'

'What do you mean — you don't know?'

'He didn't call while I was here. He might have called while I was out.'

'Oh, it's too bad!'

Her tone accused him as much as the television man.

'I'm sorry. But you did ask me — '

'There's so much I wanted to watch tonight. Oh, really!' She softened: 'You look all in.'

'Do I? I feel fine.'

'There are rings under your eyes. Definite rings. And I think you're getting a stye.'

He touched a lid with the tip of his little finger. 'Here?'

'No, no! The other one! The other eye! It's all that reading.' Most days Nigel would take himself off to the London Library or the British Museum to toil away at his twenty-year-old task of translating the *Iliad* into Spenserian stanzas. Martha herself abhorred reading.

'I can't *feel* anything.'

'You never do. Your leg might be dropping off with gangrene and you wouldn't realize it was happening.' Roughly affectionate,

16

she patted him on the shoulder. 'Well, cut along upstairs and wash and tidy yourself for supper. And tell those two girls everything will be ready in quarter of an hour. They never hear me when I call. Go on! I'll put some Golden Eye ointment on the stye for you later.'

'Are you *sure* it's a stye?'

'Of course it's a stye.'

4

Swallows twittering under the eaves to cheer each other in the winter-locked land of their mistaken migration, the two Cypriot girls, Soula and Koula, eyes ringed, not like Nigel's with fatigue and disappointment, but with eye-shadow bought from a jaunty saleswoman who had called one day when Martha was out, and fingernails the same silver as their full lips, were guzzling Turkish delight. One of Soula's patients, grateful for her alacrity with the bedpan, had given the box to her.

'Goodness, Koula, you peck at your food like a bird.'

'Won't you really have just another spoonful of these *delicious* Brussels sprouts?'

'Though I say it myself, this 'otpot is better than you'd get at any restaurant.'

The two girls bounced up and down on Soula's bed in merriment at the inaccuracy of their imitations of Martha, while Koula at the same time flicked the sugar off her fingertips with a darting scarlet tongue.

A knock at the door.

'Soula! Koula?'

They held their breaths, shaking with the effort.

'Koula! Soula?'

Soula exploded first; and hurriedly transformed her giggles to a paroxysm of coughing. Koula joined her. In her case the coughing was partly genuine, since some of the sugar was lodged in her throat.

'Girls?'

'Yes, Mr. Kingsley?'

'Girls!'

'You want us, Mr. Kingsley?'

'Supper will be ready in quarter of an hour. Miss Kingsley asked me to tell you.'

'Thank you, Mr. Kingsley.'

'We'll be down, Mr. Kingsley.'

With long fingers Koula extracted another piece of Turkish delight from the box. With stubby ones Soula followed her. Then again they were convulsed with giggles.

Tears running down their cheeks, they might have been weeping for their parental olive groves and the village *volta* and the boys who had not married them because their dowries were insufficient.

5

Martha angrily switched the television set on and off, on and off. She was stooping to examine the plug when Nigel looked up from his copy of the *Classical Quarterly* and reminded her:

'It's out of order. Don't you remember?'

'So it is. Blast.'

'Soula and Koula have gone out. You could borrow their transistor.'

Martha shook her head. She liked to talk; she did not care to listen.

'Where's the evening paper?'

'I don't know.'

'Well, haven't you seen it?'

'No.'

'You must have seen it.'

Martha began shifting piles of her unanswered letters and unpaid bills back and forth across the table.

'Perhaps Soula and Koula took it,' Nigel suggested.

Martha plucked a cushion in a purple-and-black harlequin pattern from the sofa and looked behind that.

'Perhaps the paper-boy forgot.'

Martha went on her hands and knees and peered beneath a chair.

'He may be ill. Last year he had tonsillitis at just about this time.'

Martha straightened, her face screwed up and a hand pressed to the small of her back.

'What's this?' Her eyes alighted on The Book.

'Hazel's latest.'

'*To Laugh, To Cry*', she read out, holding the book almost against her nose. She snorted. Then she began to read the blurb silently to herself.

When Helen Streater gives birth to the boy that she and her architect husband have both so much wanted, the baby looks like any other baby – except that, to them, it seems more beautiful and more intelligent than any other baby has ever been. But as the months pass, Helen senses, long before her husband, that something is subtly wrong. When a specialist confirms all her fears, the couple are faced with the most agonizing of all decisions for any parents. Are they to keep the child that will never, they have been told brutally, be anything but a 'vegetable', or are they to put it away in a home? Helen has no doubt in her own mind what they must do. But her husband . . .

'This is not a novel!'

'Of course it's a novel.'

'Don't be an idiot. This is Hazel's own story.'

'Every novel is based on someone's own story. Nothing happens in a novel that hasn't somewhere at some time happened to someone.'

Martha sank into the chair at her knee.

'Where are my glasses?' she asked without looking up from the blurb.

19

Nigel got up, crossed to the television set and plucked them off its top.

Silently Martha took them and twisted first one of the old-fashioned wire earpieces and then the other behind her large, pointed ears.

'It's incredible,' she said. 'I'd no idea she was writing about *herself*. You never told me.'

'You're never interested in Hazel's books.'

'Of course I am!'

'You've never read one, Martha.'

Martha began to read.

Nigel crept back to his chair and sat uncomfortably on the edge of it for several seconds, gazing at her. Then he jumped up. He could bear it no longer.

'I think I'll go out for a stroll.'

'In this weather! Are you out of your mind?'

'I – I have a slight go of heartburn. A walk might help.'

'Take a teaspoon of bicarb in half a glass of cold water,' she called after him, her eyes still on the page.

But he was already struggling into his overcoat.

6

Martha barely heard Nigel return or make his way upstairs. Admittedly, both operations he performed with the stealth of a professional housebreaker; but when Koula and Soula arrived back home late and crept no less furtively up to their attic nest, Martha was always aware of it. 'Oh, *do* be quieter, girls!' she would often call out, her voice sounding like that of an old woman in the absence of the teeth that grinned beside her in a mug labelled 'Strychnine', the present of a jokey daily whom they had long since sacked.

Ten o'clock struck from the grandfather clock in the hall; and since habit was her bondage, she at once heaved herself up out of the armchair, stooped to turn off the gas fire, switched off the standard lamp and the overhead lights, locked and bolted the doors back and front, made certain that the French windows on to the garden were also locked and bolted and then trudged her way up the stairs to her room. Through all these actions, familiar now from years of nightly repetition, she never ceased to read.

As she moved about the task of preparing herself for bed, she propped the book now on the mantelpiece, now on a chair and now on the bedside table, her eyes still fixed on it as though she were following some manual of instruction — How to Undress in Easy Stages. But when she had struggled out of the cumbersome old-fashioned corset of perforated rubber that pushed up her bosom to such proud effect and compressed the fat of her belly and buttocks into an armour-plated tube, and the blue-veined corrugated flesh flopped from the removal of that restraint, it was as if the restraining rigidity of habit had also been stripped off with it. She sank on to the bed, the toes of one stockinged foot crossed over the other in pigeon position and her arms crossed under the far from virginal-looking breasts that no one but herself and her woman doctor had ever touched.

She read on and on, with an occasional sharp intake of her breath or a writhing of her body, such as she might have made at the dentist when the drill seared a nerve.

It grew colder and colder in the room as the night advanced, and she too grew colder, unaware of the open window beyond her, of the bare thighs that under her bare.arms now had exactly the same glacial, rubbery feel as the corset flung across the back of a Victorian prie-dieu, of the slow, emphatic tick-tick of the cheap alarm clock on the bedside table and of the striking of the grand-father clock in the hall.

It must have been after three o'clock that, teeth chattering and lips, toes and fingers magenta with cold, she suddenly leapt off the bed and, The Book clutched to her, dashed out into the passage and banged into Nigel's room.

'Nigel!'

He sat up in bed, staring at the apparition of shuddering flesh, blazing eyes and tousled hair. He tugged the sheet and blankets up to his pointed chin, eyelids fluttering in time to the fluttering of his heart, as he cowered away from the jabs of light that, like the needles of a shower, were raining down on to his defenceless head, shoulders and hands.

'Oh!' he groaned. 'Oh!'

'This book! This *book*!' she shrilled.

7

In the years when the child had slept in a cot beside her, long after the age when any other child would have been sleeping in a bed, Hazel had repeatedly experienced the same waking nightmare. She was bound, round and round and round, mummy-like, in wet, elastic filaments, that covered her mouth and eyes and nose so that she could not cry out or see or breathe, and that pinioned her arms and legs so that she could not move. She struggled, because the child was calling for her, with those incoherent yelps, wails and whinnies that were all he would ever learn of speech. She struggled in a long-drawn-out agony of effort, snapping first one of the filaments and then another and another. And another.

But, this time, what was dragging her, gasping and twitching, out of the deep, dark pool of oblivion was not the child but the telephone by her bed.

She stretched out a hand, numb and tingling with pins-and-needles.

She croaked: 'Yes?'

'Is that you, Hazel?'

'Yes.'

She fumbled for the switch of the bedside lamp. She rubbed a heavy eyelid.

22

'Hazel — is that you?'

'Yes. What is it!'

Either she had forgotten to wind the alarm clock or it was only ten past six.

'Hazel!'

'Yes.'

'How *could* you?'

Nausea welled up from the pit of Hazel's stomach and exploded, sour, in her mouth. She swallowed hard and swallowed again.

'What do you mean?'

'Your book.'

'My book?'

'Your novel. It's so — *hurtful*. Hazel, how could you?' The voice, transmitted by the receiver, seemed to pierce deep into Hazel's skull as though to pass on that hurt. 'Hazel!'

'I don't know what this is all about.'

'Of course you do. Your novel. I thought we were friends.'

'Of course we're friends. What *is* all this?'

'No friend could write like that. Never.'

'But you're not *in* the book.'

'Of course I am. It's obvious. It'll be obvious to everyone.'

'But there's no character remotely like you.'

'This — this Major Charles. Of course he's me.'

'But he's — he's a *man*.'

'Oh, that's just a trick.' It sounded as if the trick had momentarily made Martha gulp with laughter; but Hazel, the nausea again swelling up, knew that the gulp was in fact a sob. 'You did that to cover yourself, and to make me look more ridiculous.'

'But really, Martha — '

Hazel had begun already to feel that terrible weariness that overcomes one when one must continue to cling tenaciously to a lie that will never be believed.

'The faith-healer!'

'But, Martha, do let me explain — '

'The mockery of my beliefs!'

'Martha, do be rational.'

'My lodgers!'

23

'Martha, please let me say what I'm trying to say – '

'My cookery!'

Hazel let go of the lie as a drowning man, despairing of being rescued, lets go of a spar too flimsy to keep him above the breakers.

'I'm awfully sorry – '

'After all we've done for you!'

'Of course I had no intention of upsetting you – of hurting your feelings – '

'After the way we stuck by you!'

'I'm grateful to you – eternally grateful to you – both of you. If it hadn't been for you and Nigel –'

'Oh, it's easy enough to poke fun at me in your superior fashion. I know I'm not smart and – and intellectual like you. But if I'm such a figure of fun, what do you think you were in the days when you used to push that – that monster around in its pram? You thought people were sorry for you, didn't you? Well, they might have been – some of them. But they also thought you an idiot to sacrifice everything – everything – your wretched husband included – to a – to a *vegetable*.'

Hazel gasped at the horror of it. When she had used that word herself in her novel, she had been able to bear it; she could not now, when it was spoken by another. It was the difference between picking a scab off her own body and having someone do it to her.

Martha went on: 'You were coming to coffee to meet the Palmers on Sunday. Well, don't. Please don't.'

'As you wish.'

'I do wish.'

The telephone clicked down; but to Hazel the click seemed like a crash. She rolled over on to her stomach on the bed, her hands pressed to her lips. 'Oh, God,' she said aloud. 'Oh, God.' But her horror now was similar to her horror when she had first learned of the death of the child.

What she had then fooled herself into believing would not happen and what she had, nonetheless, known, in some impenetrably dark recess of her being, must happen, had happened at last.

24

It was over. It could not happen again. The horror had shaded, then as now, into relief.

8

Koula and Soula chased each other, now one ahead and now the other, down the hill to the High Street. They wore identical coats and hats of imitation lamb; their cheeks were bright with cold and the long mascara-thick lashes under their slightly protuberant eyes trembled with the tears that the wind had pricked from them.

'Please don't chatter so! My head won't stand it at this hour of the morning!' one of them sang out in what she imagined to be an imitation of Martha.

'I slept not a wink!' the other took up in antiphon.

'Nigel, *must* you crunch your toast quite so noisily?'

'No, a glass of Alka-Seltzer is all I want this morning.'

They joined hands now and capered past a rheumy old man standing patiently over a mongrel straining in the gutter.

'I think Miss Kingsley maybe has a hangover.'

'Koula!'

Their shrill laughter made a famished robin rocket off the lawn in front of the public library.

'I think Miss Kingsley maybe has a man with her all night.'

'Soula!'

Breathless with giggles and the exertion of racing down the hill, they crashed into a parcel-laden woman tottering round a corner on her way to the Post Office.

9

After breakfast, Martha, usually so energetic about scrubbing out
the bath ('Those two little sluts have left the bathroom in a
ghastly mess again – it really is too bad'), imitating a jumbo-jet
over Nigel's head with the vacuum cleaner and answering letters
in the rounded, immature handwriting of a conscientious but
dim-witted schoolgirl, now did none of these things but instead
lay out on her bed, her eyes fixed on the lampshade that the
ice-laden wind from the half-open window slapped back and forth
above her supine body.

Nigel put his head round the door. He had been intending to
ask her for a stamp but now thought better of it.

'Aren't you feeling well!'

'I'm feeling perfectly well.'

'Then why – why are you lying there?'

'Surely I'm at liberty to lie on my own bed in my own time, if I
choose.'

'Of course.'

'I'm thinking.'

'Oh.'

He quickly shut the door. He knew that if she were thinking –
an action rare for her – then it must be about The Book; and if it
were about The Book, then it was likely that their increasingly
hysterical conversation of the early hours would re-ignite itself.
The purple rings under his eyes looked like bruises received in
that confrontation. He would have to go out to one of the lib-
raries until her frenzy had spent itself.

But her ears had always been preternaturally acute where any of
his movements were concerned; and as he tiptoed across the hall
from the sitting-room to the front door, she leapt off the bed like
a cat at the first far, faint rustle of a rodent.

'Nigel!' She was leaning over the banisters, the hair that she
usually rolled into an untidy grey croissant across the nape of her
neck now hanging dishevelled to her shoulders.

26

Nigel stared straight ahead at the handle of the front door.

'*Nigel!*'

Quickly he opened the door and clicked it shut behind him.

She thundered down the stairs, the whole house shaking, and tugged the front door open once again. She put out first her head and then the whole upper part of her body.

'Nigel!'

Unfortunately the milkman had once again been dawdling for a cup of tea in the upstairs of the antique shop, 'Serendipity', kept by a Mrs Fairfax-Wisley at the corner.

'The lady's calling you, sir,' he said as he emerged, a hand nervously testing his flies.

'Oh, not me, surely.'

'I think so, sir.'

'*Nigel!*'

He had to turn back.

'What's happened to your ears?'

'I was thinking.'

'Thinking! Well, I've been thinking too.'

A scuffed brief-case, bulging with books and the sandwiches – thick, damp wedges of steam-baked bread stuffed with Australian cheddar cheese – that he had frenziedly cut for himself, pulled his left shoulder down as though to dislocate it. On his right arm the crow of an unfurled umbrella flapped an ungainly wing in the razor-sharp wind slashing down from the polar wastes of Notting Hill.

'Yes?'

'That book can't go ahead.'

'What do you mean?'

A lace curtain twitched in the sitting-room of the house opposite where a Major-General, already on the retired list before the outbreak of the last war, eked out his nonagenarian days in an armchair at the window.

'What I say. She'll have to stop it.'

'Stop it?'

'It can't go on sale. That's all there is to it.'

'Can't go on sale?'

'Do stop repeating everything I say. It's so – so moronic.'

Mournful bloodhound eyes and a huge white moustache appeared at the window.

'Come in! Come on in! I don't want everyone in the street to know our business.'

Nigel edged in. Martha jerked the door decisively closed behind him.

'You'll have to go and see her.'

'I?'

'You're the only person whose advice she'll ever take. You know how obstinate she is. Over that child of hers — over the divorce. If anyone can do anything with her, you can.'

It was years since Nigel had done anything with Hazel. He had longed to, how he had longed to, but to no avail. He put down the brief-case; the crow on his arm was now as still as his own bleak, blank countenance.

'It's too late, far too late.'

'Nonsense!'

'Publication date is the Thursday — or Friday — after next. I can't remember which. Anyway, it's far too late.'

'That's nearly two weeks.'

'Copies will have gone out to the reviewers. Some of them will have written their reviews. And the bookshops will already have received their orders . . . '

'I can't help that. The book must be stopped. If you appeal to her . . . After all, she's said often enough that you're her oldest and closest friend.'

Nigel sank into a chair; he plucked at the crow's trailing wing.

'Why don't you get that umbrella repaired?'

Brooding, he did not answer.

'Go and see her. Now.'

'But there's — there's no *point*. At this stage of things — '

'Well, *try*!'

Nigel heaved a sigh that was almost a groan, his pointed chin retracted as though to transfix his narrow chest to the back of the chair against which he was slumped.

'I do wish that you'd take that umbrella to the little man round the corner. It looks so sloppy . . . Now go on and try. Go on!'

Nigel got slowly to his feet.

28

'And then come back and tell me what she says!'

10

Nigel nibbled at his biscuit. It was strange how Hazel's homemade biscuits always tasted so different from Martha's. Hazel, kneeling on the floor with her back to him, continued to scrub out the oven.

'She's in a terrible state. Terrible. I've not seen her quite like that since . . . '

His voice trailed off. He was recalling the time, in the war, when their mother, now dead, had commanded Martha to forget all about the pale young army chaplain, the nephew of some obscure Irish peer, with whom she had been going to concerts. (The only music Martha enjoyed now was *Your Hundred Best Tunes* on Radio 2 on a Sunday evening.) He was 'not the marrying kind', the old lady had said forcefully; and if he were coaxed or badgered into marrying, the result would not be satisfactory and might even be disastrous.

'Poor Martha.' Hazel sank on to the floor from her kneeling position. She felt genuinely sorry for the other woman, lashing out in her blind anguish and rage; but she also felt the first faint stirrings of resentment against her for making her feel sorry. 'She was quite beside herself on the telephone this morning. And at that hour − aroused from a deep sleep − I was not in the best condition to cope with her. Oh, it's awful.'

Nigel nibbled again and fragments of shortbread sprayed outwards to nestle in the hirsute creases of his Harris tweed jacket.

'I never thought she'd take it quite like that.'

'Well, let's face it − we never thought she'd take it at all.'

'What do you mean?'

'She never reads anything but the evening paper − and some,

29

just some, of her letters. We counted on that. Didn't we?' she challenged.

'I suppose so.'

'We were fools.' She got up off the floor and sat herself on the opposite side of the kitchen table from him. '*I* was a fool. Having a book is rather like having a baby. While one is pregnant with one or the other, one doesn't think of the consequences. One's one desire is to get it out. If it's a baby, one doesn't think of things like septicaemia, caesarians and eclampsia – whatever that is. Or that the baby might turn out to be – abnormal.' Her sharp face became even sharper, and she gave a little shudder as she said that last word. 'And in the same way, if it's a novel, one doesn't think of the bitchy queer reviewer who's going to say that it "reeks of femininity" (she was quoting from one of her own reviews in a Sunday paper) or of the bitchy female reviewer who will find that it has "too much heart and too little art".' (Again she was quoting.) 'Much less does one think of the dotty woman friend who is going to decide that she is a male character in it and kick up the hell of a fuss.'

Nigel examined what remained of his biscuit. 'But I suppose it was – predictable.'

'If it was predictable, why the hell didn't you predict it?'

He was silent. In a sense he had regarded The Book, brought to him in pencilled drafts, chapter by chapter, and then in typescript and finally in proof, as partly his too. Like her, he had persuaded himself –but how, *how?* – that Martha would never read it or that, if she did read it, she would see no resemblance between 'Major Charles' and herself.

'You read it often enough.'

He hung his head.

'And how did it get into her hands? That's what beats me. Did you put it there?'

He shook his head, in dumb misery.

'Then *how?*'

He began to tell her, breathless and stumbling as though he were picking his way up a rocky mountainside, of leaving The Book out on top of the television set – 'I was in this hurry, I didn't think what I was doing, she was bawling for the mackerel'

– of the failure of the television engineer to call to repair the set and of the failure of the paper-boy to bring the *Evening Standard* and of the unforeseen accident of Martha's picking The Book up and reading it doggedly, on and on, into the early hours. He had been over the whole terrible sequence of events a number of times already in his own mind; and already – since, unlike Martha, he was a person who never ceased to turn the knife against himself to cut deep into the core of his inmost motives – he had asked himself the fateful question: how accidental had, in fact, been the 'accident' by which The Book had come to Martha's notice? Perhaps, without being consciously aware of it, he had wished to precipitate the showdown between the two women, outwardly so matey with each other and inwardly so hostile, that each had shirked for the last twenty-five years or more.

'God, I am unlucky!' Hazel exclaimed at the end of it. 'God!'

'I suppose you *could* rewrite all that out,' he said tentatively, not daring to meet her cold, hard gaze.

'All *what* out?'

'Well – all the Major bit.' He hurried on, before she could interrupt him: 'He's not really such an *important* character, is he? I mean, you could – could think of someone else. Someone entirely different.'

'But the Major's *not* Martha. Any more than you're the Major's wife. Surely I don't have to tell you how a novelist sets about creating characters –.'

'Yes, I know, I know.' Her anger shocked and terrified him and yet, in a strange way, also filled him with an almost sexual exaltation. 'But Martha doesn't understand all that. You know her. She's – literal-minded. Just because the Major has some of her traits and does some of the things she's done and lives in our house on Campden Hill – well, for her that's decisive, the Major *is* her.'

Both of them stared out of the window, heads averted from each other, in total silence. Then Hazel got up. She kicked up the still-open oven door with a foot.

'It's too late,' she said.

'That's what I told her.'

'How can I – at this stage . . . ?' She hugged herself, as she

31

emitted a dry, bitter laugh. 'The irony is that that libel man Melvyn Kurtz should have insisted on those releases from Miklos and Jan — which, as you know, I never thought they'd sign — and yet we never for one moment thought that we should ask for one from Martha.' (Miklos had been Hazel's lover; Jan had been her husband.)

'Perhaps we never thought we should ask for one, because in our hearts of hearts we knew she wouldn't give it.'

Nigel, usually so pliant, so reticent, so fearful of saying anything that would cause displeasure or hint at disapproval or provoke a shock, could nonetheless from time to time blurt out some remark like this that at once homed unerringly to the target.

'Oh, it just never occurred to me! That was all there was to it.' He had succeeded in rattling Hazel; and again, mingled with his distress and fear, there surged up within him that same almost sexual exaltation of a few minutes before.

'So what am I to tell her?'

'Tell her what I'd tell her myself if she had the guts to come and see me, instead of sending you as her envoy. Tell her it's too late. *It's too bloody late.*'

'I see.'

'That's all there is to it. The subject is closed.'

11

Fortunately that afternoon Martha was distracted from her frenzy of hurt feelings and resentment — in a futile attempt to relieve them she had begun to scrub out the kitchen, the pots and pans rattling noisily as they dropped from her hands and the mop chipping off the paintwork of the skirting-boards in grubby flakes — by the unexpected arrival of one of her 'girls'.

But 'girl' was hardly an appropriate description of the demure, almost prim woman, in a light-brown overcoat buttoned up to the chin and a dark-brown felt hat sitting low on her forehead, to whom Nigel, summoned by a shout from Martha, hurried down the stairs to open the door.

The visitor withdrew a small hand, with round shell-like pink nails, from the lamb's wool muff that dangled from a cord around her neck. Nigel wondered if she expected him to shake it. He decided not to.

'Is Miss Kingsley in, please? I'm afraid I haven't got an appointment with her. I called on the off-chance.' The voice pecked at the words with dainty fastidiousness.

'Do come in. I'll go and call her. It's so cold out, isn't it?'

Evidently this must be one of the social workers, prison visitors, charity collectors or Samaritans with whom Martha 'worked'.

'Thank you.' With a nervous smile at Nigel, the woman — who must be in her thirties — slipped past him into the hall.

'Who shall I say it is?'

The woman was glancing around her. 'Oh — Maggie. Maggie Nash. Please.'

Martha straightened herself, one hand gripping the handle of the mop while the other brushed a lock of greying hair off her sweat-speckled forehead, as Nigel announced the visitor.

'*Who?*'

'A Miss — or Mrs — Nash,' he repeated. 'Maggie. Maggie Nash.'

'Heavens! I thought she wasn't due out until next week . . . Take her into the sitting-room and ask her to sit down and I'll be with her in a jiffy.' Martha began to tug off her apron — the strings were inextricably knotted — and to smooth back her hair. With Maggie she never felt wholly at her ease or at her best.

Nigel retreated upstairs as soon as he had completed his commission, leaving the visitor perched on the edge of a chair, her handbag in her lap and her hands crossed over it, as though in fear that someone might snatch it from her.

'Maggie!'

Maggie got to her feet, her small pink-and-white face drooping and troubled.

'I'm sorry to call in out of the blue like this, Miss Kingsley.'

'Sit down, Sit down, my dear.' Martha sat first, knees wide

33

apart, to draw a handkerchief out of the pocket of her tweed skirt and mop at her forehead. 'What a surprise! I'd no idea you were due out so soon. I thought you said the seventeenth.'

'No. The seventh.' The seventeenth was, in fact, the day that The Book, not Maggie, was due out.

'Splendid! ... What about a cigarette?'

Martha jumped up again, to fetch the box in which a packet of uninvitingly damp State Express, stamped 'British Airways', mouldered for visitors. Neither she nor Nigel smoked.

'Thank you.' Maggie gave a lady-like shake of her head and a little sniff. 'I don't.'

'No, of course not. Very wise of you. A drink?'

'I – I don't drink, Miss Kingsley. Don't you remember?'

'Well, let me make you a cup of tea. Or coffee if you'd prefer it.'

'Nothing, thank you. Please don't put yourself to any trouble on my account.'

'It's no trouble, dear. And if it were – well, that's what I'm here for. Isn't it?'

The younger woman, head lowered, traced the outline of the stitching on the front of her bag with a thin forefinger. 'All I wanted was a – a little chat with you. That was all.'

'Of course, dear.'

'One's glad to be out, of course, but one does miss – the company. Oh, I know it must sound odd for me to say that,' she rushed on, as though to stop Martha from making the interjection she was obviously leaning forward to make. 'When all the time I was inside I thought how horrible it was and wanted only to get out. But' – her lower lip trembled slightly – 'life seems. awfully *lonely* now.'

In the case of some of her other 'girls' tears would not have been unwelcome. Martha might even have encouraged them – it could be helpful, she often said, to get it all out of one's system in a single good cry. But the prospect of tears from this quiet, well-spoken woman was somehow unnerving and daunting. So briskly she asked: 'What are your plans?'

'Well – that – that was what I really wanted to talk to you about.' She hesitated. 'If you could give me your advice ...'

'Of course, my dear.'

Again the visitor hesitated, biting her lower lip between her small, white teeth as though to stop its trembling.

'You know I have this little boy — my little boy, Jack? He's illegitimate, of course.'

Martha nodded, her whole body tensed as though in preparation to support the burden of the other woman's distracted and desolate identity.

'Well, while I was inside he was taken into care. That was the worst part of it all, it really was.'

'I do think your parents behaved awfully harshly. Whatever you'd done.'

'It was being Plymouth Brethren, I suppose. First that trouble I had when I was bound over. Then the baby. Then this latest trouble. It was too much for them, I suppose.'

'Well, if that's their attitude — a very *un*-Christian attitude to my way of thinking — then I suppose there's nothing more to be said about it.'

'I think my mother would be perfectly willing to forgive and forget. It's my father, you see. He just can't get over it all.'

'So there's no chance of making a home with them for the child?'

'Oh no! None at all. . . . But his father, the baby's father — well, he got in touch with me just before I got out and he said that he'd take us both in.'

'Maggie! You wouldn't do that!' Martha sat bolt upright, clutching the arms of the chair. 'After all you've told me about him! Beating you up. Beating up the baby. Forcing you into all those — those criminal activities. And those — those other things he made you do. You can't go back to a brute like that. He's been the cause of all your troubles.'

'What else is there for me to do?' the visitor asked with a resigned helplessness that pierced Martha to the quick. 'It's the only way to get my boy back.'

'There must be some alternative. There *must*.'

'Well, there *is* my friend — Molly . . .' Her voice trailed away.

'Molly?'

'We met the first time I was inside. An Irish girl. Quite

simple. Without any education. But she – she was awfully good to me. Without her I really think I'd have killed myself, it was all so *awful*. She took me under her wing.'

'And why was *she* there? I don't think I've met this Molly, have I?'

Maggie shook her head. 'I don't think so. Though of course she's heard all about you – from me and some of the other women. Oh, she also got in with this man who – who was a kind of pimp to her and made her help him with a couple of jobs and . . .' Again her voice trailed away. 'She's a thoroughly decent girl at heart. Just very simple. And she was madly in love with him.'

'The old story.'

The woman opposite to her nodded.

'Where is this – this Molly now?'

'She's working in a hotel in Dundee. She's managed to break off from the man – though she says it was terribly difficult and he – he threatened her and, oh, all sorts of frightful things. . . . Well, she's got this job and she's happy and the owners – he's a retired tea-planter, I think she said – are awfully good to her.' Two circular spots had appeared in the centres of her cheeks; her eyes had a feverish glitter to them. She leant forward, clasping the bag tightly. 'Well, they need a receptionist – somebody who can also do the accounts. And Molly thought that I. . . . There's an empty flat, you see – over the coach-house, Molly says. Of course it's in a terrible state now, but they'd let us have it and bit by bit we could do it up. And then I'd make an application to have Jack released to me . . .'

Yet again her voice trailed off, as her brief excitement at all these possibilities also guttered and expired.

But Martha was enthusiastic, slapping her knees with her palms: 'I think that all sounds marvellous! Marvellous! It's just the thing for you. You need a total break. Out of London. An environment that's new to you. A proper job. Away from that creature. . . . Oh, yes, Maggie, that's perfect.'

'The only trouble is . . .'

'Yes, dear?'

'Well. . . . No.' She was suddenly decisive. 'I don't want to trouble you with all that.'

36

'With what?'

'It's better if I don't say.'

'Maggie — I'm your *friend*.' Martha leant forward. 'Tell me. Maggie, tell me.'

Maggie drew a deep sigh. 'Oh, you're always so good to me, Miss Kingsley! So understanding! You're not like some of the other visitors — so sanctimonious and condescending and — and *smug*!'

'Tell me, Maggie.'

'Well, it's the usual bother.' Her mouth twisted.

'Money?'

A mute and desolate nod.

'You've nothing?'

'Almost nothing.' She clicked open her bag as though to show Martha its contents.

Martha got heavily to her feet. Her face, irradiated by compassion, looked almost monumental as she gazed down, an ample goddess, at the neat bowed head of the suppliant before her.

'Don't worry,' she said.

She went over to a drawer, unlocked it and fumbled inside. Then murmuring 'Just one moment, dear,' she strode out into the hall to bawl up the stairwell: 'Nigel! *Nigel!*'

'Did you call?'

Nervously he peered over the banisters at her.

She beckoned and beckoned again. Reluctantly he edged down.

'Have you got ten pounds to lend me?' she whispered into his ear, clutching him by a shoulder.

He took out his battered wallet and counted. 'Only nine.'

'That'll have to do.'

He wanted to say that it was too late to go to the bank now, that he needed the fare to a lecture at the Classical Association, that she still owed him a fiver borrowed the week before; but she had already tweaked the notes from his nerveless fingers and hurried away with them.

Her face was still exalted as she held them out: 'There you are, my dear.'

Maggie took them in both her delicate, blue-veined hands.

37

'Oh, Miss Kingsley! Miss Kingsley!' Her pale eyes were suddenly brimming with tears.

'Say no more. And it's a present, not a loan.'

Martha crossed over to the desk again and pulled a writing-pad from under a pile of unpaid bills. 'Now give me the address of that hotel. We must keep in touch.'

'Oh, I'll write to you. Of course I'll write to you. Just as soon as I'm settled.'

12

Maggie's friend Molly sat slumped, Persians twittering and squawking like birds all around her, at a table in the window of the coffee-bar on High Street Kensington. Her three neighbours, hairy youths with delicate hands and flashing, bloodshot eyes, were Hazel's basement tenants; but Molly knew nothing of Hazel, only of Martha. She stirred her cup of coffee and then sipped at it, leaving a line of froth along her upper lip. She had the pulpy, battle-scarred features of a punch-drunk bruiser, the eyes small and deep in their cushions of flesh and the nose broken at the bridge.

Christ, it was hot in here! But she did not dare take off her grease-stained burberry, beneath which she was wearing two dresses, a two-piece suit, a pair of trousers and an overcoat. The sweat gleaned on her corrugated forehead. She was not Irish but Australian.

What had become of Maggie? A tremor of fear glided, an ice-cold snake, through her stomach. The trouble with that girl was that she was accident-prone, that was it. She had the class, she had the wits, she had the guts. But things that went right for other people far less gifted went wrong for her.

Molly tore at the nail of her little finger with her teeth, leaving a smear of blood along her chin. On the little finger was the signet ring presented to her by Maggie. God knows what that hand giving the blessing on it was supposed to represent; and God knows what was meant by the inscription, *'Spes tutissima coelis'*. It was a gift and it wouldn't be right to ask her how or where she had got it.

There she was! And about time too. Making one feel as if one were about to squitter with worry and yet not hurrying to tell one what had happened. Christ! Even stopping to look with love at some furs in a window.

Molly, a seemingly pregnant figure with close-cropped iron grey hair sticking up in spikes around that battered bruiser's mug, lumbered up and went and stood in the door of the coffee-bar. The cashier, dainty in a cream cashmere sweater and a double rope of pearls, eyed her with suspicion. 'Just looking for my mate,' Molly reassured her. Then she bellowed: 'Get a move on, girl!'

Maggie skipped towards her, her hands deep in the muff and the upturned collar of her coat making her long neck seem even longer.

'So what happened?'

'Let me catch my breath.' Maggie sank down on to the banquette, a slender hand going up to unbutton her collar. 'Did you see that fabulous display of mink and sable across the road?'

'Forget the mink and sable. So what happened? Come across!'

'There's this coat — mutation mink outside . . . '

Molly heaved a sigh. Everything must have gone all right; the little bitch was teasing.

'For Christ's sake, Maggie!'

Maggie opened her bag, peered into its recesses and then announced demurely, 'Nine pounds. That was the best I could do.'

'Terrific!'

A large, rough hand shot out to pat the chill, pallid cheek. But Maggie had pulled away before it could reach it. 'Not in here, Molly.'

'Don't be so bloody respectable!' But Molly was always delighted, never annoyed, by Maggie's lady-like pretentions. 'Not too difficult?' she asked.

39

'A sitting duck.'

Molly raised a stubby thumb.

'She's got some nice things in that house of hers,' Maggie went on ruminatively. 'Worth thinking about. And how about you?'

Molly indicated the shopping bags stacked on the banquette beside her and piled into a corner on the floor. She grinned, revealing small, wicked teeth tanned with nicotine.

'Oh, Molly!' Maggie exclaimed, pretending to be shocked.

'It's not mutation mink, but I've even got a little something for you.'

She bent and hitched up first the hem of the raincoat, then that of the coat, and then that of the coat-and-skirt beneath it. 'Like it?' she asked.

Maggie might have known that she would choose black silk, sequins and diamanté. She would never wear it.

13

'Poor little creature! What I can't understand is the attitude of the parents.'

'I suppose they feel they've had just about enough.' Nigel was in a sour mood after the loss of his nine pounds. 'One can hardly blame them.'

'*I* blame them. People like that call themselves Christians but they seem to know nothing of the Christian virtue of forgiveness. Her father's a bank manager or solicitor or something. He ought to know better.'

'I wonder if you'll see her again,'

'Of course I shall. She's exactly the kind of person who turns up months later to return the money. Not that I'd take it back, of course. It was a gift.'

'She must have quite a record.'

Martha compressed her lips. 'Who was it who said "The

confidence trick is the work of man but the no-confidence trick is the work of the devil"?'

'I've no idea. It sounds like one of those meaningless aphorisms of Emerson.'

' "O, ye of little faith ..." ' Martha said, as she swept from his room.

At least she knew where that quotation came from.

14

Yellow mist dotted the surface of the Serpentine like blobs of coagulating fat. Far off someone invisible whistled to an invisible dog and whistled again. The wavering note had a piercingly forlorn sound to it as Hazel paused to listen, an angular figure against the roundness of lake and mist-shrouded trees and the bridge that was no more than a shadowy hump without either beginning or end. The wings of her turned-up coat-collar jutted out sharply, as did her elbows and her shoulders, while her ungloved hands sought in vain for warmth in pockets cobwebby with the chill and moist of the late winter afternoon.

She had come into the Gardens because it had seemed easier to think over the situation when walking out like this than when staring, a coil of compressed nervosity, into a gas fire.

'Come here! Come *here*, Rex!'

The voice must belong to the same person who earlier had whistled. An Afghan hound, shaggily dishevelled, pattered out of the mist and almost blundered into her. The owner followed, a frail youth, hair no less copious and tangled than his dog's, his high-heeled boots clicking like castanets on the asphalt.

'What did I say? . . . Come here! *Here!* Now sit!'

The dog wavered past Hazel and then reluctantly came to a halt as the voice pursued it: 'Rex! *Rex!* You bloody well do what I tell you to do!'

41

The youth did not glance at Hazel as he hurried by, one hand swishing a branch in admonition at the dog.

'*Sit!*'

The dog stared up at him with hurt, bewildered eyes.

'You heard me! Now sit!'

The branch descended, with a shower of dead leaves as it struck the creature on its rump. There was a squeal.

'That's better.'

The dog had sat, quailing, its tail sweeping the path from side to side.

'All right! Come on then! *Come!*'

Hazel could hear the castanet-like clicking long after they had disappeared from sight.

That was the tone — and not only the tone, but also the faintly nasal accent — in which that psychiatrist (what was his name? Orris? Arris?) had shouted at Peter. Nigel had spoken of him, a refugee who had worked with Freud and been a friend of his during the years of his cancer-tormented exile and had then, shortly before the old man's death, quarrelled with him and repudiated his allegiance. He worked wonders, Nigel said. Children who were — who were like Peter had become his speciality. He had evolved this special technique for dealing with them and he got results that no one else could get. But she had not been able to bear hearing this previously mild middle-aged Jew barking his orders at the child, gripping him by either arm and shaking him as he did so. (The child's head flopped back and forth as though the neck had been broken.) So they had never gone back to him, though Nigel had told her that it had been silly and unfair not to have given the man a proper chance.

When she had written about that incident in her novel (shoulders hunched now, hands still deep in pockets, Hazel began to wander on, with no notion of the direction she might be taking) she had changed it, to give it — as she thought — a sharper point. Now it was Martha, in her guise of Major Charles, who had persuaded her to try out the miracle-worker; and the miracle-worker was no longer a middle-aged balding Jew of (probably) Central European origins despite his English-sounding name, but a tense and shrill American woman, barely in her thirties, who had reluctantly agreed to see the distraught mother and her vegetable-child, even though she had come to England merely to attend a conference and to make a single vehement appearance on television.

There was no doubt about it that Martha had been wonderful – yes, that was the adjective that had always somehow been used by Hazel and her friends – about poor Peter. Other people had been sympathetic about him and, in rare instances, had helped him, out of love for Hazel. But Martha's love had been, not for Hazel – whom she had never really liked – but solely and miraculously for the child. There had been that strange noise (under the dripping trees, Hazel now seemed to hear it, as far-off yet piercing as that earlier whistle) that Peter had made when he was pleased: a crowing sound, strangled and hoarse, akin to that made by normal children when suffering from whooping-cough. He had made it for only three people in all his life: for Hazel, for Miklos and for Martha. Never for his father or either of his grandmothers or for all those people who would peer nervously down at him and say what a dear little fellow he was and wasn't his smile angelic, and who would shower him with the gifts that were a substitute for the affection they could not force themselves to feel.

But in the book she had made all that clear! She shook her head angrily, as though Martha were here now beside her in the dimming light of the late winter afternoon and were arguing with her. Between Major Charles and the child of her brain, as between Martha and the child of her womb, an invisible wire had perpetually thrilled with secret messages. Yes, but that was the paradox, of course. Major Charles was silly and vain and snobbish and gifted with less, rather than more, sensibility than his wife, or the Hazel who was Helen in the novel, or than Helen's friends. Which made it all the more inexplicable that he should have established a rapport that had eluded all but two other people.

And yes, of course, reading about Major Charles, with his obtuseness and tactlessness and his boasts about his prowess as a chef and his small, mean economies and his jealous love of the wife whom he alternately bullied and cosseted, Martha had not unnaturally thought 'So *that's* what I'm like in her view.' Not unnaturally . . .

Until this moment Hazel's only feeling had been one of exasperation. It had always been poor old Martha's role to 'ruin' things. Long, long ago she had ruined Hazel's brief affair with Nigel and after that she had ruined anything else he had ever attempted, whether intellectually or emotionally. Holidays she had ruined and picnics and excursions to the theatre or to concerts: anything, in fact, that the three of them or even just Nigel and Hazel undertook together. Now, not surprisingly, she was going to ruin Hazel's triumph over the book.

But Hazel's annoyance at this (once more she was standing beside the lake with its grease-like blobs of mist, duck wings clattering in the reeds beside her) was now for the first time tempered with guilt. Well, of course, it *had* been rather beastly to show her up in that way. After all, she had been wonderful, quite wonderful (that word again!) in the way she had taken complete charge of Peter for a whole blissful ten days while Hazel and Miklos went off on that holiday of theirs, a honeymoon really, to Morocco. She had always been on call, had fussed over the child and changed his perpetually soiled clothes and somehow curbed those wild, horrifyingly inexplicable tantrums. It was difficult – impossible? – to explain to someone so wholly unliterary and literal-minded: 'It had to be like that in the book. That's how it happened and so that's how it had to happen.' Nigel could understand. Martha never would.

At the recognition of that fact, Hazel's exasperation sharpened once more. The trouble was – one had to face it – that Martha was a basically stupid woman. Like Major Charles. . .

She started, with a little gasp of alarm, as a huge figure, carrying what she at first, wildly, thought to be a coffin under an arm, emerged out of the mist on silent plimsolls and all but collided into her. Prongs of red hair dripped moisture on to a low freckled forehead. The wide, serrated grin was wolfish.

'Whoops! . . . Sorry.'

It was a battleship that this man in his forties was cradling to its secret, thrilling launching from somewhere among the duck-infested reeds. She had seen him before, usually at the Round Pond, when she had wheeled Peter out. 'Look, darling! Look at the boat!' And Peter would stare fixedly at a point that always, maddeningly, seemed fractionally to the left or the right of the chugging object at which she would be pointing

At such times it was invariably to Nigel that she turned. Jan, her divorced husband, had given him the cruel nickname 'the Waste-disposal Unit' — whatever trouble, Jan said, clogged itself within her, she would thrust down into Nigel to have him eliminate it. But on this occasion how could she expect the Waste-disposal Unit to function on her behalf? It was, after all, impossible to feed it Martha and Martha's lacerated feelings to grind up and digest.

She thought of other of her friends: of a childless woman writer, older and more successful than herself, who had been the most insistent of all those who had urged her to put Peter away in an institution; of a married doctor with whom, briefly, she had had an embarrassing affair of hasty pre-dinner couplings in his deserted consulting rooms and no less hasty post-luncheon ones in her own house; even of Miklos, her one-time lover, eleven years younger than herself, whose unspoken order when he had baled out had been, 'Don't contact me. I'll contact you.'

Then she remembered Arnold — Arnold Shaw.

His advice, let's face it, was usually better than Nigel's; and the only reason that she did not seek it more often was that, unlike Nigel's, it was so often unpalatable. 'I'm the kind of person who tells you, not what you want to do, but what you ought to do,' he had answered bitingly when once she had protested 'Oh, how cruel you are!' at some particularly unwelcome home-truth.

After some years of making money as a stockbroker, he now lived on what he called 'my modest competence' in a small flat crowded to the ceilings with possessions. The block overlooked the Park, from what others once used to call — and he still called — 'the fashionable side'. Though not a homosexual — unless he had shown unusual discretion to her over this aspect of himself — he had never married and seemed to live the life of a eunuch. But unlike most eunuchs, he had no sense of deprivation and suffered from no envy. In the thirties and the first years of the war, he had enjoyed a brief and explosive success as a surrealist poet. He had also been a member of the Party. But in the twilight that he had later entered as the shadowy head of some shadowy wartime intelligence group (he was proficient in half-a-dozen languages) both the poetic success and the political convictions had gathered dust in an attic that he had had, mysteriously, no further compulsion to enter.

Yes, she would go and see Arnold. But though his flat was so near – through the mist she could see the hazy outline of what, on clearer days, looked, not like a block of luxury flats, but one of those Christian Science Churches to which Martha had insisted on taking her at her period of acutest misery over Peter – he was not the kind of friend on whom one could drop in without the formality of a prior telephone call. Once and once only she had done that to him, saying, breathlessly joyful, as he opened the door (it was the start of her time of great happiness with Miklos): 'I was just passing and outside your block there was this man selling these gladioli – the first I've seen this spring. So I couldn't resist . . . ' He did not ask her in. 'How kind of you.' He took the bunch from her – was his small grimace for the touch of the paper, screwed round the stems, which was already frayed and soggy? – and then gave it one small shake and then another more vigorous. Petals shuddered down on to the thick emerald pile of the carpet in the corridor. 'Oh dear!' she exclaimed, and 'They're *lovely!*' he exclaimed simultaneously. He kissed her on the cheek, the lips hardly brushing the skin. 'Thank you.' Inexorably he then began to close the door on both her and what now looked like flakes of plaster from the ceiling.

At the corner where she had bought those ill-fated blooms, she knew that there was a telephone kiosk. She had attempted to use it on her last visit to Arnold, only to find that the instrument had been, not smashed, but expertly dismantled into components that littered the floor. But this time she was lucky.

'Hello.'

'Arnold?'

'Yes.'

'Is that you, Arnold?'

He sounded like a stranger.

'Yes.'

'Oh, Hazel here. It seems such ages and ages since I saw you last. How are you?

46

'Dying.'

She gave a laugh, hardly taking in the word. Then, suddenly, she felt the cold steel that had struck upwards through her vitals. The last time she had spoken to him, several days before, had he not spoken of 'a tiresome check-up' at St Thomas's?

'What do you mean?'

'What I say. It seems that a place has been booked for me on the Transcendental Express. First class, of course. Back to the engine.'

'Oh, God . . . How *awful!*'

'It's nice of you to say so. But it's not awful for me. I feel as I used to feel halfway through those parties of Miklos's. It was always so much earlier than one thought — and hoped. One wanted to be away . . . Well, this party has also gone on too long.'

'Oh, *Arnold!*'

'Don't be upset.'

'I'll come and see you soon. Soon.' (Not now. Because she must not be distracted by her own cosmically trivial piece of news from sharing to the full in the momentous agony of his.) 'Very soon. But what — what is it exactly?'

Arnold's ailments, obscure and often socially convenient, had for years been a joke among his friends. ('I've asked Arnold to come too — but I'm afraid that the prospect of seeing Martha may precipitate another of his *turns*.')

'What is it? Oh, a number of things. It's pointless to enumerate them. If they had come single spies, perhaps. . . .' His voice trailed away. 'But a battalion of them . . .'

Though she walked faster and faster back through the Park and though she huddled deeper and deeper into her overcoat, shoulders hunched and hands plunged in pockets, she could not control the shivers that passed through her body like an attack of fever. She clenched her jaws until they ached, but even so felt the tremors that shook them.

Ahead of her, in the little passageway that connected the splendours of Palace Gardens Terrace with the squalors of Church Street, she suddenly heard the castanets again, and there, striding out, was the young man, with his Afghan dog, now holding in

47

his jaws the branch with which he had been belaboured, pattering beside him.

As the pair debouched into the main road, an elderly Irish drunk, battered trilby hat askew and face mottled and fiery, all but staggered into the dog, side-stepped vertiginously, and then landed up with one foot in the gutter and the hat over his eyes. In a phlegm-clogged voice he shouted: 'You look where that bloody dog of yours is going!'

'You look where you're going yourself,' the young man retorted in surprisingly prim, refined accents.

'With a bloody silly branch like that in his jaw, he's going to interfere with some woman.' The elderly man had now pushed the hat up his forehead and was squinting at Hazel. Perhaps she was the hypothetical woman to whom he referred.

'You're more likely to interfere with a woman than my dog,' the young man hissed back over his shoulder as he continued on his way.

'Shit! That's what you are! *Shit!*' The old man staggered towards a wall and placed the palm of a hand against it, using it as a pivot. 'Shit!' he muttered again, twisting round.

The undirected venom of the whole brief exchange upset Hazel, she could not have said why, almost as much as Martha's telephone call and Arnold's news. The result was that she could not bring herself to walk past the reeling drunk and turned back to negotiate the road higher up Church Street, even though by doing so she would deprive herself of the pedestrian crossing.

'Shit!'

The epithet now seemed to be flung, not in the direction of the youth and his dog (they had vanished into the crowds), but at herself.

15

Nigel rapped lightly on the door and then, when there was no answer, overcame a cowardly impulse to do nothing further and rapped again more loudly.

'Yes?'

He opened on to darkness. Though it was barely five o'clock, the curtains had been drawn. A humped shape on the bed stirred and sighed.

'Is something the matter?'

Another sigh, deeper than its predecessor.

'Martha! Are you feeling ill?'

'I'm perfectly all right.' Bedclothes muffled the voice.

'Don't you want some tea?'

'No.'

'I could fetch you some.'

'Oh, go away. Do *go away!*'

'Is it a migraine?'

'I've told you. I'm perfectly all right. Now go away.'

'I wish . . .'

'*Please.* Nigel!'

Nigel went.

In the kitchen he sat down to a tea of innumerable slices of toast, prepared in pairs in the pop-up toaster that had been a gift from Hazel the previous Christmas, and then thickly buttered and honeyed.

To eat his way stolidly through the best part of a loaf brought a curious assuagement to his spirit.

16

Martha rose to prepare the supper. Her sense of duty was strong.

'Are you not eating, Miss Kingsley?' Koula asked, fastidiously slicing a round of luncheon meat and popping a morsel between her full lips.

'No. I'm not eating.' The tone was bleak in its stoicism.

'You are not well, Miss Kingsley?'

'I'm perfectly well, thank you, Soula.'

'Maybe your stomach is not good?'

'There is nothing wrong with my stomach, thank you, Koula.'

'In the hospital, many of the patients have the trots. Maybe there is something bad in the kitchen.'

'In *this* kitchen, Soula?' Momentarily Martha was roused from her nerveless gloom. Her voice grew jagged.

'No, no!' Soula began to giggle.

'In the kitchen of the hospital!' Koula was now also convulsed.

When the girls had gulped their cups of instant coffee, they excused themselves and hastened upstairs to round off their meal with plump, syrup-dripping fingers of baklava, the present of an Arab woman patient whose moans and cries, long before the onset of her labour, had filled the whole ward.

'Oh, those girls *are* silly!'

Martha began to stack the crockery in the dishwasher – a task that she allowed no one else to perform for her.

'They're nice. Sweet.'

'The appetites they have! Do you know that our consumption of butter has more than *trebled* since they came to us?'

'They work hard. And probably the food at the hospital isn't all that plentiful. Or good.'

'You're soft. That's the trouble with you. Soft.'

Nigel shrugged. Martha had often levelled that accusation against him.

He stirred the spoon round his empty coffee-cup, making it

tinkle, until Martha drew her breath in sharply and glared at him.

'Martha . . .'

'Yes?'

He was talking to her backside, uptilted at him as she continued to put cups into the dishwasher.

'Would you rather that – that I didn't go to Tony and Mabel?'

'Why on earth should I rather?'

'I just thought . . .'

Martha was moved by the offer, but she could never show that she was moved. Instead she said grumpily: 'I've no desire to go. But you enjoy it, don't you?'

'Of course.'

With the exception of Hazel, Tony and Mabel were now his oldest and closest friends. So many other friends of that period had been lost through Martha.

'Well, then.'

'I mean, if you'd . . .'

'To tell you the truth, I'm rather looking forward to a weekend by myself.' (In fact, humped under the bedclothes in her darkened bedroom as the dawn broke, she had been wondering how on earth she would get through the weekend ahead without him.) 'I've a lot of things to do. Household things.'

'In that case . . .'

Martha wanted to put her short dachshund's arms round his narrow, hunched shoulders and to squeeze him to her. She wanted to say: Nigel, I'm so unhappy. That horrible woman, that horrible book. It's as though she had put me in a cage at the zoo, for people to stare and poke and make fun at me. Don't leave me. Don't inflict on me the isolation in which to think that I'm really as she says. Stay with me. Reassure me.

But instead:

'I know what it means to you to pay your visits to that pair. It wouldn't be my choice, they bore me stiff. But *you* enjoy them . . .'

Nigel enjoyed so many things that Martha did not enjoy.

17

That Martha's telephone call came in the middle of dinner was not by design. She herself liked to eat at six-thirty or even earlier and she always found it difficult to accept that the customs of others might be different from her own.

Tony had just been talking about his decision, regarded as academic suicide by his colleagues, to relinquish his post at Oxford for one which took him for less than half a year to a Middle West university of which, he confessed, even he had never heard until, at a conference in Stockholm, he had been obliged to put the drunken dean of the faculty to bed in the hotel room next to his own. 'If he hadn't puked all over my DJ, I doubt if he'd have done anything. It was that little accident that really cemented the deal. Or perhaps I should say more, accurately, stuck it together.'

'It still seems to me rather rash.' Nigel savoured the delicious smoothness of the avocado mousse. Soula and Koula would by now have finished a meal of soused mackerel. Or curried beans on toast. Or spaghetti and chips. Guiltily he realized that this consideration intensified, instead of diminishing, his pleasure.

'Not at all. It was all thought out with extreme deliberation. By me. And by my good wife . . . Wasn't it, darling?'

Mabel, rings biting deep into pudgy fingers as she devoured her mousse with even sharper gusto than Nigel, nodded. 'Do you think I should have put in rather more paprika?'

'Nonsense. This is just right. Perfect . . . No, dear fellow, after months and months – one might almost say, years and years – of thought, Mabel and I decided that what we had both secretly wanted all our lives was the exact opposite of what our parents had wanted both for themselves and for us. High living and plain thinking – that's what we'd wanted. And that's precisely what we've now got.'

'We've never had more money,' Mabel said, digging deep to help herself to what was left of the mousse.

'And never had more time. It's years since I was actually able to *finish* a piece of *petit point*.'

'But if' — Nigel's tongue flickered out to remove a greyish-green gobbet of mousse from the tuck at one corner of his mouth — 'if — as rumour has it — Maurice is on the way out . . .'

'Oh, he's on the way out all right. Parkinson's.'

'Addison's,' Mabel corrected.

'Then surely — you'd have been in the running for the chair?'

'Who wants a chair? Far more work, endless trouble and tedium. With revolting students and the even more revolting Peter Pans of the faculty. And what for? Even if I enjoyed the Snovian exercise of power and influence, I'd have little more than I have now. And the increase in income would have been infinitely smaller than I've achieved in my present sinecure.'

'You were often tipped for the Mastership . . .'

'Horrors! The strain of the last sit-in gave poor old Philip his coronary. Another will finish him.'

'The lodge is a barracks,' Mabel took up, beginning to remove their plates.

'And there's talk of turning it into flats — of which the Master will have only one, an extremely modest one.'

'We're far better off here.'

'Now at last I can *work* — for at least five months of the year, when I'm not in the States.'

'And, in any case, they're using him so much on the box these days . . .'

Mabel pushed the dishes through the hatch, where her 'treasure' — an elderly widow in surgical stockings and a head-scarf — hurried over to receive them and transport them to the sink. When Martha had urged Mabel to buy a dishwasher, Tony had butted in to say that it would be even more ruinous to their china than the male Filipino au pair whom they had employed, briefly and disastrously, as an experiment.

'You'd better see to the dishing-up of the duck,' Tony whispered. Mabel went out. 'She was given the recipe by Sybille Merlier — a new girl, quite appealing, who lectures in French. I must say parsnips and duck don't sound a *terribly* promising combination. But we'll see.'

It was then that the telephone rang. Tony rose at the bird-like trilling, throwing down his napkin. 'Fuck! Why the hell do people always have to ring during meals?'

From the hall, Nigel could hear him, first snappish and then surly:

'Yes ... Yes, it is ... Oh ... Oh, yes ... Yes ... Well, yes, we were, as a matter of fact, in the middle of dinner ... No matter ... No, no ... I'll get him for you ... Nigel!'

'Yes. Is it for me?'

'That egregious sister of yours. If you'll pardon the epithet.'

Nigel picked up the receiver with a disloyal spurt of annoyance at Martha for putting him in this position. 'Martha?'

'Oh, Nigel!'

'Is something wrong?'

'No. Oh no. I just wanted a word with you.'

'We're in the middle of dinner. Shall I ring you back?'

'It won't take a moment. Nigel, I – I was thinking ...' Her voice trailed off, as if she had forgotten what she had been thinking.

'Yes?' Sharp, irritable. Nigel only spoke to her like that when he was with Tony and Mabel.

'Charles.'

'Charles?'

'In the book. Charles Kingsley.'

'I don't understand.'

'Charles – in the book. Major Charles. And Kingsley. Our surname.'

'Martha, what *do* you mean?'

'Don't be long, old fellow!' Tony bawled from the dining-room. Nigel then heard him order Mabel: 'Start! Start! I don't see why our dinner should be ruined just because that stupid cow ...'

'Don't you *see*? That's why she called that horrible man Major Charles. It was the connection with our name. Of course that was it. And what makes it even more cruel is that I used to call little Peter my water-baby. Don't you remember?'

Nigel remembered; and with the shock of remembrance, there came another shock – Martha, generally regarded as so much less perceptive than he, had on this occasion noticed something that

54

he had failed to notice. With this twin shock, he also became aware of a curious sensation of tingling in the arm that was holding the telephone receiver. Hurriedly he transferred it to the other.

'Oh, I think that's just a coincidence.'

'Of course it's not a coincidence. That was her way — her clever way — of making sure that people realize that that couple are meant for us.'

'I've never thought for one moment that that ghastly wife of the Major — ' But of course he had.

'Then you've been even more fatuous over this whole affair than I thought you had. Are you *blind*?'

'There may be one or two small resemblances — '

'One or two!'

'But that doesn't mean that — '

'We've got to stop that book. Now more than ever. It'll make us the laughing-stock of all our friends.'

'We can't stop it.'

From the dining-room Nigel heard: 'Oh, very well, put it in the oven for him! I can see he'll be stuck out there for a long time yet.'

'Have you shown *them* the book?'

'Who?'

'Tony and Mabel, of course.'

'Not yet.'

In order to dig the novel out of Martha — the process had been similar in its messiness and difficulty to removing shrapnel from a wound — Nigel had used the pretext that his Oxford friends were eager to look at it.

'Why not?'

'Well, I've not been here all that long. And we've had so many things to talk about.'

'I want to know what they think about it. I'm sure they'll agree with me. Show it to them. Now.'

'I can hardly show it to them in the middle of dinner.'

From the dining-room: 'Yes, it's much better than I'd dared to hope. Just carve me another *tiny* sliver . . . well, perhaps two . . .'

'After dinner, then. It's got to be stopped. If necessary, we'll – we'll have to do something legal.'

At that mention of doing something legal, Nigel's left arm began to tingle as his right had done. What could she mean?

'I'll show it to them. Just as soon as the right moment comes.'

'After dinner. Don't forget.'

'I won't forget.'

At that, abruptly and without any goodbyes, Martha rang off. Such was her habit when a telephone call had not fulfilled her expectations.

'I'm afraid that protracted call has ruined for you what has been, I must admit, a surprising triumph.'

'Of course I cheated by adding the orange-peel. That wasn't in her recipe.'

'Well, all I can say is that your cheating has produced a grand slam.'

'Mrs Eldred' – Mabel was at the hatch – 'could you please let me have the plate from the oven.'

'I'm afraid it's rather shrivelled,' Mrs Eldred sniffed.

'I couldn't turn down the oven,' Mabel explained. 'Because of the soufflé.'

'So what did our Martha want?'

When Tony used that 'our' of a person, it denoted a process of disowning, not of annexing.

'Oh, she's in rather of a state.'

'What's unusual about that?'

'It's Hazel's novel. The new one.'

'I thought it wasn't out.'

'I thought Martha never read. Books, I mean,' Mabel took up.

'It isn't out. Not for ten days.' Nigel raised a parsnip on his fork; it was a vegetable he detested. 'But she gave me an advance copy. And – and Martha picked it up and looked at it.' At first reluctantly and then with gathering willingness and speed he began to tell the story.

Ever since they had occupied rooms next to each other when they had arrived, Tony from Eton and Nigel from Westminster, to sit for the Classical scholarships that they had both secured so easily, Tony had regarded Nigel as yet another of the possessions

56

that his acquisitive nature had already begun to accumulate. Nigel was like the small Cotman drawing extracted from a penniless aunt; the netsuke bought for a few shillings at an auction-sale in Windsor; the David Roberts hand-coloured print of Petra given to Tony by a young usher as a timid and tortuous declaration of love. Each object had some intrinsic value but acquired even more by the mere virtue of belonging to Tony and no one else. When Tony had later married and endowed Mabel with all his worldly goods in exchange for her more copious ones, part of the endowment had been, of course, his friend. But whereas no one else would ever lay claim to the Cotman, the netsuke or the David Roberts, there were always people like Martha and Hazel to lay claim to Nigel; and for such usurpers Tony and Mabel could feel only resentment and dislike.

Lying full length on the sofa, his stockinged feet curling luxuriously in the warmth from the huge log crackling and sparking in the open Elizabethan fireplace, Tony read. Meanwhile, Nigel, perched on the edge of his armchair, watched him anxiously, from time to time rubbing his thin hands against each other as though they were cold. Mabel was knitting – a tent-like garment in purple wool intended not for herself but a forthcoming sale of work in aid of the village church.

Since he never – it was his own proud boast – bothered with reading novels, Tony did not bother with reading this one, except in as far as it had any reference to Martha. His eyes skimmed with the adroitness of a practised reviewer.

'Gosh!' It was the first of a succession of delighted yelps, gurgles and guffaws.

'Where have you got?'

'It's where she says that this Major fellow has the body of a dachshund. I had never thought of that. But of course it describes poor M. to a T.'

'I'd always thought of Martha's body being more like a camel's,' Mabel put in.

'A *camel's!* Don't be idiotic. Camels' legs are, if anything, unusually long.'

Mabel counted stitches, her evanescent eyebrows drawn together over her slightly protuberant eyes. 'Perhaps it's the way she has of sitting down,' she mused. 'You know. That preliminary crossing of the legs and then the back straight and the small head held high as she descends.'

Nigel could queasily feel the parsnips, soft and furry, still on his tongue. He put his hands between his knees and squeezed them tightly until his calves ached.

'Oh, Lord! . . . "Culinary Coué-ism". It's quite a neat phrase. Isn't it?' Tony looked over the tops of his reading-glasses first at Nigel and then at Mabel. 'When Mabel says that a dish is going to be "delicious", you know that, with luck, you're in for a treat. But when our Martha proudly announces "I've got a delicious Irish stew for you", it's the inevitable forerunner of something really dire.'

Nigel, who had previously been shivering, now felt his forehead burn. The last time, a long time ago, that Tony and Mabel had been entertained at the house on Campden Hill, it was an Irish stew that Martha had prepared for them, saying firmly in answer to Nigel's timid suggestion that perhaps a joint would be more appropriate: 'They must take us as they find us. And everyone agrees that my Irish stews are always delicious' – yes, she had used that exact epithet.

'I must say Hazel is really rather a bitch. But I always thought that. The only thing to be said in her favour is that the book makes her out to be even less attractive a character than the pair of you.'

'Oh, I don't think . . .'

'All this dreadful *meum* and *tuum*. This scene here – my eye's just alighted on it – when she complains of this Romanian lover of hers – '

'Actually a Hungarian – '

' – always using her towel instead of the one she puts out for him. What's the point, for Christ's sake, in being lovers if you can't use each other's towels?'

'I think – if you read on – that her complaint's really that he uses her towel to polish his shoes.'

'So what?' Tony flicked over some pages. 'Oh, poor Martha! No really! Cripes!'

'What is it now?' Mabel turned a row. 'What is it? Don't keep

it to yourself.' Tony was chuckling, his chin on his breastbone.
'Tony! Read!'

'Oh, it's about her passion for *cults*. "In moments of depression, Major Charles would go out shopping for a new system of beliefs in the way that women go out shopping for a new hat or coat" ... Is she still on that Rudolph Steiner jag, by the way?'

'I've no idea.'

'The last was Subud surely?' Mabel intervened.

'Oh, crikey!' Tony now almost fell off the sofa on to the floor in a convulsion of merriment.

The log had long since been consumed and Mabel's purple tent had collapsed around her knees at a final casting-off, when Tony at last came to the end of his reading.

'Well ...! I *must* say ...! Blimey!' He lay back, exhausted, on the sofa.

Nigel choked back that ever-recurrent furriness of parsnip. His joints were all aching and burning as from a long sojourn on the rack.

'Yes, Hazel's a bitch,' Mabel said, staring into the dying fire. '*Whatever* one may think of Martha ...'

'We've all said things like that about her *in private*. But to pillory the poor soul in a book.... Not to mention you.'

'Oh, I don't mind. I'm like that, I know I am. And in any case, the character isn't *me*. It just happens to have a few of my attributes. That's all.'

'You're such a masochist, Nigel,' Mabel said. 'You *enjoy* being hurt.'

'Not at all.'

'Of course you do.' Tony was firm. 'But you can't blame Martha if her reactions are a little more — shall we say? — normal.'

As though she had heard her name spoken at that moment far away in Oxford, Martha had sat up in bed, muzzy from a sleeping-pill that had failed to make her sleep, and had then thrown her short legs over its side and reached for her dressing-gown. Then she had deliberated, hunched over the arms she had clasped across her stomach. Finally, wheezing and sighing, she had got up and padded round the bed to the telephone.

'Is that the phone?'

'Who on earth can be ringing at an hour like this?'

Nigel knew already that it could only be one person.

Tony stretched out a small, plump hand, its skin pink and smooth.

'Martha! ... Yes, my dear ...' His tone was far more friendly than on the previous occasion; and now it grew progressively warmer, just as previously it had grown progressively chillier. 'No ... No, we haven't even *started* to go to bed. As you know, we're later retirers – and later risers – than you. As a matter of fact, we've been having what could best be described by that old-fashioned phrase "a reading-party" ... Yes, dear.' (Nigel had never heard Tony call Martha 'dear' before.) 'Yes, that's right. The book. Our dear Hazel's book ... Well, yes, I must say, I *do* agree ... Yes, beastly. The exact word. Beastly ... Yes, a laughing-stock ... Quite ... In the old days you would have had to challenge her to a duel ... No, I think it *horrid*, quite horrid ... I was shocked. *We* were shocked ... Yes, I know, but you know what Nigel's like.' Tony glanced over at Nigel and, meeting his misery-stricken gaze, winked at him. 'Such a glutton for punishment.' He put his hand over the mouthpiece and while the receiver continued to quack, commented: 'She's going to go on till the cows come home.' He put the receiver back to his ear: 'What was that, my dear? ... Well, yes, if the word libel has any meaning at all, I should call it libellous. Certainly. Quite definitely. A hundred per cent ... Well, we can't speak for the young man – the Romanian or Hungarian – perhaps he enjoys the spectacle of their dirty linen being washed in public ... Nor can we speak for all her other friends ... But for you ...'

At last the terrible call had ended.

Tony replaced the receiver on its cradle.

'Oh, she is in a stew! Oh, she is in a tizzy! Golly!'

'What did she say?'

But Nigel knew already most of what she had said.

'She's determined to get the book stopped. And I can't say I blame her.'

'She can't do that!' Nigel cried out in pain.

60

'Of course she can. For a start she could take out an injunction.'

'You didn't say that to her?'

'You heard that I didn't. But any lawyer will tell her that. I
presume that she just wants to stop the book, not to make any
money?'

'But poor Hazel . . .'

'Poor Hazel has asked for it.'

18

'Undo my necklace, darling.'

Tony loved the little crease of fat where the clasp of the pearls
rested. Tenderly he eased the diamond-encrusted catch and then
lowered his mouth, as though to bite.

'Umm!'

'Poor Nigel!' The words were part of the touch of his lips on
her skin.

'O-o-h! . . . Yes, poor Nigel.'

'I knew no good would come of his friendship with that bitch.'

'Of course a lot of it *is* rather clever.'

'It's not difficult to be clever at the expense of Martha.'

'Fancy getting oneself caught in the crossfire between two such
women . . . Darling – it *is* awfully late. Do you really want to?'

'Yep. . . . He's lived like that for years. Twenty at least.'

'Let me take the bedspread off.'

'Shall I clean my teeth?'

'Mmm?'

'Shall I clean my teeth?'

'Later . . . Did I put too much garlic in the duck?'

'Nope. Perfect.'

'Wait! . . . *Wait*!'

In the room next door their soul-child, so wayward but always
so easily brought back to heel, was staring out of the window at a

garden glittering spikily with rime. The motionless tear at one corner of his right eyeball might have been a fragment of the same ice painfully embedded there.

19

Martha tried to raise the crystal vessel and tip it forward (on the high brass bedstead the muscles in her neck and short plump arms tautened) just as that saint, Bronislaw Mozoomdar, had instructed her to do. But it was like trying to heave an old-fashioned trunk, all leather straps and brass-bound corners, on to a narrow luggage rack. Staring up at the light dangling from the ceiling, she could see the vessel superimposed on it. But, so far from being translucent, its sides were smeared and darkened with a filthy residue. The phrases at which Tony had laughed so heartily and at which Mabel had smirked with so much pleasure, stuck there, slimy and malodorous, and no effort of hers availed to dislodge them. THE FUTURE IS ALSO IN THE PAST, IT IS NOT WHOLLY CONTAINED IN THE PRESENT. Tears of exasperation and exhaustion formed at the corners of her eyes as she repeated the incantation. Then, when it failed in that form, she tried it in the other. THE FUTURE IS ALSO IN THE PRESENT, IT IS NOT WHOLLY CONTAINED IN THE PAST. Which was right, oh, which was right? The Master had no telephone. She would have to go round to see him to enquire.

Oh, but she was not like that, no, she was *not*. Perhaps she did sometimes speak harshly to Nigel and perhaps she did sometimes order him around. But she was devoted to him, everyone knew that. He was the only person who had ever really counted in her life for years and years. Except, of course, for that poor dear little child. Nigel had never complained or criticized — after all, he was a free agent, they weren't married to each other, and had he wanted to, he could have walked out, just like that. So if he hadn't complained or criticized, what right had She to do so?

But the ingratitude of it! And so underhand! There She was, eating their food (and whatever She said to the contrary, it was good, wholesome food) and turning to them in every trouble (She was the kind of person who was never out of trouble, of one kind or another) and even, more than once, borrowing money from them (it was always easy to earn Her kind of reputation for generosity, if usually one was being generous with money not one's own); and then all the time secretly She was watching them and despising them and laughing at them behind their backs and noting down everything for later use.

She called herself a novelist and novelists were supposed to *invent*, weren't they? But the trouble with Her was that She had no invention. Everything She wrote had really happened at some time or other to someone or other. That was not what *real* novelists did. Real novelists used their imaginations.

Oh, it was a bitter day when Nigel had first met Her at Oxford all those years ago. She'd seen at once the kind of person She was, but Nigel wouldn't listen to her. Infatuated, that was it. And She was, even then, sleeping around. Nigel refused to believe it but of course She was. She'd always been something of a nymphomaniac, mad about men. There was that Pakistani at Balliol. He'd never have given Her that opal ring (October was her month) if he hadn't got something in return. You could bet your life on that! And so it had gone on, man after man, until even Nigel had had to admit that he wasn't the only pebble on that beach.

And how patient they'd both been about that awful Hungarian of Hers! If she herself hadn't had a word with the manager and so got him that job in that Knightsbridge shop, where would he be now? Oh no, it was she, not Hazel, who had got him started. What a fool She'd made of herself over him, a man almost young enough to be Her son! You'd think She'd want to forget about it, instead of now spilling the beans to the world at large. But that's what She was like. An exhibitionist, a regular little exhibitionist. She'd always remember that afternoon at Kew, when in the middle of the hothouse, with people all around them (children too!)

63

they'd suddenly started smooching in the most blatant and revolting manner. Couldn't wait. Lips glued together. His hands all over Her. Just like a dog with a bitch on heat . . .

Again she raised the vessel; again she struggled, lips clenched and eyes screwed tight, to tip it forward. Oh, how, how could the universal odic force well up within it (she strained to hear the Master's voice, faint and far-off, retreating, from somewhere beyond the lightshade but could not catch the words) if it was crammed and clogged with all this *filth*?

A knock at the door.

Another knock.

A stifled giggle.

Oh God! Those two must be wanting their supper.

'Yes!'

Koula's head appeared around the door.

'Are you still unwell?'

'No, I'm not unwell. Thinking. Just thinking.' Martha continued to stare up at the ceiling.

'Thinking?' Koula edged into the room and Soula followed.

'Yes, thinking. A process that may be strange to you.' She gave a dry, bitter laugh. 'I suppose you're hungry.'

'It's gone seven, Miss Kingsley.'

'We are to be at the cinema at ten past eight.'

'Oh, heavens!' Martha sat up on the bed, a hand to her forehead. 'Well, I suppose I'd better attend to you.'

'We can get something for ourselves. If you prefer.'

'You'll only burn the pan. Like you did the last time you had that idea.'

'No, no. We are careful! This time we are careful!'

Martha hesitated; then sank back on the pillow. 'Very well,' she half-sighed, half-groaned. 'Macaroni, a tin of macaroni. And the rest of the milk-pudding from the lunch. In the fridge. And there should be a tomato or two. And cheese. And – oh – anything else you find.'

She closed her eyes.

Soula and Koula scampered down the stairs.

Soula turned: 'Sh!'

Koula responded: 'Sh!' slim finger to lip.

On tiptoe and in slow motion they negotiated the last three or four steps and then scurried into the kitchen.

Koula pulled open the refrigerator door and removed four eggs. One fell out of her grasp and smashed on the floor. Soula mopped it up with the oven-cloth, which she then put to soak in the sink.

Meanwhile Koula was routing out tomatoes, potatoes, garlic, olive oil (precious in Martha's eyes, to be used only for constipation), pepper, salt.

Soul's eyes lit on a tin of tongue. She snatched it from the shelf.

Koula's eyes lit on a tin of mangoes. She snatched it too.

The frying-pan sizzled on flaring gas.

Soula's eyes lit on a tin of tongue. She snatched it from the fingers turning round the tins so that she could read the labels on them.

Koula sniffed and wiped mascara off on the back of a hand as she stripped the skin off an onion.

Upstairs Martha also sniffed. And sniffed again.

Oh God! Those two little sluts! Something was burning! Heavily, like a whale emerging from the cold dimnesses of ocean, she struggled into an upright position. 'Koula! Soula!'

Neither of them answered.

'Soula! Koula!'

She sank back on to the pillow.

Oh, what was the use!

20

Minette sat huddled, lost in the depths of a voluminous fur coat that had a stiff, high collar and wide turned-back sleeves, on a spindly gilt Empire chair at the back of her Church Street shop. There was steam on the windows and the one customer, an elderly

American tourist in search of Bohemian glass, had beads of sweat above her wide, thin upper lip.

Minette gulped from a mug of tea she clasped in both mittened hands. She shivered.

'The fug in here!'

Martha had pushed open the door and left it ajar.

'Oh, do close the door! I'm perishing from this cold.' Putting down the mug, Minette hugged herself and stamped tiny feet in green suede bootees that sprouted fox-coloured fur at their tops.

'It's not *cold* dear. Invigorating.'

But it was not the freshness of the sunlit winter morning but the fact that she had taken a decision and begun to act on it that had invigorated Martha.

'There's a small hair-crack here,' the American woman pronounced, holding out a goblet for inspection.

'Yes, there's a small hair-crack,' Minette agreed in her metallic French accent.

'Then would you – ?'

'The price takes account of the crack.' To Martha: 'Sit down.'

'I'll think about it. Last week at Christie's there was this quite beautiful glass, with a picture of Alexander the First – '

But Minette was not interested. 'You'll have a cup of coffee?' she said to Martha.

Martha shook her head. She tried to avoid drinking coffee, ever since a doctor had told her that it was bad for her migraines.

'Thank you,' the American woman said, going out.

Minette ignored her.

The friendship between the diminutive middle-aged Frenchwoman and Martha, two people so different in every way, puzzled and exasperated their separate sets of friends, who were always asking each other 'What *can* she see in her?' What, in fact, Minette saw in Martha was the stability that her own capricious, erratic life had always lacked; what Martha saw in Minette was the romance for which she had never had either the physical attributes or the moral courage.

'*Ces Americains!*' Minette exclaimed contemptuously, edging the goblet back into its correct position on its shelf. Nonetheless it was from '*ces Americains*', the majority of whom were less obser-

66

vant about hair-cracks, that she made most of her money. 'You look tired,' she said. 'Pale.'

'I've not slept well. Something's been on my mind.'

Minette raised pencilled eyebrows in interrogation. 'Those girls?' (In fact, Minette rather liked those girls.)

'Oh, they're always giving trouble of some kind or another. But I'm used to them.'

Martha, who had sunk on to a Victorian chaise-longue, its velvet sheeted in polythene, now stooped and withdrew a wad of papers out of her green canvas shopping bag. She had laboriously copied certain passages from *To Laugh, To Cry*, before allowing Nigel to take the book with him to Oxford.

'No. It's *this*.'

Minette, too vain to wear her glasses except when it was absolutely essential, peered, her triangular face lowered close to the sheets. 'What is it?'

'Hazel's latest. I've copied the worst bits to show you. You were right to warn me against her. You never trusted her, did you?'

Minette, whose moods and attitudes tended to be simulacra of those of the people in whose company she found herself — this was the key to her general popularity — only did not trust Hazel when she was with Martha. At other times she approved of her and even liked her.

She shrugged. 'What is it about?'

'*Us*!'

'Us?'

'Not you. Fortunately for you. But me. And Nigel. And all sorts of other real people — like that ghastly Miklos creature and that girl of his — that Canadian who was once my lodger and who took him away from Hazel — and, oh, those two pansies who live down her road . . .'

'Adrian and Eardley?'

Martha nodded.

Minette knew them: they bought antiques from her and she from them.

'Then it's not a novel?' Minette said.

'It's *supposed* to be. But of course it isn't. It's just a — just a slice

67

of her own autobiography. It's so utterly *treacherous*.' She scrabbled among the pages. The references were already indelibly marked, in livid scar-tissue, on her mind. 'For example,' she said. She held out a sheet, thumb on the passage; the polythene crackled beneath her thighs. 'Read this.'

'Just one moment.'

Reluctantly Minette put down her mug of coffee and got up to find her glasses.

'Behind you! On the commode!' Impatience gave Martha's voice a peremptory edge. *'Behind* you!'

Minette put on the glasses. Thick-framed and studded with rhinestones, they seemed far too heavy for the bridge of the fragile, beaky nose on which they rested halfway down. She began to read: slowly, lips moving slightly, because though so fluent in speaking English, she still had difficulty with the written word.

'Isn't it *monstrous?*' Martha prompted.

Minette had read only a sentence. But she nodded.

'Even if it were true, it's such bad taste — such bad manners. You don't eat meals at someone's house and then write like that about the food.'

Minette had eaten some memorably revolting meals at the Kingsley table, but she had only talked of them to others, never written of them. Again she nodded.

'Then there's this.' Martha snatched that sheet from Minette, while she was still stumbling over a phrase about 'dehydrated mashed potato served up with many of the granules still dehydrated', and again her hand pawed the leaves. Page 23. She thrust it out.

'I know I suffer from superfluous hair. And it's got far worse since the change. But it's so *cruel* to remark on it.'

Minette screwed up her eyes to read again.

'Cruel,' Martha repeated, a murmur of true agony, as she gazed intently at her friend.

Minette looked up bewildered. 'But this — this is about a man. No?'

'Yes, yes, of course. Don't you see? That's what so diabolical of her. But she means it for me, of course she does. Why else should she write of his "wispy moustache"? It is "wispy", isn't it? In the

68

book I mean. That *is* the adjective she uses?' But Martha knew that it was. That piece of scar-tissue had also already formed irremovably.

'I can't see how a *man* —'

'Oh, don't be silly, Minette! And the wife in the book — the wife, this Nanette woman — well, that's Nigel. A nice way to pay *him* back, after all he's done for her. But that's what she's like. Treacherous. Completely treacherous.'

Minette, who was unliterary, even ill-educated — her writing, backward-sloping and all extravagant loops and swirls, was that of a showy child — was nonetheless gifted with common sense. Had she not been, she would not have been able to make enough of a living from her shop to send her son to St Paul's. 'But, Martha, I do think. . . . If it's a man and if he has a *wife*. . . .'

Yet, as she spoke, her own personality seemed to dissolve — a sandcastle first eroded and then swept flat by the rising tide — at the onslaught of Martha's. Within five minutes she, too, was flushed and trembling with indignation.

'*Mais c'est vraiment exécrable!* This woman! And she says she is your friend. *Ah non!*'

'Well, she says she's *your* friend too. But you should hear some of the remarks she makes about you behind your back. You remember when you bought those sixteenth-century miniatures?'

'The stolen ones?'

Martha nodded. 'The ones from that house in Gordon Place. Well, she more or less said outright that you were far too shrewd and experienced not to have known that they were stolen.'

'She said that!'

Minette, the insecurities of whose earlier years had given her a perpetual sense of hidden enemies lurking in ambush all around her, was appalled.

Martha nodded.

'*Ah non!*'

'I didn't want to tell you before. I knew how upset it would make you. But now you see the kind of person she is. *Poisonous!*'

Minette found herself unable to read on, though Martha was again thrusting another of the scrawled pages at her.

'What will you do?'

69

'The book must be stopped.'

'But is that possible?'

'Of course it's possible. I know in France – and even in America – writers and journalists can get away with writing any kind of lying filth they like about real people. But in England the law is strict. As it ought to be. We have this feeling about privacy, it's a peculiarly English thing. Two of our closest friends – you've not met them, they live near Oxford, he's a *most* distinguished scholar – agree with me *utterly* – a hundred per cent. They say it's a scandal. They say I ought to sue.'

'Sue?'

'But of course I don't want to do that – unless I'm forced to do it. If she stops the book, once and for all, well, there's an end of the matter.'

'But how *can* you make her stop it?' Minette turned with an impatient gesture to a new customer, a large woman with a tiny hairless dog tucked under an arm, who had just swept into the shop. 'Yes?'

The woman said that she was looking for a silver toast rack – 'nothing too expensive' – as a wedding present for a niece.

Minette shook her head with an angry little toss. 'Nothing of that kind.'

'Nothing?'

'Nothing.'

The woman left the door open behind her as she waddled out.

'*Merde!*'

Minette half got up and put out a green-booted foot to kick the door shut.

'I must see Roddie. I must ask him for his advice. He'll know how I should set about it.'

'Yes, of course, my Roddie will know.'

Roddie, Minette's only child by an Englishman who had been killed at El Alamein, worked in a firm of solicitors in the Brompton Road. Martha had consulted him in the past about an uncooperative neighbour whose cat made a habit of urinating in the flower-beds, about a rate assessment with which she had not agreed and about some shirts, a Christmas present for Nigel,

70

which had failed to arrive from the mail-order firm in Scunthorpe, though paid for in advance.

'Roddie's so clever. Old Agar' – this was the Kingsley family solicitor – 'is hopeless about anything but wills and mortgages and trusts.'

'Yes, I am sure my Roddie would know what to do. And he knows so much about books.'

'That's exactly what I thought myself.'

'He's doing wonderfully well. It's a great relief to me. After all that trouble.'

For a while they continued to talk of Roddie, who had recently moved out of his mother's flat into a larger one with a smarter address that he shared with a friend; who had inherited a collection of English watercolours from an elderly client ('Roddie was so kind to her all those months when she was dying'); and who always looked so elegant and always managed to be so amusing and clever. In this ceremony, often celebrated by the two women, of praising the paragon, they forgot for a while the bitterness of their indignation.

When she finally got up to go (Minette had telephoned to make an appointment with Roddie for her, for that same afternoon) Martha was serene, even benign.

'Oh, Minette, you're always so *good* for me, I don't know why. Just the opposite of that dreadful creature. Whenever I'm with her I have this feeling of – of, well, *unease*. But with you . . .'

'What does Nigel think?' Minette asked as she went, shivering, with her fur coat pulled around her, to open the door for Martha.

'Nigel? Oh, he agrees with me, of course. Up to the hilt. A hundred per cent.'

Martha believed that. She usually believed what she wanted to believe.

21

'You're back! I didn't think you'd be back as early as this!' Martha was not pleased.

'Tony had to drive into Oxford for a meeting and so it seemed the most convenient thing for him to take me to the station at the same time.' Nigel rested a foot on the bottom stair and his suitcase on the foot.

'I've no lunch for you.'

'That doesn't matter. I can make do with a boiled egg and some toast.'

'I was going to open a tin of baked beans for myself. I haven't the time to cook.'

'Baked beans will be fine.' Mabel, when he had said goodbye to her, had been in the process of preparing Chicken Waterzooi.

'It's only a small tin. Curried.'

'Then, as I said, I'll make do with an egg.'

'You see, I'm in a hurry, I've got to dash out again.'

Nigel went upstairs and humped his suitcase on to his bed. He shivered and put out a hand to the oil-filled radiator. Martha had turned it off. He took out his things one by one from his case and began to arrange them, lingering over the whole operation in order not to have to descend to another confrontation.

'Nigel!'

'Yes?'

'Three and a half minutes?'

'Please.'

'Then it's ready.'

Heavily he trod the stairs, fingers blue as they slid down the banisters.

'You shouldn't have bothered.'

'No bother.' Martha was brisk, almost joyful. Perhaps, he thought with an exhilarating access of relief, she had forgotten all about The Book by now. She whacked the top of his egg with the spoon, then snatched the saucepan of sizzling beans off the cooker.

'How were Tony and Mabel?'

'Much as usual. Except . . .' He faltered.

'Except?'

'Something seems to have happened to Tony.'

'What do you mean?'

'I'm not sure.' He had realized it only now. He hesitated. 'A loss of nerve.'

'Loss of nerve?'

Years before Nigel, too, had suffered a similar loss of nerve and had never regained it. He could recognize the symptoms.

He shrugged.

Martha hurried on: 'I rather wish I'd gone with you. It's years since I saw them.'

'You saw them last February.'

'Well, months. They cheer me up.'

Nigel was astonished; he had never heard Martha say a good word for either of them before.

'Yes,' he agreed. 'Both of them can be – amusing.'

'Tony's always so sensible, that's what I like about him. And a good friend. He's the sort of person to whom one can turn in any trouble and know that one will get good, *disinterested* counsel.'

Energetically Martha mopped up the gravy from her beans with a piece of bread on the end of her fork.

She popped the saturated piece of bread into her mouth and rose.

'Put the things into the dishwasher when you've finished, there's a love.' It was seldom that she accorded him this privilege; it made him feel uneasy.

Nigel nodded. 'Aren't you going to eat anything else?'

'Haven't time.'

'Where are you going?'

'To see Roddie.'

'Roddie?'

'You *know* Roddie. Minette's Roddie.'

'Oh!'

'She's made an appointment for me. He had to fix me in during his lunch-hour. Sweet of him.'

He did not, as she expected, ask her why she was going to see

Roddie. Instead he went on doggedly excavating the already empty interior of the eggshell.

'It's about The Book.'

He did not answer, head still bowed and spoon scraping, scraping.

'If you're not prepared to do anything about it, I am!'

Still he did not look up.

'Tony agreed with me. One hundred per cent,' she said, pulling on her powder-blue overcoat. 'And I'll trouble you to go and get me the copy from your room. Nigel! You heard what I said! Move!'

22

Roddie, his feet up on the desk and his chair tilted so far back that it seemed to be in imminent danger of tipping over, lifted the edge of his sandwich and peered inside. He groaned:

'Not salt beef again!'

'I thought you liked salt beef,' Irene said, dragging open a filing cabinet.

'Sometimes. But not day after day after day.'

'There was ham. And cheese and tomato. And egg of course . . . Who was that old crow?'

'*Old crow!* That's no way to speak of one of my mother's oldest and dearest friends. That, Irene, was Miss Martha Kingsley. And I think that we're going to handle a libel action for her.'

'A *libel* action!'

'There's always got to be a first time. Hasn't there?'

Irene nodded. Her first time had recently been with one of the senior partners in the back of a Triumph 2000 in a layby near Guildford.

'Who's libelled her?' she asked.

'A woman – or should I say lady? – novelist. By name of Hazel Saunders.'

'I've read something by her. Or about her. I can't remember what. So what did she say then?'

'Well, among other things she said – or says – that Miss Kingsley looks like a dachshund.'

'A *what*?'

'A dachshund. Well, as you can see, that's a very grave thing to allege about anyone. And particularly about anyone as highly regarded and respectable as Miss Kingsley. So the book must be stopped.'

'Stopped?'

'That's what I said, Irene.'

'Is that possible?'

'You'd be surprised.'

23

In the wind-swept, empty foyer (as she speeded past, Hazel happened to glance in) the slightly hump-backed figure, trouser legs short enough to reveal thick grey woollen socks rumpled about the ankles, was poking a finger, as though to clear a blocked drain, into the recesses of a purse haggled over (how many years ago?) in the *souk* at Meknes. The girl at the guichet waited patiently, arms folded.

'Nigel!'

He turned and the recalcitrant coin jumped up and rolled towards her.

She stooped.

'Thanks.'

'The cinema – at this hour!'

'I was at a loose end. Nothing to do. And I wanted to see this –'

'But you couldn't! Everyone says it's absolute trash.'

When he was worried or unhappy – when, as he would put it,

things got him down – Nigel invariably adopted one of two courses. Either he produced a cold, streaming at the eyes and coughing and gasping into a catarrh-saturated handkerchief, or else he retreated to the cinema, often to sit through the whole performance twice or even three times over. Sometimes he availed himself of both these funk-holes simultaneously, spattering a darkened auditorium with sneezing-fit on sneezing-fit.

'But I like trash. The trashier the better. You know that.' He was edging away from her, as though from some invisible contagion. 'Front stalls, please.' He tapped two coins in front of the girl.

'Did you have a good weekend?'

'Weekend? Oh, yes.'

'Did Tony have any message for me?'

'Just – just – oh, he sent his love, of course.'

'I like the way you transport back and forth between us something that neither or us ever really feels.'

Nigel was now edging towards the entry, ticket in hand.

'Nigel! What's the matter?'

'Matter? Nothing.'

'Something's on your mind.'

'Why do you think that?'

'Because I know you. I know you, Nigel.'

Unhappily he stared at a scuffed once-pink rose on the carpet at his feet.

'Tell.'

He gave a small jerk of the head, like a horse refusing the bit.

'It's Martha,' Hazel said. Silence. 'Isn't it?'

The head nodded, a hand went to the door that led to the empty, darkened cinema.

'Is she still upset? . . . Nigel!'

Now at last he looked at her, the eyes sorrowful in their reproach, heavy with what might have almost been a weight of unshed tears. 'Very. I think I'd better warn you. She's – she's gone to see a lawyer. She's on the warpath.'

'A lawyer?'

Again the nod.

'But *why*?' (Of course she knew why.) '*Why?*'

76

'You know – The Book. She's determined – determined to get it stopped. She's on the warpath, I can tell you.'

'But she can't! Not now. There are only ten days to go. How *can* she?'

'I don't know.'

The outstretched hand pushed the door. (Out of the darkness an American woman's voice hurled: *'Get back to your fancy-woman then! Get back to her!'*)

'It's too late.'

(*'But honey, be reasonable. Don't you understand . . .?'*)

'Roddie. Minette's Roddie. She's gone to him.'

'Roddie! But he's more of a friend of Miklos than of Martha.'

'I don't know,' he repeated.

He slipped through the doors and was lost.

'Nigel! Just one moment!'

The doors swung back and forth and then juddered to a halt.

24

The robust contralto voice hooted 'Speed, bonnie boat' as the robust legs thumped down the stairs.

Startled on the threshold of the front door, Koula and Soula craned up.

'Hello, girls! Back already! We're going to have a joint this evening!' Martha announced in overflowing joy and love.

'A joint!'

'A joint!'

The girls gazed at each other as though they did not know what the word meant.

'Pork. A lovely leg. With crackling. C-R-A-C-K-L-I-N-G. You know crackling?'

'I do not know crackling.'

'Who is crackling?'

'You'll see. Delicious!'

Martha sailed past them into the kitchen. As they mounted the stairs, they could still hear the contralto voice hooting:

> *Speed* bonnie *boat,*
> Like a *bird* on the *wing* . . .

25

'I still think the Athenaeum would be more suitable,' Jerry said. His own club was the Travellers.

Erwin, whose club the Athenaeum was, replied: 'Do you? Do you really? The food there is always so – so *debilitating*.'

'But the Travellers – wouldn't that be a little too *flighty* for him?'

Nephew and uncle stared simultaneously at the neat grey head of their female editor of many years, as she pored over the typescript of a jumbo historical novel about the loves of Genghis Khan. Eileen's office, literally a landing in the narrow Georgian house with their offices on either side of it, represented the no-man's land across which the two men usually confronted each other.

'What do you think, Eileen?'

'Yes, give us the benefit of your invaluable advice, Eileen love.'

'Well, I must say, the only time I ate at the Athenaeum, the food *was* rather unexciting. On the other hand' – with Eileen there was always another hand – 'I wonder what a man like that would make of all those coloured waiters at the Travellers.'

'I don't see why they should worry him. Make him feel at home. He *is* from West Virginia, isn't he?' Erwin adjusted his bow-tie with small, nervous twitches, peering at his reflection in a tarnished mirror propped above the filing cabinet.

Jerry ran long-nailed fingers through long hair. 'Every American has heard about the Athenaeum. It has a cachet.'

'Well, I suppose Mary and I *could* put on a dinner for him at home,' Erwin said. 'But Wimbledon. ....'

'Well, for the matter of that, *we* could do something too in Blackheath. But the children ...'

They were about (nephew and uncle hoped) to sell the dwarf family publishing house of Barlow and Braintree to the American giant Thalberg McCorquodale. A week ago they had taken Lotte Thalberg to dinner at the Athenaeum and the week before that they had taken Herman Thalberg to dinner at the Travellers. It was now a question of where they were to take Monty McCorquodale.

'We're so nearly there,' Erwin sighed.

'It would be a shame if, at the last moment, we mucked things up.'

'How about a restaurant?' Eileen looked up to ask.

'Rules?'

'Walton's?'

'Chez Noel?'

'Chez Nico?'

'Chez Lui?'

'Chez Moi?'

'You get an awfully reasonable meal at the Swiss Food Centre,' Eileen interjected, to be contemptuously ignored.

'If only one of us belonged to the Beefsteak!' Erwin sighed again, wiping his eyeglass on a shirt-front that was grubby from the manuscripts that had leant against it.

'Yes, the Beefsteak!' Jerry agreed, excavating one nostril with the fastidious nail of a forefinger.

At that moment the seventeen-year-old youth with the unbroken voice to whom both partners referred, even in his presence, as 'our indispensable dogsbody', knocked on the door and rushed in before any of the trio had had time to tell him to do so. He waved a letter at them as though shooing away invisible wasps.

'Special delivery. By taxi. He wants you to sign for it.'

'Can't you sign?' Erwin hissed. 'Must you waste our time with these trivialities? It's probably only some unpublishable manuscript.'

79

'Hardly — if it's in an envelope as small as that,' Jerry yawned.

'Said it must be signed for by one or other of you. The partners, he said.'

'Who said?' Erwin demanded, drawing out a heavy gold pen from the recesses of his frayed velvet jacket.

'This bloke. S'pose he's the taxi-driver. On instruction, like.'

'Oh, give it to me!'

Jerry snatched both envelope and receipt, brandishing a biro heavily scored with the marks of his teeth.

'I'll sign!' Erwin cried out.

But Jerry had already done so.

'Let me open it!' Erwin then cried again.

But a stiletto-sharp nail was already ripping.

'God!'

'What is it?' Erwin asked.

Eileen rested the two-and-a-half stone of the typescript on her knees and looked across at Jerry. 'Bad news?'

'What a bloody bore!'

'It's not that printer, is it?' Erwin uncrossed his legs and began to rise.

'A final notice about the electricity?' Eileen surmised.

'This is just what we need! This is just what we need at a time like this!'

Briefly Jerry extended Roddie's letter; then he decided to read it aloud to them instead.'

'Gentlemen,' he began, in a voice that rumbled seismically deep in his narrow, pointed chest. (He was rather proud of that voice, having once been an amateur actor.) 'It has come to the attention of our client, Miss Martha Kingsley, that you are about to publish a novel that can only be regarded as a highly damaging and libellous attack on her reputation and character. I refer to . . .'

26

Hazel was one of Jerry's authors. In fact, all of the novelists on the Barlow and Braintree list – with the exception of an octogenarian friend of Erwin's who, year after year, pupped yet another vain attempt to repeat the worldwide success of a book published in 1921 – belonged to him. This did not mean, of course, that he always read their books – Eileen did that – but it did mean that it was he who took them out to lunch, countered their objections to their dust-jackets and blurbs and attempted to persuade them that advertising and parties never, of themselves, sold a single copy.

'Helen? I mean, Hazel?' Ever since he had read The Book (she was, after all, considered to be the brightest star in the dim firmament of the Barlow and Braintree fiction list and he had therefore felt himself obliged to do so) Jerry had been perpetually confusing the two names.

'Yes.'

'It's Jerry here, love. Jerry. Your devoted and admiring publisher. Remember?'

Hazel had the sensation that a lift in which she had been standing had all at once begun to hurtle downwards.

'Oh, Hello, Jerry.'

'Long time, no see. I've been so hellishly busy. Erwin was saying only the other day – we must all meet for a lunch. ... But look, love, something rather boring has happened. That's why I'm ringing.'

'Boring?'

'A bit of a drag, in fact. Yes. Does the name Martha Kingsley mean anything to you?'

'Martha Kingsley? Of course. She and her brother have been friends of mine for, oh, for years and years. You've met them.'

'Have I?'

'Yes. Don't you remember? At Covent Garden – *Cosi fan tutte*. I introduced you to each other.'

'She was wearing a Spanish shawl with a rose embroidered on it?'

'That's right.'

'Oh, Christ! *That* woman!'

'What's happened? What's the matter?'

'Well, as I say, love, it's all rather a bore. It seems that your friend – this Martha Kingsley – has decided that she's your Major –' he glanced down at the note on his blotter to remind himself – 'your Major Charles.'

Silence.

'Are you with me love?'

'Yes. Yes, I'm with you.'

'Has she raised the matter with you?'

'Yes.'

'And?'

'Well, the whole thing's absolutely absurd! How *can* she be a man?'

'That's what I said to Erwin.'

'I did my best to smoothe her ruffled feelings. I told her she was being, well, ridiculous. But the trouble is . . .' Her voice faded.

'Yes?'

'Well, she's a basically *stupid* woman. And obstinate.'

'I could see that when I met her.'

'She's been in touch with you?'

'Not she. Her solicitor.'

'Oh God!'

'Well, as I said, it's a bit of a bind. Isn't it? I mean, she hasn't a leg to stand on, but when you get one of these crackpots on your hands. . . . Well, you never know where it will end, do you? They can make the most godawful nuisance of themselves.'

'I suppose the best course would be simply to ignore her?'

'Ignore her? Oh, we couldn't do that, love. No, I think we'll have to send her a solicitor's letter in reply. All formal and official.'

'Is that necessary?'

'Yes, I know it *is* a fearful drag. But the thing is – Erwin and I have made an appointment with Alec Forbes for tomorrow at eleven. He's *the* libel man, you know.' (Until this new emergency, Jerry had always referred to another, older solicitor, Melvyn Kurtz as '*the* libel man'; but after Kurtz's account with Barlow and Braintree had remained unpaid for over a year, he had declined to continue to act for them.)

'Oh, it does seem a lot of fuss about nothing!'

'Better to be safe than sorry. The point is — we'd like you to come along.'

'I?'

'I think you'd better, love. You know the old cow. You can fill in the background for Alec better than us.'

'Oh, very well.'

'Yes, I know, it *is* a drag. A godawful bore in fact. But it'll be nice to see you. We might even have a bite together after it is over. How about that?'

'Thank you.'

'Then let me give you Alec's address. The firm is called Cobbold, Rosenberg, Tweedale, Forbes. Got it? No? Well, let me spell it out . . .'

27

Hazel had stayed in cheap hotels on the Continent that, stairs uncarpeted and paintwork murky, had entrances like this. Had she had any luggage with her, the elderly porter with the creaking boots and the silvery hair parted, as though by an incision, exactly down to the middle of his shiny forehead, would undoubtedly have expected her to carry it. She shivered as they mounted past one grass-green door after another.

Erwin sat, red-nosed and diminutive, at the end of a long conference table, with a wide, high window behind him that gave on to a wider and higher brick wall. He was frowning down at *The Times* crossword puzzle.

'Hazel!' He rose, one hand plucking at the end of his check bow-tie. 'What a nuisance all this is! As though one weren't busy enough already.'

'I'm sorry.'

'Sit down, dear girl.'

She sat. 'How are things?'

'Oh, worrying. Worrying.' He continued to gaze at the crossword for a few seconds with melancholy eyes; then he pushed it from him. 'Tiger,' he said.

'Tiger?'

'Tiggy. You remember Tiggy. It's a hair-ball. Or so the vet *says*. But he's getting on, as you know. Mary thinks it might be — something worse.'

'Oh. I'm sorry.'

He sighed. 'Well, we're none of us getting any younger, I suppose.'

'Is Jerry not here yet?'

He shook his head. 'Always late. *You* know that, I'm sure. Fortunately Alec has the reputation for being always late as well.... Yes, this is all a dreadful nuisance. Silly woman!'

'I still think our best course would be completely to ignore her.'

He drew in his lips. 'No.' He did not elaborate.

The door opened.

'Hello. Helen — uh, I mean Hazel love! ... Erwin ... Sorry to be late ...' After he had breathlessly kissed her, first on one cheek and then on the other, Jerry wriggled round to spin his brief-case across the table. 'It's one of the kids,' he explained. 'We think the little bastard may have caught mumps.'

'Oh, lord!' Erwin backed. 'I've never *had* mumps. And one's always told ...'

'Well, *I'm* not contagious ... Alec not ready for us?'

'Got a client. Or so he'd have us believe.'

'I'm afraid this is all rather a drag ... Sit down, love, why don't you? You'll make us all feel restless.'

Hazel sat again; but she had to rise a moment later when the porter returned.

Alec Forbes's hands were bright red in contrast to the pallor of the rest of his rambling body; when she held one in hers, she could feel the sweat warm and sticky on its palm. A middle-aged baby, with teeth that seemed to have become prominent from too long and too persistent a sucking at the teat, and wispy blond hair, he flapped in the direction of the chairs ranged round an enormous desk piled high with files and papers.

When they had settled themselves, Erwin cleared his throat. As he did so Jerry asked:

'Shall I put you in the picture?'

'If you would.'

But it was Erwin who began. 'I have here' – he was fumbling in his brief-case – 'another copy of the – er – work in dispute. You have, of course, already had one sent to you. It was, I may say, read by Melvyn Kurtz, who – um – recommended that we should publish it *only* if we secured releases from two individuals on whom two of the – er – characters might have been thought to have been based. Which we managed to do – rather to our surprise.'

Without looking up, the lawyer continued to scribble on a pad. 'And who were these two people?'

'One was Mrs Saunders's former husband,' Jerry answered.

'And one was a – um – friend of hers. From Hungary,' Erwin added. 'Perhaps at this point' – frantically Erwin tugged with both hands at the bow-tie as though to dismember it – 'I should explain why we have come to you rather than gone back to Melvyn. We have of course – who hasn't? – the highest regard for him. But we did feel – in a situation as tricky as this – '

'With so much at stake – ' Jerry interpolated.

'Dealing with someone who is obviously not entirely in her right mind – '

'A paranoiac – '

'With a real nuisance potential – '

'Well, we felt we must go to the top. Right to the top.'

'I'm flattered.' The solicitor punched in a full stop, as though in an attempt to drive the point of his pencil through the pad. Then he looked up, not at either of the two men but at Hazel, to give her a little smirk.

At that, suddenly, inexplicably she felt safer. Adrift in a

shark-strewn sea, she had glimpsed — admittedly far off — a lifeboat bearing down on her.

Antiphonally nephew and uncle continued, as they put it, 'to fill in the picture', turning to Hazel or each other whenever they wished to have something confirmed or amplified. From time to time the lawyer would raise a red-palmed hand, like a policeman halting traffic, to interpolate some query.

'So that's it,' Jerry said at the end.

'That's about it,' Erwin said.

Both of them looked expectantly at the lawyer.

Forbes lowered the pencil he had been balancing between two spatulate forefingers. Again he smirked at Hazel, the smooth babyish face creasing into unexpected fissures.

'I've read the copy of the book you sent me last night. At a rush of course. And I must say — this woman's complaints seem to me *extremely* far-fetched.'

'Absolutely!'

'She's off her head!'

'I'm so glad you think that!'

'I knew you would!'

'Utterly far-fetched!'

'Preposterous!'

Again the lawyer raised a hand, crimson palm outwards, to halt uncle and nephew.

'I have never, in all my experience, heard of a woman claiming to be libelled in the guise of a man. Or, indeed, vice versa. Never. In fact' — he got up, went to the window and peered out at the same brick wall that, at a lower level, provided the only view from the conference room — 'when my literary clients have qualms about this or that possible danger of identification, my advice is always the same: change sex!' He turned and confronted them. 'But — let's face it — such people can be nuisances.'

'Certainly!'

'How right you are!'

'Let us therefore fire a whiff of grapeshot across her bows.' He returned to the desk, picked up Roddie's letter and scrutinized it with vague distaste. 'The name of this firm of solicitors is, I must confess, unknown to me. But that's neither here nor there

... The letter *seems* to be signed by one' – he peered, holding the letter up to the grey light filtering down from the window – 'Rodney ... Templeton, is it?'

'That's Roddie,' Hazel said.

'Roddie? You know him?'

'A little. His mother is – well – an acquaintance. She has an antique shop around the corner from where I live.'

'And he's acting for this – woman?'

Hazel nodded. 'The mother and she are bosom friends.'

'I see.'

'He's only twenty-five or six.'

Forbes considered. 'In that case, a telephone call might be in order. What do you say?'

'Excellent idea,' Jerry agreed.

'Splendid,' Erwin said.

'While our Miss Peabody is getting the number – or attempting to get it,' Forbes said, as he returned from the cell in which his secretary was incarcerated, 'let me switch on this little machine for you. It may amuse you to listen in to our conversation ... There!' He straightened himself, nostrils dilated from the effort of stooping down to flick on the switch. 'I always mean to have the switch moved. Absurd place for it. If one of these time-and-motion chaps were to work out how much energy I expend on just – '

'Your call, Mr. Forbes!' Miss Peabody's voice fluted from the loudspeaker.

'Ah, yes ... Yes ...' Forbes winked at them as he picked up the telephone, gripping it between shoulder and jutting chin until one hand had reached out for pencil and the other for pad. 'Hello ... hello ...'

Listening to the two voices, the one from the chair on her right and the other from the loudspeaker on her left, Hazel had the sensation that halves of two entirely separate conversations had been clumsily spliced together. Both were talking about the same subject, The Book; but neither seemed to be aware of what the other was saying.

'... frankly absurd ...'

'... grave exception to these unwarranted innuendoes ...'

'. . . would hardly wish to go into the witness box and invite Counsel to address her as Major Charles . . .'

'. . . if a novel is a work of invention, then by no stretch of the imagination could this publication qualify for . . .'

'. . . can only view with amusement the prospect of your client saying Yes, I'm stingy, Yes, I'm a bad cook, Yes, I'm a bore, and therefore this egregious character *must* be none other than . . .'

'. . . malice . . .'

'. . . vexatious . . .'

'. . . infringement of privacy . . .'

'. . . paranoid delusions . . .'

'. . . disloyalty . . .'

At first Roddie seemed to be holding his own; but as Forbes's voice swooped and soared more and more histrionically, one hand gesturing before his face when it was not using the pencil to slash in a series of geometrical patterns on the pad, Hazel realized, with mounting exhilaration, that into Roddie's voice there was seeping a note of anxiety, even defeat.

'. . . I shall wish to put this before my client and ask for further instructions.'

'Naturally, it would only be wise to do so.'

'She is, I may say, highly incensed. Highly incensed.'

'If she is, then I can only say that it is extremely silly of her. There are, after all, only the most tenuous of links between her and this — entirely fictional character. She knows Mrs Saunders, she has shared in many of her past experiences. Those two facts of themselves can hardly be said to establish identification.'

'With due respect there is more to it than that.'

'Precious little more, Mr Templeton. With due respect.'

All at once the two halves of the conversation had become congruent.

'As I have said, my client is highly incensed — '

'And as I have said — '

The end of the conversation resembled a series of volleys and half-volleys delivered by Forbes, which Rodney, scurrying hither and thither, had increasing difficulty in lobbing back over the net.

'I think that's the end of that,' Forbes said, blowing out his cheeks as he returned the receiver to its cradle.

Game, set and match.

'Splendid,' Erwin said, rising to his feet.

'You made mincemeat of him,' Jerry added, also leaping up.

'Would you mind . . .?' Forbes indicated the switch of the 'little machine'. Jerry stooped. 'Thank you.'

Erwin picked up his brief-case off the floor. 'Do you think . . .?' He held it to his pear-shaped torso with one hand, while the other caressed the end of his bow-tie.

'It looks as if . . .?' Jerry took up.

'I hope that we shall not be bothered any further. One never knows, of course. But I *hope*. It all depends on whether Mr Templeton can make his client see sense or not.'

'No one can ever persuade Martha to see sense if she decides she doesn't want to.'

But none of the three men was listening to Hazel. They had begun to discuss some mutual friend, apparently with the name of Bunty (male or female was not clear):

'That cruise was a great mistake.'

'Apparently it was at Yokohama that things really reached their nadir. I do mean *nadir,* don't I?'

'Yes, nadir is the only word to describe the simultaneous re-drafting of wills and cutting of wrists.'

'Such a messy business.'

'After the bingo session. Apparently.'

'It didn't make mama turn a hair, of course.'

'Of course.'

'The next morning she and that Liberian banker — who was once such a close buddy of Onassis — were buying kimono in Tokyo. Apparently.'

'So heartless.'

'But then she *is* heartless.'

The three men guffawed.

In the street, Jerry looked at his watch.

'God! I must dash. You know how impossible it is to get a seat at the Travellers, let alone a table, once it has passed the hour of one. And I'm supposed to be talking about his new novel to R. P.

Maxton. I haven't read it — which I mustn't, of course, let him know. Ah, there's a taxi!' He raised his briefcase aloft. 'During the journey I'll have to dust off the old superlatives.'

Erwin also looked at his watch. 'Is it past one? Hell! I'm going to be late for the dear old Bish. He's just announced that he has a new book for us — *The Big Guns of Faith* can you imagine? Superlatives for him too.'

'You'd better hop in with me,' Jerry said to his partner.

'That was just what I was about to suggest,' Erwin concurred.

'Hazel!'

'Love!'

Jerry grabbed one of her arms, Erwin the other. She thought that they were going to guide her up into the taxi but gently yet forcefully they were pushing her away from them.

'Lovely to have seen you.'

'I don't think we need worry for a moment longer.'

'Alec knows his stuff.'

'Thank God we went to him. Melvyn's such a defeatist.'

'Best man in the business. Better than Melvyn.'

'*Much* better than Melvyn.'

'We must have lunch together *soon*.'

'The three of us. Not in either of our dreary clubs but in some really exciting restaurant.'

'Inigo Jones.'

'Carrier's.'

'Bye, love.'

'Goodbye, Hazel, dear.'

In the pub it took Hazel some time to jostle her way through dark-suited lawyers to a ham sandwich and half-a-pint of lager.

28

Koula and Soula sat side by side on Koula's bed, their arms round each other. Koula sniffed, chewed on the end of her handkerchief and then used it to wipe the smear of a tear off the side of her nose.

'He won't wait for me,' Koula said.

Soula peered over her friend's shoulder at the letter – Greek characters now modestly cramped together and now blatantly self-assertive – that had caused their distress. The paper was pale-blue, soggy, faintly lined.

'You need not go for long,' Soula said. 'A week, two weeks.'

Koula shook her head. 'If I go, I'll never come back. Yes. I know that.'

'But why? Why?' Soula, however, knew it too.

'Because they did not wish me to come. I send them money – as you send money – but they would prefer me to be there to work on the farm.' Koula had, in fact, only once sent money, on her brother's twenty-first birthday; Soula was always intending to send money but never had. 'If they get me home, then . . .' She bit again on the handkerchief, the tears welling from her eyes and rolling down her cheeks. 'He will forget me,' she said.

'No, no,' Soula comforted. 'No, *koukla mou*. He loves you. How can he forget you?' But both knew that Ralph, the mortuary attendant with the full, fleshy lips beneath a luxuriant glossy black moustache, had already forgotten many other foreign nurses.

'He will forget me.'

Martha, on her way to see Minette and Rodney, rapped on the door at that moment, pushing it open before either of the girls had time to answer. She had come in to tell them that they would either have to get their own supper this evening or wait till her return; but when she saw them both sitting on that divan bed, bought second-hand as the result of a telephone call to an adver-

91

tiser in darkest North Kensington, she at once forgot her original intention.

'Oh, girls! Really! Not – not – *not* on that lovely Foamspring mattress. I've told you. Time and time again. You'll wreck the springs! Apart from dirtying the bedspread.'

It was only then that she noticed that Koula and perhaps even Soula had been crying.

'What's the matter?' she asked. 'What's happened?' Unimaginative but kind, she was slow to detect the misery of others; but once detected, it met with her immediate sympathy, consolation and advice.

'Nothing,' Koula said, sniffing again; but simultaneously Soula explained: 'Koula has had a letter from her elder brother. Their mother is ill.'

'Ill? Something serious?'

'She has a stone,' Soula said. 'Many stones. She must have an operation.'

Koula burst into passionate weeping; Martha rushed to her.

'There, there, darling! Stones are *nothing*. She may not even *need* that operation. I had stones once, the doctor said my gallbladder was absolutely choked with them. Dozens and dozens. But I stood out against an operation, I put myself on a regime of olive oil *every* day three times a day, and – hey presto! – they just melted away.'

Whenever any of her friends had an illness, it was Martha's practice to encourage them with stories of how she had suffered from exactly the same illness in a far more serious and painful form and, by a combination of will-power and self-doctoring, had overcome it.

'But I do not wish to go home! They say that I must go home and I do not wish to go home!'

'Then you shan't go home. But surely it's only for a short period? In no time at all your mother will be up and about again.'

'That is what I tell her,' Soula said. 'She will go for two, three, four weeks and then she will return.'

'It will be *forever!*'

These Cypriot girls gave way to hysteria so easily; but fortunately they recovered with no less ease. Martha gave a little snorting laugh, patting Koula's shoulder. 'Now, now. What's all this? I think you're making too much fuss altogether.'

She went on attempting to encourage the girl in the same brisk, no-nonsense manner; and the strange thing was that her encouragement, unlike Soula's, was soon effective.

'Look what a mess you've made of your make-up,' Martha said, getting to her feet a few minutes later, with a final reassuring tap. 'You've no idea what a sight you look, my dear.'

She said it good-naturedly and both the girls burst into squeals of laughter, which intensified when Koula rose to examine her face, shiny cheeks smeared with mascara, in the mirror on the dressing-table.

Martha explained about the supper. 'I have an interview – a very important interview – about something I don't honestly think I can discuss with you both now. And I simply can't postpone it. I don't know what's happened to Mr Kingsley but tell him I've left a little note for him on top of the bread-bin. If he's hungry, he can make himself a Marmite sandwich. Now what about you both? Do you want to get yourselves something or do you want to wait till I return?'

'We must go to the Town Hall.'

'There is a dance.'

'We are meeting Geoffrey.'

'And Ralph.'

The two girls were now radiant.

'Very well,' Martha said, though she would have preferred them to wait for her. 'Then I suggest that you warm up the macaroni cheese that you'll find in the fridge. And' – suddenly she felt generous, they were dear girls after all, for all their silliness – 'there's a tin of steak-and-kidney pie. I'll leave it out for you on the kitchen table.'

'You are very kind, Miss Kingsley.'

'You are very good to us, Miss Kingsley.'

For once, Soula and Koula meant it.

Hurrying down the hill, towards Minette's shop and the flat above it, Martha began to whistle to herself – 'Speed, bonny boat'. It was lucky that this was an evening when Roddie was having supper with his mother. Otherwise, he might have been

93

at Covent Garden or even, as he put it, slumming at the Coliseum or going to one of those parties in Earl's Court which, in the days when mother and son had lived together, had always made Minette so inexplicably nervy and unhappy.

Minette, of course, was possessive over Roddie; but that was understandable and one had to forgive it, because after all he was all that she had. Perhaps she herself (a rare flash of self-insight) was similarly possessive – though not, of course not to the same degree – over Nigel. That was always the danger for a lonely woman. Not that she was lonely, not really, not in the way that poor Minette was. She'd always filled her life to the brim, her cup had indeed run over. Whereas poor Minette . . .

When she had telephoned and said that she had just missed Roddie at the office and had been unable to get him at his home, Minette had been reluctant, yes, actually reluctant, to admit that he was, at that precise moment, already on his way over to her; and when she had admitted it at last, she had been even more reluctant to suggest that Martha should come across to have a word with him. After all, it *was* an emergency; one could not afford to lose any time. When in Minette's own life similar emergencies had risen – like that drunken, one-legged ex-naval officer from Ilfracombe – Martha herself had always pushed everything else aside in order to help in dealing with them. But Minette, dear and charming creature though she was, *was* selfish, one had to face the fact. Much take and little give . . .

Oh, poor little Koula! She was a sweet girl, there wasn't an atom of badness or meanness in her. But she was shallow, they were both of them shallow. It was anguished tears one moment and the next moment convulsions of giggles over something so childish that no other adult would even smile at it. Koula was as fond of that mother of hers as she could be fond of anyone. But the thought of a dance and a boyfriend was enough to put her out of her head. Well, she was probably far happier to be like that.

'We haven't quite finished our supper,' Minette greeted Martha, a crumb of Bresse Bleu cheese on one side of her pointed chin. 'But come in, dear! Come in! The room is just beginning to get warm.'

Martha began to pull off her coat and fur-lined gloves; the heat

94

was already assailing her like the sudden onset of one of those flushes from which she had suffered for so many — four, five? — years during the change. She searched for a coat-hanger or even a peg that was not already occupied beside the door in the cramped little hall; Minette had already left her, the door ajar into the living-room, where she could glimpse the firelight and the laden card-table set up beside it. Nigel called that living-room Minette's Aladdin's Cave. He liked it; but to Martha it seemed fussily, even vulgarly overcrowded.

Roddie half-rose at her entry, in one slim hand a Romary biscuit piled high with cheese. 'Hello, Martha. Take a pew. We'll be finished in a minute.' His mother was pouring some claret into his glass.

'Hello, Roddie. I hope you don't mind my coming to see you like this after office hours? But it *is* rather urgent — if we're going to get that book stopped in time.'

'Anything to oblige a friend,' Roddie said, popping what was left of the cheese-laden biscuit into his mouth.

As Martha seated herself in a Georgian tub-chair badly in need of re-upholstery, her stomach rumbled mournfully. If Minette ever called on her during a meal, she always asked her to take pot-luck. Many was the time when she had opened a tin of beans or sardines for her or boiled her an egg. But that was not Minette's way. She just never thought of such things.

'Roddie is telling me of this villa that he and some friends are thinking of renting in Marrakesh.' Minette spread another biscuit with a liberal amount of butter. 'He says that now Tangier is *out*. Only the dregs go there. Is that right, Roddie?'

Roddie nodded.

'Surely there are still some very nice people in Tangier?' Martha said, staring at the ruby glow of the wine in its goblet as the firelight flickered behind it. 'We have some very nice friends who've settled in Tangier.'

'He says that Tangier is full of the kind of people who are no longer acceptable in Athens or Torremolinos or Hammamet or even Brighton. But Marrakesh is something else. Isn't that so, Roddie?'

Again Roddie nodded.

95

'We are eating early because, instead of spending the whole evening with his poor old mother as he promised, he has to go on to a party. Can you imagine – a party that starts at ten or eleven? And in Limehouse!'

'Limehouse?' Martha was startled. 'I thought that that was where all the Chinese live.'

'If so, they're very smart Chinese these days,' Roddie answered. He let the wine he had just sipped rest on his tongue. 'I think this Nenin not at all bad. I don't know what you're complaining about.'

'I prefer the Villegeorge. And it's cheaper.'

Deep within Martha a subterranean express rumbled to its destination. She licked her lips, tongue scraping over tissue granular from the winter wind through which she had thrust her way. 'I wonder,' she said. 'To warm me up. Perhaps a glass . . .'

But Roddie's chair was snarling back. He wiped his mouth against the back of a hand on the little finger of which, weighting it down like some physical excrescence, he wore a huge jet intaglio ring. 'How about some coffee, Mumsie?' he asked.

Minette got to her stockinged feet, leaving her bootees to continue to snuggle beneath the table. 'Of course, darling.'

'Perhaps Martha could do with a cup?'

'Oh, no, Martha never drinks coffee – you know that, sweetie. It gives her one of her horrid migraines.'

While Minette was busy in the tiny little kitchen, among her copper pans and jars of spices and a jumble of old newspapers, empty cartons and half-empty bottles of rancid wine and medicines reduced to brackish syrup, Roddie stretched himself out in the least uncomfortable of the armchairs, in a position that mercifully shielded the blaze of the fire from Martha's already blazing cheeks. He took from his pocket a flat gold cigarette case, with a monogram not his own on it, and extracted an equally flat cigarette. Automatically he held it out. Martha shook her head: 'I don't.'

'Of course not, silly of me not to remember.'

'So what happened?' she demanded with sudden urgency.

He raised surprised eyebrows as his lighter, also gold and also bearing a monogram not his own, clicked open.

'I got your message,' Martha went on. 'But all those silly girls could tell me was that you wanted me to get in touch. They'd scribbled it on the back of a letter – a rather important letter, as a matter of fact – and they spelled touch, believe it or not, t-u-t-c-h.'

Roddie laughed.

'They're nitwits, absolute nitwits. But one can't help liking them. . . . So what was it? Have we got somewhere?'

Smoke spiralled down through Roddie's aristocratically long and thin nose. 'I had a chat on the telephone with Alec Forbes.'

'*Who?*'

'Alec Forbes. You've heard of him?'

Martha shook her head.

Minette entered, a tarnished Georgian silver tray, with two thimble-like coffee cups on it, borne in a shaky hand.

'Thanks, Mumsie. Smells divine.'

'Who? Who did you say? Roddie!'

Roddie sipped. 'I know him from yore,' he lied. 'He's always been rather good to me. He's one of the top men – *the* top man perhaps. A solicitor. He represents – the others.'

'The others? You mean that dreadful woman – ?'

'No, no. The firm. Barlow and Braintree – or Braintree and Barlow. Whatever it is.'

'Oh, I see . . . And what did he have to say?'

Roddie drew in his breath. 'It's pretty tricky,' he said. 'Libel actions *are* tricky. And as he said – the fact that it's a *man* . . .'

'But that man's *me*. It must be obvious to the meanest intelligence that it's me.'

'You see, it's not enough for *you* to say that it's you. Other people have got to say that it's you. And the portrait – if it is you – has to be shown to have held you up to ridicule and contempt.'

'Well, of course it has! Of course. I'm – I'm respected in this neighbourhood, respected in my work. There's even been talk about – about my work being – being recognized in some way. In the Birthday Honours. Or the New Year Honours. Well, if that kind of libellous picture of me is allowed to be disseminated . . .'

Wearily, Roddie closed his eyes. He thought with longing of

the Mercedes coupé in which Hans and Fiedl and Gerda had promised to fetch him, of the wide plate-glass window over the oily Thames, of the amusing talk and the amusing people and oh, none of this ghastly *shop* with this ghastly woman . . .

He made an effort: 'Quite, quite. But nonetheless it is *tricky*. Libel actions are the most tricky things there are. Any lawyer will tell you that.'

'Nigel saw *at once* that it was me. And so did these friends of ours. Responsible friends, friends of many years. He's a don, a highly distinguished Classics don. She used once to review for *Country Life*. Or the *Sketch* in the days that it existed. I can't remember which. So that's three people straight off who haven't an atom of doubt that that cruel, cruel picture is of *me*.'

Roddie again closed his eyes. 'Well, that's something.' he agreed.

'And you yourself must have seen. I mean, it's obvious, blatant. When Minette reads the book from cover to cover, it'll *horrify* her. By the way, you *have* still got the copy, haven't you? It's the only one at present. And I'm going to make jolly sure that it remains the only one,' she added grimly.

'Oh, yes. It's safely in the office.'

'Good. It wouldn't do to lose it.' Minette and Roddie were always mislaying things like railway tickets and spectacles and propelling pencils. 'I'm sure I won't be the only person to kick up a fuss. There are these two pansies with the antique shop – you know the pair. *They* won't care to have the whole world know they're pansies. And then that Canadian girl, Lydia – she's become Laura in the novel, as though that disguises her! You remember? *She* won't care to have her affair with that Hungarian described in all that squalid detail, now will she? And, oh, all kinds of other people, like that dear old soul in the Post Office, the one with the droopy cardigan, who is in that wretched book *to the life,* cardigan and all. That's not fiction, that's not what the great novelists did, did they? Dickens and Thackeray and George Eliot thought up their people!'

Minette huddled closer over the fire, wriggling her toes in their sheer grey stockings. '*Mais c'est vraiment scandaleux*, Roddie!'

'Roddie, you remember that girl, that Canadian girl, you *must* remember her? Don't you remember how she was my lodger and how that dreadful sex-obsessed Hungarian creature first met her when he was my lodger too – long before he and Hazel started their affair. And then she moved out – because it embarrassed her that Nigel and I should know *exactly* what was going on – and took this room in the house of that sister of Lord Wooler. And then Lord Wooler's sister asked her to leave because of all that was going on and the little slut then consulted you – on Hazel's advice – on the grounds that the old girl hadn't any right to evict her. And you – so clever as always – got a court order or something.'

Roddie nodded as each of these events was detailed in sequence, and Minette, staring into the fire, nodded in time with him.

'Well, it's all there. If you've read the book, you'll know that it's all there, hardly disguised at all. There's this Lydia, but of course, as I say, she's become Laura – or is it Linda? – and she's been made into an American instead of a Canadian. And Lord Wooler's sister is there to the life, complaining – quite rightly – that she can't have that kind of thing going on under her roof. And there's *you*, yes even you. It's all there, all of it.'

Roddie considered, his half-finished cup of coffee resting above the third button of his flowered silk waistcoat as he stared into the fire. Minette stared at him, waiting for her cue.

'Well, yes,' he said. 'Yes. There is that. Of course. Yes.'

'You must put all this to them!' Martha cried out. 'You mustn't knuckle under. *We* mustn't knuckle under.'

'I'm not knuckling under. Far from it. But there are certain forms of procedure . . .'

'Right. But let's get moving. We haven't any time to lose.'

Roddie smiled. 'I can hardly do anything *now*.'

'Not *now*. Don't be silly. But tomorrow. First thing tomorrow.'

Roddie nodded. 'Of course.'

Minette rattled a poker along the grate. 'If anyone can stop this book for you, Martha, my Roddie can.'

29

'It's the Pelham Mixture you like best, isn't it? Or would you prefer to try this Oolong I was brought by a professor from Hong Kong?'

'Anything. It doesn't matter, Arnold. Anything at all.'

'But of course it matters. You must have the tea you like.'

'Let's try the Oolong.' Hazel went to the kitchen window and looked over the tops of trees dishevelled by wind and rain. 'It can't be that final,' she said. 'It can't, I feel sure. How many people have you consulted?'

'Too many. Far too many. And having examined the entrails, all the soothsayers come up with the same prognosis. Bad.'

'But there must be *something* . . .'

'Nothing.' He smiled sideways at her, pouring the hot water into the teapot with an unfalteringly steady hand. 'So don't let's talk any more about it . . . Come.' He picked up the tray. 'Perhaps you'd be very sweet and bring the biscuits.'

Seated in the sitting-room, his small feet crossed before him and his small hands folded in his lap, while his cup of tea gathered a pallid film across its surface, he said: 'Now what is all this about your book?'

Hazel told him, from time to time nervously gulping tea or nibbling at an edge of her biscuit.

At the end, he shook his head and sighed: 'Oh dear.'

'It's a nuisance,' Hazel said. 'A worry. But I suppose that's the end of it. I'm sorry, of course, to lose her friendship – she *has* been good to me – and it's going to make things rather difficult with dear old Nigel.'

Again Arnold shook his head, making her feel suddenly panicky and cold. 'No, I'm afraid that I don't think that *is* the end of it. I never liked her, as you know – what little I saw of her. And I've never *really* taken to the brother either. A dangerous couple.'

'Dangerous!'

100

'The combination of weakness and stupidity is always bound to be dangerous. Isn't it?'

Hazel again raised the cup of highly scented tea; but it now made her feel nauseated merely to smell it. She sipped and sipped again and then swallowed with an effort.

'She'll get over it, I suppose.'

'I hope you're right. I hope so, Hazel.'

'But you don't think so?'

'No. I wish I did but I don't. Your book has infected her with an illness from which I doubt if she'll recover – any more than I'll recover from mine.'

'Then what am I to do?'

He shrugged. 'You'll have to fight her. Weak people are easy to fight. Stupid people aren't. She's the stupid one.'

There was cruelty in his clarity, for all the kindness with which he looked at her across the low table on which he had set down the tea.

'I hope you're wrong,' she said.

'I hope I am ... Poor Hazel.' The calm, steady gaze held her frightened one. 'You've never let me read this book. Why?'

'I've brought you a copy. It's in the hall, in my bag.'

'Your other books you've shown me in proof – even in type-script.'

'Yes.'

'Why didn't you show me this one?'

'Because – because I knew that you were unwell and I – I didn't want ...' But that was not it; she knew now, as she had not known before, that that was not it.

'Did you think I'd disapprove?'

'I don't know what I thought. You have this – this marvellous reticence. And it's – it's rather a self-indulgent book. Do you remember that someone once made a remark about Edna O'Brien washing her dirty knickers in public? Well, perhaps that's what I've done too. And you wouldn't approve of anything so – so – well, in such bad taste.'

He smiled, with that same gentle, wistful gaze across the table at her. 'You make me out to be such a prig when you say things like that.'

'Anyway you must read it now and tell me what you think. Probably you'll hate it. I don't know.'

'I don't think I'd hate anything you wrote. What you write is too much a part of the person I love for me to hate it.'

She said slowly: 'I think it's the best thing I've ever done. I *know* it is.'

'I look forward to reading it.'

Soon after that he began to flag, resting his head at an angle that seemed curiously uncomfortable, far back in his chair, and speaking in what was little more than a whisper between grey lips that hardly moved.

Hazel got up and said that she must go.

'Yes, I'm afraid that you must. A little now tires me a lot. But come again – soon. You will, won't you?'

'Don't get up. Please!'

But he was dragging himself up out of the chair, as though out of some invisible quagmire.

At the door she said: 'Oh, Arnold, this makes me feel so sad.' The unshed tears were heavy behind her eyes; her forehead throbbed with them.

He took one of her hands in fingers that were horribly dank. 'You mustn't feel sad. Please. It'll be quite a relief to cease living on borrowed time – and borrowed blood.'

On an impulse she was going to embrace him; but as though mysteriously forewarned, he suddenly withdrew from her with a jaunty wave of a hand and a brilliant smile.

As he vanished into his bedroom, he called out in a voice suddenly deep, loud and clear: 'Leave the book on the hall table, there's an angel. I'll read it as soon as I feel equal to it.'

She prepared to let herself out after complying with his instructions.

'Goodbye, Arnold!'

From the bedroom: '*Moriturus, te saluto.*'

30

From upstairs came the sound of desolate keening. Koula had received another letter, this time from her father instead of her brother.

'Where's that book?' Nigel asked.

'What book?' Martha's scissors snipped, as crisp as her voice. She leant back from the vase: 'Aren't these daffs a treat? One feels spring is really just around the corner now.'

'Hazel's book.'

'You know where it is. It's with Roddie. And as soon as he's finished with it, I want Beryl to have a look.' Beryl, who ran a shop for a variety of charities concerned with animals and children, looked, with her pert puppy-dog face and her little-girl manner, like an uneasy compromise between the two. Martha shuttled between her and Minette, now favouring the one and now the other as her 'special' friend.

'Beryl? Why should she want to read it?'

'I didn't say that she *wanted* to read it. Did I? I think she *ought* to read it. Which is another matter.'

'Ought to read it?'

'Ought to read it. Because Roddie says that, to stop the book, it's essential other people should recognize that that vile man is *me*. Oh, I've told you all this already. Do you take nothing in?'

'I want that book. I want it back. It's mine.'

'You'll have it back just as soon as I've finished with it. Anyway what do you want it for? To gloat?'

'Why should I gloat?'

'To see me held up to ridicule in that fashion.' Martha's lower lip began to tremble, making Nigel feel as if a chisel had suddenly been smashed deep into his forehead. He could not bear to see her cry; even as a boy, he had not been able to bear it. Soon her whole face would crumple up and disintegrate, the eyes shrinking to holes, the nose elongating itself and the chin seeming about to come away in flakes, as though fashioned from putty. 'How *could* you have let her write things like that without a word, a single word of protest, unless you took a secret pleasure in it? Yes! (He was about to demure, his mouth was gaping, fish-like.) 'Yes! Nothing you can say can ever, ever alter that. To have sided with *her* against me . . .'

'There was no question of taking sides . . . Anyway, I want the book back.'

'You'll have it back like I said — when we've done with it.'

He remembered the humiliation of when, in their childhood, she would appropriate his toys. Then, too, her overweening answer had always been the same; and then too he had given way to her, with the same cringing patience. The pattern was set; one did not break it now.

He shrugged. 'It's *my* book,' he muttered sulkily.

Martha jerked at a daffodil, as though she were extracting a tooth, the violence of the movement causing two other daffodils to hop across the table, spattering it with water. 'Damn!' She turned, daffodil in hand: 'Roddie says you'll have to sign something.'

'*Sign* something?'

She nodded and the daffodil in her hand nodded. 'What do they call it? An affidavit.'

'I'm signing nothing. You do as you please. But count me out. I don't want to get involved.'

'You're involved whether you like it or not.' (Their father, the sour-faced headmaster, was saying to them: 'You're in this together. One of you is quite as much responsible as the other.') 'It's nothing much. You just have to put your signature to some document or other.'

'I won't do it.'

'Roddie says you'll have to. It's essential apparently.'

'Essential for *what?*'

'Well, to get that filthy book stopped, of course. We have to have these sworn affidavits. From you. Minette. Beryl. Oh, yes, and from Mabel and Tony.'

'Mabel and Tony'll never sign.'

'Of course they will. Why shouldn't they? Tony was most

sympathetic to me on the phone. He agreed with me one hundred per cent.'

'You wait and see.'

'They're old friends. It's not a great deal to ask them to do for one after all these years.'

'Well, *I'm* not signing!'

Blandly Martha replaced the daffodil in the vase. 'You'll have to talk to Roddie about it,' she said.

31

Each day, for the past five weeks, Hazel had been going to her typewriter with a sense of relief and even joy. She was at work on a long short-story, a form so unfashionable that she doubted if she would ever see it published. But the fact that its ultimate destiny would probably be to end up in the guest-room chest-of-drawers, among the two unperformed and unperformable plays, the adolescent poems and the novel-abortions of the long, dry years of caring for the child and simultaneously precipitating and attempting to halt the erosion of her marriage, curiously in no way made her fashion it less meticulously or take less pleasure in that fashioning.

Today, however, as she placed a fresh sheet of paper in the typewriter and hammered out the number of the page, she experienced not that old sense of exultant celebration but a dragging fatigue. She forced herself on; but it was like pinching at an exhausted toothpaste tube.

Twelve o'clock.

Well, perhaps (she rose from the typewriter) it would be better to have an early lunch and then come back to the story later, when her mood might have changed. But at that moment a change of mood seemed as bleakly unlikely as a change of the weather that caused the laburnum tree outside her window to drip with a melancholy plop-plop-plop into the butt, moss-grown and beginning to rot, that collected rain-water which no one had ever used since Miklos, always vain about his appearance, had moved out and started to wash his long, silky blond hair in the washbasins of other, younger women.

She took two eggs from the refrigerator; but as she cracked the first of them, it was all too much bother. Perhaps she would, after all, go out for lunch, even though to eat out alone, a solitary middle-aged woman, was something she always found singularly cheerless, with the head waiter pushing her into the darkest and draughtiest corner of the restaurant and the wine waiter delaying to bring her her Martini until halfway through the meal and the other customers (or was this simply what her husband, Jan, used to call her 'writer's paranoia'?) eyeing her with amusement, lechery or contempt.

Well, she'd better face it. But she wouldn't go to a smart or expensive restaurant but to a pub or a snack-bar or perhaps even to Barker's Penthouse, where the female staff were always solicitous to another female and few males penetrated.

In the event, however, she found herself passing the Hamburger Haven and, remembering that she and Miklos would sometimes go there for a hurried lunch (thirtyish, he always gravitated to clothes, bars and restaurants favoured by the twentyish), she suddenly turned in on an impulse, even though she could see through the partially steamed-up plate-glass window that it was already crowded.

An attractive waitress, whose eyes looked myopically somnolent from the weight of mascara around them, smiled and said: 'Perhaps you could squeeze in over there?'

It was, indeed, a squeeze, past the chairs of a group of youthful businessmen, too eager to talk against each other to notice that she was trying to pass; and 'over there' was a table with two other women, mother and daughter, up from the country no doubt on a shopping spree, silently and even morosely making their way through double portions piled high with tomato ketchup.

The waitress handed her the menu: 'Perhaps you'd rather have sat with your friend: I forgot he was here.'

'My friend?'

106

'Isn't that him over there? It's a long time since you've been here — the two of you together, I mean.'

Hazel looked over to the corner to which she was pointing; but it was only by leaning forward (inadvertently her knee touched the bony knee of the pale girl busily munching lettuce opposite her no less busily munching mother) that she could see the two tables that had been put together and the people around them, their anoraks and coats thrown back untidily over their chairs and their elbows propping chins among a litter of coffee-cups and ashtrays. Yes, there he was, excitedly pointing with his pipe (an affectation of his English years) at a slim, blonde girl whose laugh sounded like silk being ripped apart. He had changed not at all. But why should that surprise her? It was only three — no, four — weeks since he had last dropped by.

'Yes, that's him. But I won't join him. He's with such a crowd. And they look as if they've finished.'

'Oh, they'll be here for an age yet. They always are. It makes the boss mad ... What shall I get for you?'

'Oh ... I don't know ... Ranch Style, I think. That's with an egg on top, isn't it?'

'Yep. That's what you always used to have.'

'You've got a terrific memory.'

'For some things.'

Yes, it was natural that the girl should remember, because it was natural that she should remember Miklos: most women and many men did. Whether they were attracted by him or not or whether they even liked him or not was irrelevant. They noticed him, they remembered him.

On each table there stood a revolving silver stand, each of its partitions containing a separate kind of sauce; and now, as Hazel leant forward again, to take another surreptitious glance at Miklos and his gang (yes, that was the right word for the people who anchored themselves around him, like brightly painted boats around a flashing buoy) another girl, beautiful, pallid and untidy, with a low bun of lifeless black hair, put out her hand to this stand, toyed with it momentarily and then sent it spinning like a roulette wheel.

There were shrieks; chairs shot back. The blonde girl put a

107

hand to her hair; the man next to her, prematurely bald, mopped at his scalp with a paper napkin; another man yelled 'Christ!' as he leapt to his feet. Miklos, his tie bleeding ketchup and a blob of it on his chin, threw back his head and roared with laughter.

Taking their cue from him, everyone else in the restaurant, previously revolted or disapproving, also began to laugh.

'You have never heard about centrifugal force,' Miklos shouted out. 'You are beautiful girl, very beautiful, but you are not very well educated.'

'Centri-*what?*' The girl was sucking barbecue sauce off a stiletto-sharp fingernail.

'Never mind!'

It was then, a paper napkin screwed up in one hand, that Miklos saw Hazel.

'Hazel!'

She waved across the restaurant, wishing that mother and daughter, each now scooping into identical ice-creams blanketed in steaming chocolate sauce, would not both fix her from under lowered lids.

Miklos hurried across.

'What are you doing here?' he demanded in delighted incredulity.

'Having lunch.'

He laughed, pulling at the fourth of the chairs at the table, twirling it round and then sitting on it with his arms crossed over its back and his thighs, wide apart in their narrow brown velvet trousers, gripping its seat. 'What luck!' he said. 'I knew today was a day for a surprise, because my horoscope said so.'

Mother and daughter now had identically pursed lips.

'Miklos!' the blonde girl called, shrill and nasal.

He flapped a hand at her in a dismissive gesture.

'What about your share of the bill? We're off.'

'Pay for me, Hilda, and I'll settle with you as soon as I get back to the office.'

'Am I keeping you from them?' Hazel asked.

Again he flapped a hand. 'I see them almost every day. Hilda and Jack – he's the one with the beard – both work with me.' He leant forward. 'But I rarely see you.'

'That's not my fault.'

He had the rare ability to focus one person alone in the brilliant beam of his attention and to exclude everyone else. It was exhilarating – until one became one of those excluded.

'*Ciao!*' Hilda touched his shoulder, a warningly proprietary gesture, as she passed the table.

'*Ciao!*' He did not even look around; the return of greeting was perfunctory.

'Bye, Miklos!'

'Same time, same place tomorrow!'

'See you, Miklos. Don't be too late back!'

'*Ciao!*' (Hilda again.)

Then they were gone.

'Oughtn't you to be getting back to the office?' She had said that so often to him in the past, with the afternoon sunshine filtering through the drawn blinds on to the huge Victorian brass double-bed, bought by the two of them together at an auction sale in Clapham; and langorously he would turn towards her, murmuring into her tangled hair 'Plenty of time. All the times in the world.' Employers would balance the advantages of his charm and creative originality against the disadvantages of his unreliability and unpunctuality, and would eventually decide that he must go, as the scales tipped down inexorably in the wrong direction.

'Plenty of time. All the times in the world.'

'Time, time,' she corrected. 'Why *will* you always use the plural? Your English would be perfect if only you'd take a little more care with it.' Her irritability was not for the recurrence of the mistake, however, but for the recurrence, in this totally different context, of a phrase she would always associate with that high bed and the feel and smell of him near her.

By now she was eating her hamburger and mercifully mother and daughter were gathering up the shopping bags piled around them. Miklos first glanced at the girl's face, her legs and her buttocks – how well Hazel knew that process of swift but systematic appraisal – and then, obviously dissatified, with that unsleeping curiosity that they both had in common, at the name on the bag in her right hand: HABITAT.

Eagerly he leant forward, his mouth only two or three inches away from Hazel's munching one.

'Did I tell you of this wonderful name that I thought of for the shop that I might open?'

'What shop?'

'Shabitat.'

'Shabitat?'

'Don't you get it? Shabby. Tat.' He laughed, tilting the chair backwards and forwards while the legs and back creaked dangerously.

'Yes, I get it. Hasn't it been used before?'

He shook his head. 'I thought of it. Yesterday in the bath I thought of it – when I wasn't thinking of you.'

'You never think of me – not for weeks and weeks on end. Come off it . . . Anyway – what is this shop?'

'I want to go back to antiques. Or junk – as you prefer to call it.'

'I don't regard anything as an antique unless it's at least a hundred and fifty years old. You know that. But why on earth should you want a shop? I thought you were doing so well in the travel business.'

'I am. I always do well. Don't I? But you know me – from time to time I feel a need for a *changement de décor*.'

'Oh yes, I know that all right.'

'So there's the possibility of these premises off Chelsea Green –'

'And the money?'

'The money?'

'For your rent. And for your stocks.'

'I have my savings.'

'They would hardly secure you a showroom near Chelsea Green and stock it with antiques – even your kind of antiques. Unless, of course, you've been even more successful lately than I had imagined.' It was curious that, though to others she had the reputation of being so encouraging, to him she always adopted this tone of almost contemptuous discouragement.

'And I'll take a partner.'

'Hilda?'

He threw back his head and laughed. 'No. Not Hilda. She has no money. The other one.'

'The blonde?'

He nodded. 'That one. She looks so young but she's a widow. She has lots and lots and lots of money.'

'A sleeping partner, in fact.'

She had meant it to be sour; but as he laughed again, she too found herself laughing.

'But yourself!' Again he leant forward. She had always hated this habit of his: it was difficult to talk into a face so close to one's own that one could not focus on the eyes. 'Tell me about yourself. The novel comes out in ten days?'

'*If* it comes out at all.'

'What do you mean?'

She began to tell him, soon pushing aside the half-eaten bun, soggy with juices from the meat, to lean her elbows on the table, her chin in her hands.

'God, that woman!' he exclaimed at one point; and later, 'I always told you, Hazel – she's no good, and he's no good either!'

'It's a worry,' she finished her account with a sigh. 'She can't *do* anything – or, at least, this lawyer says she can't. But you know what she's like. There was that endless dispute, months and months of it, almost years and years, over that neighbour's cat that came over the wall to pee. Until the cat died. You remember?'

He nodded. He remembered.

'And think how implacable she was to Lydia' – even now it was an effort to get out the name – 'demanding all that rent and going round to her new lodgings over and over again to see that she got what had been owing.' She gave a little shudder, even though the atmosphere in the crowded little restaurant, with the rain sheeting down outside, was uncomfortably muggy. 'I know there's nothing really to worry about but I *am* worried. With her you can never be certain.'

He considered, completely serious now. Then he said: 'The book *must* appear. It *must*, Hazel.'

She shrugged.

'It's the best thing you've ever done. It's a little masterpiece.

111

Yes!' he halted the protest she was on the point of making. 'I know you think I know nothing about English literature and very little about literature in general. But I can say "This is a little masterpiece" and know that it is right.'

'Oh, Miklos! How encouraging you always are! You're so good for me! Always!'

In the book, disguised as a Romanian instead of a Hungarian refugee, he was so often shown in a light that illuminated only his deficiencies: his selfishness over small things, his vanity, his unfaithfulness, his unreliability. But despite that he could nonetheless say with total sincerity: 'This is a little masterpiece.' It was in this magnanimity, not in his sexual attractiveness, that he was really exceptional. His moments of moral grandeur – there was no other word for it – might be intermittent; but at least he had them, whereas Martha, so much his moral superior in so many petty ways, never had and never would.

'Don't worry, Hazel. Whatever happens, the book *must* come out.'

'How good you are! How good!'

He shook his head, smiling down at the knife with which he had been fiddling.

Out in the rain, without either umbrella or coat, Miklos turned up the collar of his jacket in the doorway of the restaurant.

'Shall I see you home?'

'No, no. You'll get soaked. And you'll probably get sacked, too, for being late again. But' – she struggled to open her umbrella into the wind – 'come and see me, Miklos. Soon.'

'Of course.'

'And – thank you.'

On the way back, picking her way among the puddles and fighting to keep her umbrella aloft, she wondered why she had said No to that suggestion that he should see her home. Probably the walk would have ended on the high Victorian brass bed on which she had so often lain sleepless, wishing that he were there on it beside her. But she had rejected the opportunity; and his rain-spattered face had briefly shown, as he had scowled up the street away from her, his bruised vanity and chagrin.

But she had not wanted (suddenly, with a joyful shock of

112

self-congratulation she realized it) to set that kind of trivial end, however long awaited and however much desired, to an encounter that had (there was no other word for it) been so momentous. For a long time she had loved him and for a long time − perhaps forever? − she would go on loving him. But only today, in the crowded steamy restaurant, had the source of that love been fully revealed to her.

32

'This is really rather serious,' Erwin said, examining the second letter from Roddie.

Jerry peered over his shoulder. 'Yes, it's rather a bore.'

'It's worse than a bore. It could be a disaster. McCorquodale asked far too many questions about that wretched Mafia book. If he thinks there's another case like that in the offing, the deal will certainly be off.'

'Regardless of the rights and wrongs.'

'And regardless of whether we're advised that we're likely to win.'

'Which we have been.'

'And which we were over that wretched Mafia book.'

Erwin stared gloomily out of the window. Jerry stared gloomily at the cape, bought that day in the sales, that Eileen had proudly hung up on the peg beside her desk. Eileen stared gloomily at her typewriter.

Jerry shook himself.

'The character's a minor one,' he said.

'Extremely minor.'

'He could be changed. We might even be able to do it without a rebinding job.'

'It's a possibility.'

'He could be made more − sympathetic.'

'These references to his petty meannesses and snobberies could be toned down.'

'I think it's the best course.'

'Unless we withdrew the book altogether.'

'Which might be even better.'

'And easier.'

The two men grew suddenly cheerful. Jerry, hands in pocket, had left the window to stride up and down the narrow office, while Erwin, hands to his bow-tie, began to feel less pained by his contemplation of the grey-and-mauve flared cape.

Eileen looked up from her typewriter.

'You're going to have a job persuading Mrs Saunders,' she said.

'Ah – Hazel!' Erwin sighed.

'She's an obstinate bitch!' Jerry muttered.

Eileen looked from one to the other of them, glad that she had been able to rob them of their temporary joy.

'Yes, you're going to have a job there,' she said.

33

'Oh, it's awful. Just awful,' Nigel said. *'Do* withdraw the book.'

'Certainly not.'

'You don't *want* a lawsuit. You know you don't.'

He stood over Hazel, a shopping bag dangling from both hands, as she worked, in the faint spring sunshine, at a straggly herbaceous border.

'Of course I don't. But I'm not going to give in to that kind of blackmail. You know and I know – and *she* knows – that she hasn't a hope in hell of winning.'

'She might win. Roddie thinks it's a certainty. A lot of people have already agreed to give evidence for her.'

'A lot of people? Who do you mean? No one's *seen* the book apart from you. And Roddie, I suppose.'

'Beryl.'

'*Beryl!* But she's illiterate. She never reads anything but romantic novels. Whenever I see her, her idea of a literary talk is to ask me if I've read this or that work by some female of whom no one has ever heard. *Beryl!*' Angrily she rose to her feet. He backed away. 'And how did she get hold of a copy of the book?'

'Well — it was the one — of course, it was the one you — you gave to me.'

'I see! So not content with starting all this trouble by letting Martha get her hands on the copy, you're now allowing her to use that copy to kick up even more fuss.'

'What was I to do, Hazel?'

'Show some guts!'

'She *is* my sister.'

'You might have thought of that when you read the book in manuscript. And in proof.'

'I never thought . . . Oh, we've been into all this already. Do withdraw the book! Please!'

'No!'

'Oh dear.' He half-turned to go, shoulders hunched in his worn burberry, mouth sagging. Then he rotated slowly back to face her. 'She means business.'

'So do I.'

'And all of them are encouraging her.'

'All of them? All of whom?'

'Minette. Roddie. Beryl. Tony and Mabel.'

'Tony and Mabel?'

'They've never liked you, you know that. They're jealous of our friendship.'

'They've never liked Martha.'

'No. But that's the whole point.'

'The whole point?'

'They'd like to see you both destroy each other. Russia and China. That's what they'd like.'

Hazel felt a fury so intense that she could hardly see Nigel cowering before her, or the azalea bushes behind him, or the black-and-white cat that was watching them from the wall. 'Well, I must say! I must say! You're a fine crowd!'

'I'm on your side, Hazel. You know that. How could I be on any other side? But – in a way – I'm also on Martha's side. After all – she *is* my sister – and we *do* live together – and – and – if anything comes between us, well, it would kill her.'

She wanted to scream out 'Well let it kill her – and good riddance too!' But she controlled that impulse, surprising herself by the mocking calm with which she told him: 'The trouble with you, dear Nigel, is that you're always on everyone's side. It makes for – complications.'

'You could change the character,' he gabbled, staring down at the hands, purple with the cold March wind, that were clutching the strings of his shopping bag. 'Couldn't you? It would be easy. I could help you. You could make it into a totally different kind of person. The character's not that important, after all.'

'Yes, it *is* important, it's very important. And if you haven't realized that, then all your praise of the book was utterly meaningless. The Major has to be like that because he has to provide a contrast with the three main characters. With Miklos – and Lydia – and me. In many ways those three are far from admirable people. But the point about them is that they are *big*. Whereas the Major – Martha – she's small. Just how small I've realized only now.'

He nodded his head miserably; and of course, he had known all along that this was the point of the character, so that she was revealing nothing new to him.

'Well, I'd better go,' he said. 'Martha needs some of these things for lunch.'

'I don't want to quarrel,' Hazel said, suddenly relenting at the spectacle of his abjectness. 'I never want to quarrel with you, Nigel. If only . . .' She wanted to say 'if only you weren't so weak' but she checked herself.

'If only things could be different,' he finished for her with a sigh.

'Yes, if only that.'

'You know' – they were now at the side gate that gave on to the road from the garden and his hand fiddled with the latch – 'Martha's not a bad woman. Really she isn't.'

'I know that, Nigel. I know that well. After all, we've been

116

seeing each other two or three times a week for years and years and years.'

'She's not very imaginative. And she doesn't understand much about the creative process. But she's — she's really a decent sort. We all have our weaknesses, after all.'

'Yes, how true.' The irony of her tone seemed to be lost on him; and it was this apparent failure to feel this first shaft that impelled her to drive home an even more brutal one. 'You know, Nigel, you've always seemed to me to illustrate one of the saddest things in life.'

'And what is that, Hazel?'

'The cruelty of the kind.'

'The cruelty of the kind?'

'Yes. The terrible cruelty of people who are terribly kind. People like you.'

'Yes. Well.' His eyes fluttered from side to side, his head lowered. 'Well. Goodbye.' Slowly, as though still deliberating what she had said, he began to make his way up the hill, the shopping bag swinging as his arm swung. Then he ambled back.

'Hazel!'

'Yes?'

She had been examining a bush of berberis in the front garden, wondering if it had survived the winter.

He said nothing.

She straightened: 'Yes?' she repeated, her tone as razor-sharp as the March wind.

'I think you ought to know ... I may have to ... It may prove necessary ...'

'Yes?'

'Oh, nothing. Nothing really. Yes. Well. Well, I suppose I had better be on my way.'

'What are you trying to say?'

'Nothing really. Nothing.' He stared at her, his pale eyes watering in the wind and his tongue moving over chapped lips. 'Goodbye, Hazel.'

'Goodbye, Nigel.'

She already knew that he was saying goodbye to her for a long time.

34

Martha was floating in an empyrean of euphoria, her spirit a silvery balloon that mounted higher and higher with each day that passed. The approval and support of her friends were like intermittent shafts of sunshine that turned the balloon incandescent. An occasional jerk on its string – from Roddie, from Nigel – might halt its ascent for a moment but could not bring it lower.

For once she felt completely in control of every circumstance of her life and of everyone associated with her. She knew with total certainty – though she could not have said from where that certainty derived – that she would conquer Hazel and obliterate that malicious, lying novel. She was the tennis player who suddenly finds a form previously denied to him and knows that he can beat the champion; the bridge player who, miraculously, feels a calm confidence that every finesse, however risky, will go his way; the singer who is all at once undaunted by the prospect of bringing off an elaborate *fioritura* and, to his astonishment, realizes that he can not only bring it off but can bring down the house with it.

'It's in the bag,' she would say to all and sundry – for already the milkman and the little man who kept the greengrocer's shop around the corner and that nice Jamaican girl at the cleaners' had heard of the beastly way in which she had been ridiculed by that woman up the road who had *called* herself her friend. 'She's on the run,' she would add – even though it was Jerry and Erwin, not Hazel, who had started running.

Hearing her boom out from the bedroom next door '*Speed*, bonny boat, Like a *bird* on the *wing* . . .' Nigel would pull the bedclothes over his head and draw his knees up to his chin. 'Oh, gosh! Oh, golly!' he would moan. And then, in a curious regression to his days at prep school: 'Oh, fart, tits, knickers, bum!'

Though she was kinder to the girls than ever in the past, no longer nagging them about lights left on or the bath unscrubbed or powder on the carpet of their room, they both sensed with a

118

mixture of bewilderment and hurt that they had ceased to matter greatly in her life, pushed now from a position near its centre to one far out on the periphery. When she jollied them along these days, it was not as in the past; nor when she listened to Koula's agonized doubts about whether to obey her father and return to Cyprus or not and to Soula's angry complaints about a sadistic and sarcastic ward-sister. From habit she said what she was expected to say; but her mind, they knew, was really elsewhere, drifting far up above them in that blue heaven to which it had escaped.

Eventually, after tears and even an attack of hysterics, after an 'uncle' (in fact, a second cousin once removed) had deserted his restaurant in Bexhill to come and see her and there had been an almost inaudible telephone call from Cyprus and a number of letters in flimsy pale blue envelopes covered with stamps of small denominations, Koula decided that she would have to be a good daughter and go back home. There was a midnight farewell with Ralph, her mortuary attendant, on a bench in Holland Walk (no, not even now, when she would probably never see him again, would she consent to return with him to his digs in Willesden) when, stopping and starting for the late walkers of dogs and the occasional raincoated plain-clothes policeman, they fumbled their way to the only kind of satisfaction that she was prepared to procure for him. 'You're hard, real hard,' he said at the end, smoothing the long ends of his ginger moustache with his fore-fingers; at which she cried out passionately, so that a startled queen under a lamp-post bolted away: 'You do not understand! You *cannot* understand.'

Later she and Soula — Soula had been walking up and down outside the Commonwealth Institute, her nose pink with cold — wept on each other's shoulders in their room, among the wrapping-paper and the carrier-bags and the suitcases, and agreed that their friendship was more important than any man.

Martha called the taxi next morning and offered a battered hold-all, in fact the property of Nigel, to replace the paper bags and parcels, a couple of Kwells and a pot of home-made rhubarb-and-ginger jam — 'to cheer your mother up in hospital'. She was, she announced, going to accompany Koula to the air terminal.

119

Soula snivelled into a handkerchief ('Now come along dear –
you're not really helping poor little Koula by doing that, are
you') while Koula answered Martha's questions. Yes, probably
her father would be meeting her, but it might be her brother or
her uncle who had a shoe-shop in Nicosia or even a cousin. No,
she didn't think she'd forgotten anything, and yes, she had her
ticket and her passport. Of course, she would write, just as soon
as she had a moment.

Martha's sense of invincibility, more potent that morning than
ever before, swept the two girls, one now noisily distraught and
the other dumbly resigned, through all formalities. Somehow offi-
cials attended to them before people who had preceded them in
the queue; somehow a willing porter, young and handsome and
with a Glasgow accent, appeared out of nowhere to handle the
suitcases and the hold-all and the parcels and paper bags (not all
of them had been eliminated), while elderly women looked
around in despair for help. 'Now you've got your passport?'

Koula nodded. They were by the barrier that led to the bus.

'And you'll swallow these two little pills at half-past ten? That
should be half-an-hour before your departure.'

Koula nodded again.

'Where's Soula?'

'I do not know. Maybe she has gone to the toilet.'

'She was here a moment ago.'

Soula arrived, eyes still red, just as the queue was about to
move down to the bus.

'Goodbye, dear. Now remember to write to me just as soon as
you can. I shall be worrying about you.'

'I shall write tomorrow,' Koula said, really believing that she
would.

Martha embraced her in a sudden access of joyful tenderness.

'Dear Koula, Dear, dear Koula. What shall we do without you?
. . . *Bon voyage,* dear!'

'Madam,' said an American voice behind her, 'if you are not
getting on this bus, do you think that my wife and I might pass?'

'I'm not preventing you,' said Martha, moving aside.

Koula waved.

Then Martha saw Soula.

'Soula! Where *are* you going?'

'I am going with Koula. I have bought a ticket.'

'To *Cyprus?*'

'No, no,' she giggled hysterically. 'To Heathrow. I will be back to lunch.'

Soula waved, as Koula waved again.

'But you never said ... We could all have ...'

They had gone. She was talking to the back of two African heads, one surmounted by a panama hat with a mauve-and-green ribbon around it.

What strange girls! Quite dotty. No order, no discipline. Oh, well. That was that.

Jauntily she made her way back into the main hall and then, on an impulse, dashed into a phone booth just before an elderly holiday-maker on his way from Bootle to Torremolinos managed to enter it.

'Roddie?'

'No. I'll put you on to him. This is Tim.'

She had no idea who Tim might be. She waited.

'Hello.'

'Roddie?'

'Yes.' He sounded guarded.

'Martha here.'

'Who?'

'Martha. Martha Kingsley.' (Why did he always pretend not to recognize her voice?)

'Oh, Martha. Martha. Hello, Martha. What can I do for you?'

'I just rang up to check if there were any further developments.'

'Developments? No. I don't think so.'

'The affidavits?'

'We shan't need those unless we have to apply for an injunction. No point in doing anything about them yet a while.' He had told her all this the evening before.

'You've had no reply?'

'Reply? No, no reply. After all, our last letter only went off yesterday morning.' He had told her this too.

'Then there are no developments?' she said, reluctant to end

121

the conversation but not knowing how to prolong it further.

'No, no developments.'

'I might call in this afternoon. Just to see. In case anything has transpired.'

'Oh, I'm afraid I'll be out on a case.'

'All afternoon.'

'Yes, all afternoon. A divorce case. An extremely complicated one.'

'Then I'll drop by tomorrow.'

'Might still be out then.'

'Well, I'll chance it.'

'Well, goodbye, Martha. Nice of you to have called.'

'Goodbye.' But he had put down the telephone even before she had had time to get out the word.

She waltzed gaily round the holiday-maker on his way from Bootle to Torremolinos and then waltzed out through the swing-door.

'Taxi!' she called, although there was a long, disgruntled queue for taxis.

It caused her no surprise when, miraculously, a taxi drew up before her. The long queue glowered and muttered in her all-conquering wake.

35

In the no-man's land of Eileen's office — she was filing her nails, a practice that always put Erwin's teeth on edge but which he had failed to devise any tactful means of stopping — uncle and nephew all but collided, each on his separate way, oblivious of the other, to the massive filing cabinet.

'Whoops!'

'Sorry!'

'I've just been thinking, Jerry – perhaps it would be better if *you* were to give Hazel a ring.'

'I thought we agreed ... In fact, I thought that by now – '

'She's far fonder of you than of me.'

'I think you're probably right. But she *respects* you far more.'

'Do you really think so?'

'Definitely. No doubt about it.'

'Well, in that case – I suppose ...'

'Besides – you're so much more tactful than I can ever be.'

'Oh, I wouldn't say that.' But in fact it was something that Erwin often said when his nephew wasn't present. 'Oh, very well ... Eileen, dear – see if you can get Hazel on the phone for me.'

Hazel had to dash in from the garden, where she was still working on the rain-sodden herbaceous border, at the sound of persistent ringing.

'Blast!' There was a trail of muddy footsteps down the hall, swept only an hour or two previously by her char. She grabbed the receiver: 'Yes?'

'Hazel? Hazel dear?'

'Yes.'

'Is this a bad moment?'

'Oh, Erwin. No. I was just. In the garden. Must. Get my breath.'

'Sorry. It was just that I wanted to talk over one or two things with you. As you know, *if* we're going to do anything about the novel, we've got to do it soon. Almost at once in fact.'

'We're not going to withdraw it.'

'Well, I know how you feel, Hazel. And I have the – the utmost sympathy with you. But at the same time – we have to take whatever advice our legal counsellors give us. It would be foolish not to do so.'

'How can you possibly withdraw the book at this stage of things?'

'I agree it will be difficult. Costly. A nuisance for all concerned. But we've got – what? – another ten days in hand. That would just about allow us to contact all the booksellers – literary editors ...'

'Those reviewers will be delighted at suddenly having their

123

copy spiked and being obliged to read some other novel instead to make up space.'

'Well, yes, I know. But that's really only a minor consideration.'

'I really can't see why we have to give the matter another thought.'

'No. No, I see what you mean. But at the same time. Our legal advisers. The best legal brains we can get. What, in fact, we've arranged, Hazel — are you with me? — is for us all to have a little conference with Derek Maybury. You know, of course, who Derek Maybury is?'

'I've no idea at all.'

'Oh.' Erwin had also had no idea at all, until he had talked to Alec Forbes earlier that morning. 'Well. Surely you must have heard of him? He's the absolutely top libel man. The best of them all. The Nureyev, as it were, of the legal profession.'

'I thought you said that Alec What's-his-name was that?'

'Oh, Alec is a *solicitor,* dear. The tops in *his* field, of course! but a *solicitor.* Derek Maybury is a barrister — a silk.'

'Yes?'

The sharp, upward inflection made him realize that, oh dear, this was going to be even more difficult than he had feared. How shrewd — and how typical — of Jerry to flatter him into making the call.

'Well, *if* we had to go to court — *if* we had to — then Derek Maybury is the man we should want to brief to appear for us. We couldn't do better. So it would be an excellent idea to get his opinion now. Don't you agree?'

'I honestly can't see how — '

'Now be reasonable, Hazel. We've got an appointment with him at one-thirty in his chambers tomorrow. It's extremely good of him to see us at all, as it'll be a Friday, he's got a case on and he wants to fly over to Paris for the Rugby match.'

'What Rugby match?'

'*I* don't know. Does it matter?' Suddenly Erwin was fretful. 'Anyway — could you possibly meet us there — at his chambers — at about one-twenty?'

A pause. Then 'I suppose so.'

'Good. Good girl. And perhaps afterwards – we might have a bite together. There's this excellent restaurant – is it called Beano? – that's quite near at hand. Patronized by the legal profession in large numbers, I gather. We might all go on there for a bite, if you liked.'

'Thank you.'

'Then let me give you the address of the chambers. You know Lincoln's Inn?' There was relief in Erwin's voice.

When Hazel had taken down the address, scribbling it with a blunt pencil on the back of what, she later realized, was a cheque for a review, Erwin cleared his throat: 'Oh, Hazel.'

'Yes.'

'One other thing. I thought – Jerry and I thought – that in fairness we ought to remind you of clause number eight in your contract.'

'Clause number eight?'

'So few writers ever bother to read what a contract actually says. And even an agent as good as Ernie doesn't always draw attention to the – er – minutiae.'

'What *is* clause number eight? I've no idea.'

'It's the clause – standard in almost every writer's contract – about the Author hereby warranting that there's nothing obscene, scandalous, indecent, blasphemous, objectionable, libellous or defamatory in his work and agreeing to indemnify and keep the Publishers indemnified against any loss, injury or damage that is a consequence of a breach of the said warranty.' He took a deep breath, loosening his collar with a forefinger. 'Or words to that effect.' He pushed the contract form from which he had been reading away from him.

'Spell it out to me.'

'What do you mean?'

'Briefly, what you're trying to tell me is that if anyone is going to lose on this deal, it's got to be me?'

'Well. Yes. Yes. As our American cousins would say, that's how the cookie crumbles.'

'Charming!'

'It's in the contract.'

'Shit!'

125

'It's in every contract.'

'I've no doubt it is. You publishers can never lose.'

'Oh, we lose, we often lose. You should examine our books
. . . Anyway there it is, my dear. There it is. I thought – Jerry
and I both thought – '

'That in fairness. Yes, I've got it. Thanks a lot.'

'See you tomorrow then.'

Hazel banged down the receiver.

'How did she take it?'

'Well, not exactly with a smile and a song.'

'But she'll come tomorrow?'

'Hm. At least, I *think* so. She took the address.'

'The trouble with that woman' – it was from that moment that
Hazel ceased to be poor Hazel or even Hazel to either of them – 'is
that she's so bloody pig-headed.'

'You remember the trouble we had with her first book? You
told her and I told her and Eileen told her that it was far too long.
But she wouldn't cut it. And then all the reviewers said that it
was far too long.'

'And that awful lesbian scene in the second book.'

'God, how often we all said that it would make endless difficulties for the travellers in the North. But no, she wouldn't listen.'

'She has such a deceptively sweet and gentle manner.'

'Well, look how she clung on to that Romanian of hers when
the poor bastard was struggling to be rid of her.'

'Hungarian, actually . . . And how she refused to put away
that child.'

'And wrecked her marriage for her obstinacy.'

'Well, one thing she's *not* going to wreck is our deal with T.M.
That's for sure. You drew her attention to clause seven, I hope?'

'Clause eight, actually. Yes, I did.'

'Good. And you didn't, I hope, tell her that it was unlikely we
should ever be able to enforce it if she dug in her heels?'

'I'm not a total lunatic. She's always prided herself on her
honesty and integrity.' As he named them, the two qualities
might have been dirty words. 'They mean a lot to her.'

'Which means they could mean a lot to us?'

126

'Exactly.'
'I don't like it, for all that.'
'*I* don't like it. But it could be worse.'
'Could it?'

36

'What *is* it?' Martha asked. 'Is it a rat?'

Soula, who had been kneeling disconsolately by the cage when Martha had come in to tell her about the bath again not having been scrubbed out after she had used it, shook her head. 'No. It is called a jerbil.'

'A *what*?'

'A jerbil. That is what Sidney told me.'

'Sidney?'

'The new night porter. He breeds them. I bought it from him.'

Martha stared, as the revolting brown creature sniffed through its bars at Soula's pointed fingernail and then scuttled back into its nest. She gave a little shudder. 'What are you going to do with it?'

'Do with it? I shall feed it.'

'Not *here*!'

Soula raised huge, desperate eyes. 'You do not like?'

'No, I do *not* like – not at all. This room will be stinking in no time at all. It must be a kind of rat, of course it's a rat. And rats are known to be dirty and to spread diseases.'

'Sidney says it is very clean. It does not make water.'

'Of course it makes water. All rats make water. And other things too. No, I'm sorry, Soula dear, but I must insist –'

'*Please,* Miss Kingsley!'

'No, it's thoroughly unhygienic. In the room in which you sleep. Above the kitchen. Next to the linen cupboard. I'm sorry, dear, but I must insist –'

127

Soula suddenly began to shudder with convulsive weeping, gripping the bars of the cage and shaking her head from side to side so that her thick black hair swung back and forth. 'No, no, no!'

'Sh, dear! You'll disturb Mr Kingsley. He's hard at work upstairs. Soula! *Soula!* Stop that now! There's no need to get hysterical.'

The hair, a glistening curtain, swung faster and faster. The voice rose to a wail. Then it sank to disconnected sobs. Martha heard: 'Koula ... lonely ... no friend ... Koula ... kill myself ... lonely ... Koula ...'

Suddenly compassion pierced her like an arrow shot from an unseen bow. Martha almost doubled up with the sweet and unexpected agony of it.

'There, there,' she said. She bent down, then kneeled, almost keeled over, put a hand on the cage to recover her balance. 'Never mind. If it means *that* much to you, well, of course you can keep it. But remember, dear, that the straw must be cleaned out *every* day. We don't want damp straw making this room and then the whole house stink.'

'But it does not *make* water,' Soula wailed, but on a lower and less desperate note.

'Of course it makes water, dear. Don't be silly. Every living creature *has* to make water. That's a rule of nature.'

37

Just as, when she had to go to the dentist, Hazel's subconscious somehow contrived that she failed to notice that her watch had stopped, boarded the wrong bus or, taking what she told herself would be a short cut, managed to lose herself, so now a series of trivial disasters brought her, panting and dishevelled by a keen, blustery wind, more than a quarter of an hour late to the appointment in Lincoln's Inn.

'Ah, there she is!' Erwin hurried forward.

'Hazel! Love! We were giving you up for lost!' (They had, in fact, just decided that the silly cow must have changed her mind about coming to the conference at all.) Jerry took both her hands in his: 'What cold hands!'

'I'm terribly sorry. There was this stupid bus conductress who told me that I ought to get off . . .'

But they were not listening to her excuses.

'Never mind, never mind! Sir Derek hasn't arrived yet.'

'You know Alec, of course.'

'Yes, indeed.'

'I'm afraid that this is the worst possible time for a conference,' the solicitor said. 'But as you probably know, Sir Derek is on a case. Rather an important one. He's appearing for that Arab sheikh – no doubt you've read about it in the papers?'

Hazel nodded, growing conscious of the grey-faced men in grey suits ranged, some seated and some standing, around the room. Were they all here to proffer advice? And would she have to pay for all of them? She had been a fool not to ask the price of this consultation in advance.

'This is one of Sir Derek's juniors.' Forbes had taken her above the elbow with forefinger and thumb and was now gently but firmly turning her round.

This man did not have a grey face; and his suit, modishly cut with wide lapels and flaps to the jacket-pockets, was a shade of tobacco brown. He smiled, as Forbes said 'Mr Rossett', and then held out a hand surprisingly broad and strong for one so willowy.

Hazel took it.

'I was up most of last night with your book. Marking for Sir Derek what seemed to be the relevant passages.' Jewish, with a high colour on the cheekbones above a jaw that had a bluish sheen to it, he spoke with a slight lisp.

'Oh, dear. I'm sorry.'

'I enjoyed it.'

'*Isn't* it a good book?' Jerry said.

'Yes, isn't it?' Erwin took up. 'The old firm's proud to be publishing it.'

'If it ever gets published,' Hazel put in.

'Oh it must,' Rossett said.

At that moment there was a flurry of doors being opened and closed and feet running up and down the narrow staircase that had led to the waiting-room. A voice boomed, nasal and commanding: 'Put it down, somewhere! Put it *down!*' There was a heavy tread on the stairs, reverberant in the silence that had suddenly blanketed the whole room. The door opened.

'Gentlemen! Good morning! Or should I say — Good afternoon?' Smiles and even discreet laughter followed this query.

The man who had come in was tall and stout, with untidy grey hair that had tumbled — no doubt displaced by the high wind outside — across a narrow forehead covered with freckles. The same freckles stuck, like grains of sand, to the saddle of a low nose, the nostrils flared, and to the backs of chubby hands that were clutching a sheaf of papers across swelling embonpoint.

Introductions were hurriedly made by Forbes. Hazel came first.

'Ah, so this is our lady novelist!'

It was a term that she detested; but it was obvious, as he grinned — one eye-tooth, she noticed, was capped with gold — and gripped her hand in his, that no malice was intended.

'Well, let's get moving. Unfortunately we have little time for the social niceties.'

Someone opened a door for him into an inner room and he sailed in ahead of them, gown billowing, and made his way over to a huge, ramshackle desk. Some of the grey-faced men in grey suits brought up the rear. Hazel wondered, fleetingly, why the others had been present.

'Please sit! Make yourselves comfortable!' There was little comfort in the straight-backed chairs; Erwin pulled a small face at Jerry as he shifted in one. Maybury was busy looking at a foolscap sheet of notes which had been tucked between the pages of what, Hazel saw, was a copy of the novel.

Then he looked up, placed the tips of his tubby fingers together on the desk before him, and, leaning forward, proceeded to summarize the whole situation with astonishing lucidity. Hazel doubted if she could have done it better herself.

'Now have I got all the details right?' he asked at the end.

They all nodded, except Rossett, who cleared his throat and said: 'The rank is not Colonel Charles, I think, but Major Charles.'

Maybury glanced down at the foolscap sheet. 'Ah, yes. Yes. That's right.' He obviously had not cared to be corrected. 'I had to race through the book during the brief journey from Hayward's Heath to Victoria this morning. And I wasn't exactly helped by the garrulous old bore who wanted to talk about the weather and his rheumatism to me.'

There were more smiles and appreciative chuckles.

'Now, Mrs – it *is* Mrs isn't it? – Mrs Saunders . . . Yes . . .' He hesitated, like a butcher deliberating where to make the first incision in a carcase, while Hazel steeled herself. 'I hope you won't be embarrassed by these questions, will you? The object of them is, of course, to establish the degree to which your – ah – novel is based on actual facts. Now, to begin with, have you yourself got a child similar to that described in the book?'

'I had such a child. He died.'

'Drowned? In the book he's drowned, isn't he?'

'No. Not drowned.'

'So his death was not due, as in the novel, to the negligence of his mother and her – her lover?'

She licked her lips, wondering why the taste of them should be so strangely bitter. 'No. No, I don't think there was any negligence. He had this – this perforated appendix. He couldn't easily explain, you see, how he felt. If there was any negligence it was the doctor's. For failing to make the diagnosis.'

'And at that time, you were also living with a man?'

'That's right.'

'A Romanian?'

'A Hungarian, in fact.'

'And your husband had by then left for Australia?'

'No. In the book it's Australia. He left for Japan.'

'He's a physicist?'

'An architect.'

'This girl-friend of the – the lover.' He peered at the sheet. 'Laura. Was she based, like these other characters, on someone real?'

'Yes. I suppose you could say that. Remotely.'

'After the child's death, the lover goes off with this girl. Did something similar happen in your life too?'

They had all been looking at her; now no one was. Except for the grey-haired man with the freckles, a genial butcher leaning across his counter, his fingernails and fingertips slightly pink with blood.

'My lover left me, yes. For another woman.'

'Would you say that this woman in real life and this woman in your book would be easily identifiable?'

'No. No, I don't think so. No.' (She was lying. She could not say: 'I decided she'd never sue because she comes from a North Country family of Methodists and she would never want them to know of her having lived with a man, much less of having to have an abortion because of it.') He was staring closely at her. 'No,' she repeated, shaking her head.

'So, that brings us to this Colonel – sorry, Major – Charles. We must get that right, for Mr Rossett, mustn't we?' There were again smiles and even laughter. 'To what extent do you think that this friend of hers is right in claiming that she is this character?'

'She can hardly be a man.'

'No. That's true.' He spoke thoughtfully, as though this had occurred to him only now. 'But you see the difficulty, don't you? If a jury is told that A in a book is, to all intents and purposes, A in real life, and so are B, C, D and E, it's puzzling for them if they are then told that F in the same book is entirely a creation of the imagination.'

'Yes, I see that.'

She could hear Erwin heave a deep sigh; she could even see him, out of the corner of her eye, glancing at the sharp toe of his black glacé-kid shoe and then sucking in his lips.

'If only you hadn't set your novel in Kensington,' he said, staring down at the cover of the book.

'Does that make such a difference?'

'Of course. Since this woman – this Martha Kingsley – lives in Kensington. And is a neighbour and old friend of yours. . . . I gather that some of your mutual friends have already claimed to recognize her?'

'Because she has prevailed on them to do so.'

'They would hardly perjure themselves, would they?'

'No – perhaps not. But she put the idea into their minds. She's a very dominant personality.'

'Forceful,' Jerry echoed from a corner.

'She sounds just the kind of person who has the maximum nuisance value. Not enough to occupy her – looking for some crusade. Dangerous.'

There was a long silence, during which Hazel became conscious of the burning of her cheeks and eyes and of that strange bitter taste – as of the aloes that her mother, years and years ago, had put on her bitten fingernails – on her dry lips. She felt vaguely sick; she ought to have eaten something before she came out.

Maybury looked up again, the butcher now beaming across his counter at his favourite customer.

'May I ask you an impertinent but rather necessary question?'

'Certainly.'

'How much money have you got?'

'How much . . .?' She frowned, groping towards the question.

'It's always necessary to know that before one gives advice.'

Disjointedly, muddling the figures and going back to correct them, with none of his lucidity and none of his command, Hazel tried to answer. There was the house, she said; her husband had made it over to her when they were divorced but it was not freehold, only leasehold, with almost eleven years to run. Apart from that? Well, she had a small private income from some money left to her by her father – oh, about four hundred pounds a year – and she let the basement flat, furnished that was, for twenty pounds a week. People said she could get much more for it, perhaps she could. Then, oh yes, there was her income from her writing. Very little from her books (she caught Erwin and Jerry exchanging a glance). But she read for publishers and she did an occasional broadcast talk and the *New Statesman* and the *Literary Supplement* occasionally sent her books for review. The total from her literary earnings? Oh, about four or five hundred each year.

As he jotted down these figures, she realized how paltry and

133

pitiful they must seem to the people ranged around her, even to Erwin and Jerry.

He began to do a sum; and while she watched him, she noticed with surprise how his lips moved as he added one digit to another. 'Hm,' he said at the end, still staring down. Then he looked up at her and smiled, revealing that costly gold cap over his eye-tooth. 'The trouble is that you're not really rich enough.'

'What do you mean?'

'To put it brutally.' He looked round the assembled company and they all, of one accord, shifted in their seats and gave little sighs and smiled (this time no one laughed), not at each other or even at him, but straight ahead or down at their feet. 'You see, Mrs Saunders, if you were richer, well, you might not mind so much if you went down a few thousand. But in your present position . . .?' He sucked in his cheeks and his nostrils flared still more widely.

'You think I'll lose the case?'

'I didn't say that. No, I didn't say that. I think that we have the probability of winning it, in fact. People are literal-minded by and large, and that means that the average jury is literal-minded. If a middle-aged woman goes into the box and says "I'm Colonel — sorry, Major — Charles", they're likely to believe the evidence of their eyes and decide she's talking rubbish. Yes, we *could* win, we *should* win. And if we didn't win, there's a distinct possibility that she would be awarded derisive damages. A penny, say. But the trouble is — the costs.'

'The costs? But surely I'd be getting those back if I won?'

'Part of them. Only part of them. Let's say you had to pay out six thousand' — he saw her wince involuntarily and assured her: 'Yes, it could easily be as much as that, perhaps far more — and let us say that you won and were awarded your costs. Those costs would only be what we call *taxed* costs — a part, no more than a part, of your *actual* costs.'

'I don't understand what you mean by taxed costs.'

'I'm not surprised, it's very complicated. But briefly what happens is that, after the action, solicitors for both parties argue the merits of each item on the bill, and what we call the taxation

134

master rejects or reduces any items he considers unreasonable or excessive.'

Rossett cleared his throat, with a loose rattle of phlegm: 'The costs, for example, incurred by the plaintiff in deciding whether to bring the action or not are unlikely to be allowed.'

'Or' — Maybury gave a sly smile — 'the amount that the winning side can claim for a barrister's fee might well be reduced if they have chosen a more expensive barrister than was strictly necessary.'

'So if I had to pay out six thousand, what might I recover — if I won, that is?'

'Four thousand, four thousand five hundred.'

'But that's terribly unfair!'

'Yes, I'm afraid the law often *is* terribly unfair. You know what they say — the poor cannot afford to litigate and they cannot afford not to litigate.' He smiled: 'I am, of course, in this case using the word "poor" only in a comparative sense.'

'But I must go on if I feel I'm in the right.'

'That's the spirit that's lost a lot of people a lot of money.'

'So you think that I should chuck in the sponge?' Suddenly she was furious, not merely with him, smiling across the desk at her with that faint, not unkindly condescension, but with all of them, so knowing and so cynical and so obsequious and so lacking in any guts.

'I'm not saying that. But I think you should weigh the pros and cons very carefully. If an injunction is sought, then that'll hold up publication in any case. If an action is started, then the book will have to be withdrawn until it's been heard. Otherwise, if you didn't withdraw it and you subsequently lost the action, you would suffer punitive damages. The action might take eighteen months to come before the court. You might lose it, it's not impossible. You might win. It all might end in a draw. Whatever happens, you'll have to count on saying goodbye to *at least* fifteen hundred.'

'I could conduct my own case.'

'You could. But you know what they say — the man who represents himself has a fool for a client.'

'But why the hell should I give in if I *know* I'm in the right?'

135

'Because in balancing the two evils, you may decide that to give in is the lesser.'

'If it's a question of the money, I could always sell the house. Prices are soaring on Campden Hill. I could get a lot for it.'

'And where would you get another house? I don't advise that.'

'I don't care where I live.'

He shrugged; then glanced at his watch. 'Well, time is getting on. I think we must leave you to think about it. I gather that Mr Barlow and Mr Braintree are both in favour of withdrawing the book and seeking Miss – Miss Kingsley's agreement to a revised version. Am I right?'

Jerry nodded, tugging at a cuff. Erwin said 'Correct', staring at the pointed toe of his glacé-kid shoe and wiggling his foot as he did so.

Hazel was dumbfounded. They had never said anything of this nature to her.

'Since I have to pay the piper, I think that at least I should be allowed to call the tune,' she said in a voice trembling with the rage she tried in vain to muffle.

Maybury nodded. 'Yes. That seems fair. And that,' he went on calmly, 'is precisely why I suggested that you should think about it. Carefully. Calmly.' He rose to his feet, twitched his gown irritably and then began to shuffle at his papers.

Finally he turned to Alec Forbes: 'How soon must a decision be made?'

Erwin lumbered out of his chair. Hazel noticed that his forehead and sharp, jutting chin were glistening with sweat. 'If we are to withdraw the books from the shops and stop the reviews, then we must reach a definite decision by Monday morning at the latest. Even then it's going to be an extremely tricky business.'

'Extremely tricky,' Jerry echoed, also rising.

'Well, then, Mrs Saunders, that gives you the weekend for your deliberations.'

'I want the book to appear. I want to go on.'

'Think about it.'

'I don't have to think about it.'

'Think about it till Monday.'

He was pushing his way through the crowded room to the

136

door. Erwin, Jerry and Forbes had almost flattened themselves against the wall at his passing.

'Goodbye, Mrs Saunders ... Goodbye, gentlemen ...' Outside in the corridor he turned to Rossett, who had followed at his heels: 'I'll never make that match. That Arab's so stinking rich he's impossible to handle,' Hazel heard him say. Evidently it was easier to handle someone 'poor' like herself.

Jerry hurried over: 'Hazel, love ... Do follow his advice. Think about it, think about it very, very carefully.'

In her fury she did not answer, turning away her head.

'Yes, my dear,' Erwin took up, 'remember that discretion is often the better part of valour. I know it's hell to have to give in to a cow like that. But why inflict all those ruinous expenses on yourself just to get even?'

'It's not a question of getting even. Don't you understand? It's a question of my book. I want the book published as I wrote it.'

'I'm sure she'd agree to the smallest of cuts,' Forbes put in soothingly.

'I reckon it would be about six or seven pages,' Jerry said.

'If that,' Erwin took up.

'You could do it over a weekend, no trouble at all. And we could tip in the new pages and have the book out by late summer or the autumn.'

'No one would be any the wiser.'

'Why *should* I give way to her?' Suddenly her eyes had filled with tears.

'The alternative would be to withdraw the book until her death, I suppose,' Jerry murmured.

'*What?*'

'It's good enough to be put down like a wine for the future,' Erwin said.

'But she may live for years and years and years. She's tough. She'll probably survive me.'

'It was just an idea.'

'If you felt the text was sacrosanct.'

They were now making their way out into the corridor and down the narrow, creaking stairs.

137

Erwin looked at his watch. 'Got to be at the dentist at two-thirty. And on an empty stomach! God!'

Jerry said: 'Well, in that case, I suppose I'd better dash back to the office to hold the fort. I'll have to send out for a sandwich. Eileen's gone to talent-spot at Essex. Some hope!'

'We must have that lunch together soon.' Erwin pressed her arm. 'Promise?'

'Yes, Hazel love, let's make it a glorious threesome. At somewhere really swanky.'

'Can I give you a lift?' Erwin was asking Forbes.

Jerry was hailing a taxi.

Hazel saw Maybury in the back of a chauffeur-driven Daimler. He was poring over some papers.

Suddenly she was alone. She felt sick, frightened, lost.

Rossett emerged from the door at her back, banging his furled umbrella impatiently on the pavement as he looked up at the sky.

'D'you think it's going to rain?'

'What?' She shook herself and managed at last to focus on him. 'It might, I suppose. The forecast said it would.'

'Oh, the forecast!' He laughed. 'Well, I think I'll walk, I'll risk it.' He took two steps away from her, then turned: 'I meant what I said about your novel. I started to read it last night, thinking "God, what a labour!" And then I was absorbed, yes, totally absorbed. It's terrific!'

'Do you really think so?'

'Yes, I do. It would be a tragedy if it didn't get published. He's not a very important character after all. Is he?'

'He is really. Like the Porter in *Macbeth* or the Gravedigger in *Hamlet*. He doesn't appear much but he's, well, a key to what I'm trying to say.'

'Oh. I see.' For a moment he sounded vaguely offended. Then, with real friendliness, he drew closer to her: 'Anyway – whatever you decide – I hope the book has lots and lots of success and makes you lots and lots of money.'

'Thank you.' She felt a strange pang pass through her, like the first premonition of a long illness.

'I'm going to read everything else you've written. Truly.'

'There isn't much of it.'

He waved the umbrella in salute and then, stepping out jauntily, one hand in the pocket of his beautifully cut, tobacco-coloured trousers, he vanished round the corner.

38

Martha awoke that Sunday morning, finding unaccountably that instead of still floating high up in the empyrean, she was dragging along the earth. She took a number of deep breaths at the open window (she was always nagging at her foreign lodgers that is was unhealthy to sleep with windows closed) but even that failed to reinflate her. It may have been that by some unconscious feat of psychic divination she had sensed that at precisely this same moment Hazel was also standing at her bedroom window, in this case both double-glazed and shut, a brush in her hand, fully resolved that whatever Jerry and Erwin might want and whatever Alec Forbes and Derek Maybury might counsel, she would carry on the fight.

Nigel, who had already brought Martha her early morning cup of tea, was seated in his dressing-gown at the kitchen table. He had had a night of intermittent awakenings, confused dreams, most of them concerned with Martha and Hazel, and sweats and chills. At four-ten he had had a strange vision of the Mediterranean as he might have seen it on that ill-fated classical cruise that he had made with the two women (Martha so obtusely garrulous whenever in the company of people who knew so much more about antiquities than she did, Hazel perpetually seasick or sick of Martha), brilliant water with black pools, as of ink, in its shifting blue identations; and simultaneously there had come into his mind, half-awake and half-asleep, that phrase of Homer ἔπι οἴνοπα πόντον at which he had so often fretted over the years of his translation, until now at last, at long last, he knew how it should go: not 'wine-dark sea' but 'wine-*stained* sea', because that, in his vision, was how that sea looked, a rumpled bright blue tablecloth with stains of red wine, spilled who knew how many nights before, blackening it here and there. 'Oh, if only I could ask Hazel what she thinks about it,' he had thought, punching at his pillow, which had worked itself, or been worked by him in his tossings and turnings, into a tough, hard ball; for already he also knew, deep within himself, that he would not see Hazel again, not to talk to, for several weeks, perhaps months or years or even forever.

But now, as he sipped his cup of bitter Nescafé (two reckless teaspoons instead of one) and again tried out the phrase, saying it to himself half-aloud, 'Wine-*stained* sea, wine-*stained* sea', he could no longer feel the same surging exhilaration, like a ship-wrecked mariner's when from his drifting lifeboat he sees far off on the horizon a small puff of smoke.

'Where's the girl?' Martha asked without a good-morning.

Nigel shrugged.

'Hasn't she been down?'

'I don't think so.'

'It's too bad. If she wants her breakfast, she must be on time for it. Mrs Mungeam will be here in less than forty minutes' – she had peered at the kitchen clock – 'and you know how she hates not to have the kitchen clear. Besides, isn't this one of the days when she has to be at the hospital at nine? She's going to get herself the sack, if she's not careful, that's what's going to happen.'

Soula was whistling in her room, something that irritated Martha even more than her singing. She could hear the piercing notes long before she had reached the girl's door.

'Soula!'

'Yes, Miss Kingsley.'

'Do get a move on, there's a good girl. You're going to be late again for the hospital.'

'I do not want breakfast.'

'You must have breakfast. It's bad for you to go out without any breakfast. There was an article in the *Observer* only two Sundays ago, saying how important it was to have a good breakfast before a day of work. By one of our leading dieticians. Besides,

140

Mr Kingsley has made lots and lots of toast and I don't want it wasted.' (Nigel had in fact made no toast at all.)

By now Martha was in the room, in which Soula was standing by the mirror in brassière, girdle and stockings. Clothes littered the floor and bed and tumbled from the chest-of-drawers and the built-in cupboard in the corner, as though a burglar had been ransacking the room. One wooden-soled boot (what a clatter they always made) lay under the dressing-table and another was dangling out of the waste-paper basket. The curtains had not been drawn and the only light was from the bedside lamp, across the shade of which Soula had, for some obscure reason, balanced a box of paper tissues.

Martha wrinkled her nose. There was a smell of scent; there was a smell that she identified as coming from the overripe banana that lay on the bedside table among hair-curlers and Greek magazines printed on soft, beige paper; and there was also a smell far less agreeable, faint but insinuating.

'I hope you're remembering to keep that animal's cage clean, Soula?'

'Oh, yes, Miss Kingsley,' Soula lied as she stepped into the skirt of her hospital uniform. 'Of course. Every day.'

'Good . . . You know you really must give this room a good doing over. I'm afraid Mrs Mungeam just refuses to touch it — and I can't say I blame her.' She gave a laugh, to take the sting out of the words. 'Now do put aside one evening, or part of your day off . . .'

'I am planning to clean it out this evening after work,' Soula lied again.

'Good girl! *Very* good girl! Now nip down to breakfast just as soon as you can.'

'All I want is a cup of coffee!' Soula called despairingly after Martha, through the half-open door. Her shoulders were aching and the backs of her calves were aching and when she had first lifted her head off the pillow the room had bobbed, shuddered and then gone round and round. If Koula had still been with her, the two of them, respectably outraged, would never have stayed for more than a few minutes at a party of that sort.

'That girl's going to pieces,' Martha announced.

141

Nigel was now examining the 'Despatches, Hatches, Matches' columns of *The Times*. 'She misses Koula, ' he said, in a low voice in case Soula should hear them.

'Yes, I know. But I don't *at all* like this Egyptian with whom she's taken up,' Martha boomed back.

'Have you met him?'

'No. But I've seen him. I happened to be looking out of my window when she went out yesterday evening and there he was – waiting for her at the corner of the road, outside the launderette. He looked as if he could do with some laundering himself – and I don't mean just his clothes. Hair to here.' She indicated a shoulder. 'Moustache. Skinny. One of those smelly sheepskin jackets from Morocco – or is it Afghanistan? It worries me. A real lounge-lizard. A girl like that could so easily get in with the wrong crowd.'

'She seems well able to look after herself. And in any case – it's not really our business, it it?'

Suddenly Nigel had recovered what he had lost and had, subconsciously, been fretting to find ever since he had got out of bed: the key to those interminable confused dreams about Hazel and Martha. But having recovered it, he wanted to throw it away, far out of sight and mind. The key had inscribed on it: You hate your sister.

'Not really our business? What an extraordinary thing to say! She's a foreigner, a girl of barely twenty-two living in our house. As Christians, if as nothing else, we have a responsibility towards her.'

'I am not a Christian, Martha. You know that.'

'I thought you were fond of the girl!'

'Of course I'm fond of her – of both of them.'

'Well, then!'

'But that has nothing to do with – '

'Oh, do stop arguing. Do stop this ceaseless senseless arguing. Why do you have to be so argumentative? My head is reeling, positively reeling with it. You really are *the* most tiresome person I know.'

'More tiresome than Hazel?'

'What did you say? *What* did you say?'

Nigel was mercifully saved from having to answer by the sound of the front door slamming shut.

'What was that?' Martha went out into the hall.

'Soula. Going. That would be my guess.'

Martha hurried into the sitting-room. She tugged back the curtains, which ought to have been drawn by Nigel but had evidently been forgotten, and peered out, her small eyes screwed up.

'He's there!' she called.

'Who's there?'

'That Egyptian. At this hour. By the launderette. And he doesn't even work at the hospital.'

'Perhaps she got tired of going out with mortuary attendants. Perhaps she found them too — cold.' He smiled at his little joke; but Martha ignored it.

'I bet he's on drugs. He has that look. He has a car too. I bet he's going to drive her to the hospital. Perhaps Soula pinches drugs from the hospital for him. One day he's going to smash up that car of his and smash up Soula with it.'

'Have your breakfast.'

Martha scooped into the tin of Nescafé; then she peered. 'What *has* happened to the Nescafé? I bought a new tin only on Monday. What *on earth* has happened to it?'

39

'Don't you love my view of the gas-works?'

Hazel stood at the huge plate-glass window, feeling the warmth that came through it like a piercing remembrance of summers that she and Arnold had spent seated out on his balcony, misty glasses in reach, or wandering through Kew Gardens (a hired Daimler, the one he always hired, waiting at the Gate) or staring at architectural fantasy after fantasy at Portmeirion.

Across the Thames from St Thomas's the Houses of Parliament – 'the gas-works' as he had called them – glittered up at her.

'Beautiful. And I suppose you pay a fortune for it?'

'I'm afraid so. There's a young American on this floor opposite – such beautiful silk pyjamas, such a very proper Boston manner – and he wandered in here one afternoon and told me that he was paying *a queen's ransom*' (briefly and brilliantly he caught the exact camp New England tones) 'for a room *half* this size. Well, you know me. I was brought up to expect nothing but the best in life. And death.'

Hazel turned from the view. 'It's like a luxury hotel.'

'Better. And since one never goes out, one doesn't have to worry about whether one's shoes have been cleaned or not. The only trouble is – I don't seem able to enjoy it.'

'Poor Arnold!'

'It's rather like when – many years ago – I decided to blue a legacy – a very *tiny* legacy – by staying at the Danieli for three weeks with someone of whom I thought I was very fond.' (How typical, thought Hazel, that it should merely be 'someone' and not a girl or a boy.) 'But though everything about the hotel was perfect – or so it seemed to the rather unsophisticated youth I then was – I couldn't *enjoy* it, any more than I can enjoy this hospital now. That person ruined it all. And I couldn't get away, we were tied to each other.' He put out an emaciated, grey hand and took a small sip of lemon barleywater. 'Well, that's how it is here too. I've brought this companion with me. Someone quite as boring and demanding and draining and malevolent as that person. And so – so I just can't enjoy myself.'

Again the emaciated, grey hand extended itself; and now Hazel noticed for the first time how the wrist was encircled by what looked like a bracelet woven from brass picture-wire. Arnold sipped again, tipping the glass up and bringing his pale lips to meet its rim with what was obviously a punishing effort.

'Can I help you?'

'No. But do come away from that window. You seem so far away.' Hazel approached the chair by the bed. 'What's troubling you?' he asked.

'Well, I hate to see you like this.'

144

'Yes, but there's something else. Tell me. Tell me, Hazel, I'm interested. Don't you understand that? *I'm still interested.*'

The sincerity was so obvious and undeniable that she sat down and began to tell him. With dark, huge eyes, the skin under them taut and glistening, he gazed at her, from time to time again reaching out for the glass of barleywater or nodding his head or muttering 'Yes. Yes. I see.'

'So that's it,' she concluded. 'Whatever course I take, I lose. But I'd rather lose fighting that beastly woman than giving in to her.'

'Yes, she *is* a beastly woman – I could never really understand why you had anything to do with her, as I've told you before. But if you're beastly to people yourself, you can't really be surprised if they're beastly back to you.'

'No, I suppose not.' She was stunned.

'I know and you know that your novel is worth far more than the hurt feelings of a Martha Kingsley. But she doesn't think that. Why should she?'

'Yes, I suppose I *have* behaved badly?'

'Oh dear. Poor Hazel. You always *were* accident-prone.'

'Yes. I've never achieved anything by luck in my life. I've always had to fight for whatever I've wanted. That's why I feel I must fight again now.'

He looked at her with sadness in the huge, moist eyes.

'You think I'm a fool?'

'I admire your – courage.'

'But you think I'm a fool?'

'I didn't say that. All I do think is that perhaps you ought to be more, well, prudent. If you fight this action, you may win a technical victory over her. But your losses will in fact be greater – far greater, perhaps – than if you appear to give in.'

'But why the hell should she get away with it?'

He gave a small smile. 'Because people are always getting away with it. All one can do is to see that they get away with the absolute minimum.'

'But if I give way, then it means that it's all that easier for another Martha Kingsley to come along and muck up another writer's novel.'

145

'Yes.'

She jumped up and again went to the window. 'I persuaded myself this morning – I was lying in bed, about seven, feeling suddenly convinced that I must fight her – that what I'd do would be to conduct my own case. Of course, I wouldn't have all the expertise but don't you think that a jury might rather warm to a writer fighting to save her book and lacking the means to hire someone like Derek Maybury to fight on her behalf?'

'Yes, they might indeed take to you in the role of female David against that appalling Goliath. But then they might not. I shouldn't think, by and large, that the average jury feels that a book is all that important in the scheme of things. Would you? If you were fighting for a cat or a dog – or even for the custody of some brat – or for your right to build a monstrosity at the end of your garden . . .'

'You *are* discouraging.'

'But you'll fight on?'

'Oh, I don't know. I just don't know.' Suddenly weariness engulfed her.

'Hazel . . . If you do decide to go on – and if you do need money – you will – you will remember that you can call on me for help?'

'Oh, Arnold . . .' She felt, strangely, not pleasure nor even gratitude, but merely that a difficult situation had suddenly become totally unmanageable.

'I mean it. I have enough to die in the state to which I've always been accustomed. I could sell the Dufy – that should bring in enough, shouldn't it?'

'Oh, no, not the Dufy! Not the Dufy!' It was a bright, crisp scene of boats bobbing in the harbour of St Tropez. The Riviera was where he had almost always gone for his holidays.

'What good is it to me now?'

'No, you mustn't sell it. I wouldn't want you to sell it.'

'All my capital – such as it is – is now tied up in my pictures and furniture.'

'I'd hate you to go home from here and find no Dufy opposite your bed . . . Oh, in any case, you know how I have this horror of *owing* anything to anyone.'

'You wouldn't *owe* in this case. I'm not proposing a loan.'

'You know what I mean. An obligation. I hate obligations. That's why I wanted to take only a minimum from Jan. The lawyers said I could have got far more than just the house.'

'That kind of pride's not good,' he said seriously. 'You're rather proud of having that kind of pride. But it's not good, honestly it isn't.'

'I know. But I can't help it. I'm sorry.'

'Well, there it is. The offer stands – should you change your mind.' He was sinking back among the pillows; and as she looked at him, she had a panicky sensation that the narrow, pale head was becoming a part of the crisp linen fabric behind it, that they were merging, that the head would vanish forever.

Fortunately at that moment a nurse came in with yet another vase of flowers to set among all the others in serried ranks before him. 'You *are* popular!' she said brightly. Something – a bunch of keys? – clinked as she passed between the bed and Hazel. She smelled babyishly of talcum powder. 'Tired?'

Arnold's head nodded on the pillow; he closed his eyes.

Hazel rose: 'I'd better go.'

'Perhaps he *has* had enough,' the nurse said pleasantly, as she prepared to leave. 'He had a lot more tests this morning.'

'I'm so tired of all these tests. What use are they? They merely confirm that I'm following the proper procedures in dying.'

'Dying? What are you saying?' the nurse cried gaily. 'I've never heard such nonsense. We've people in far worse shape than you on this floor.'

'Then I can only feel sorry for them.'

The nurse had gone. Arnold put out his hand and Hazel took it. 'Yes, I think I'd better go,' she said.

'Perhaps it would be better. I'm not much fun now.'

As she held the cold, damp fingers, she noticed once again the curious bracelet. 'What's that?' she asked, pointing.

'That? Oh, it's such a nuisance. My Mrs Toomey brought it to me. You know she's a Roman? Well, she and Mr Toomey went on a holiday to Marbella – one of those package things, I treated them to it – and she picked up this bracelet at some shrine or other. She thinks, poor soul, that it might work a miracle for me.

147

It's awfully uncomfortable — too big and far too heavy. But I suppose it would hurt her feelings if I . . . So I wear it.'

As she stood at attention in the crowded lift, Hazel thought of that bracelet, clumsily made as though from twisted picture-wire, around the fragile wrist and the image suddenly brought into her eyes the tears that, she knew only now, she had been wanting to shed throughout her time in the hospital room.

40

She would take the 170 bus outside the hospital, she decided, and then walk across Battersea Park to see the bulbs, returning to Kensington on the 49. She did not want to hasten her arrival home, where she would busy herself with a number of trivial tasks — sorting letters and tidying drawers and washing underclothes — while her mind leapt and scuttled around its little cage, looking in vain for an exit. Either Jerry or Erwin — it would probably be Erwin, since they had obviously decided between them that he was the one better able to 'handle' her — would telephone in less than twenty-four hours and she would then have to have her decision, whether defiant or compliant, ready for them. If, despite their having agreed that, since she was to pay the piper, she must have the right to call the tune, they nonetheless now refused to stand up to Martha, then Hazel would be faced with a war on two fronts: one with them (could she force them to fight the case?) and one with her persecutor.

On the top of the bus she thought alternately on the one hand of Martha exulting in her victory and on the other of the sale of her house, the lengthy preparations for the case and the ordeal of the final appearance — eighteen months, two years hence? — before a judge and a jury who would, no doubt, each be equally shocked by the revelations of the curious isosceles triangle that she, Lydia and Miklos had formed, with him at the apex. Poor Miklos!

Except that he would not mind at all. When she had asked him for the release demanded by Jerry and Erwin at the instigation of Mervyn Kurtz, he had signed with a flourish: 'I have no taboos. Say what you like about me.' But what about Lydia and the others? Suddenly she remembered that hapless American, met at some literary party, who had written a book about Italy. No one had thought of suing until one over-sensitive or over-greedy woman had decided to do so; then the writs had rained down on him. When she herself had met him, he had just made an unsuccessful suicide attempt, his book and himself both ruined and his publishers, a small firm, almost so . . .

Oh, what was she to decide, what *was* she to decide?

She clenched her fists and gritted her teeth, leaning forward to look out of the top of the bus at a desolate riverside scene of stalking gantries above the blackened ruins of a warehouse gnawed by fire. A guard-dog was weaving back and forth along a high barbed-wire fence, from time to time lowering its head to bay through it at the traffic.

She had thought that she was alone on the top of the bus but now a squat middle-aged man, with disproportionately long arms, was making his way, swinging from bar to bar, with each jerk and sway of the bus, towards her. His face was round and soft and above it he wore a tartan cap, pulled low over his forehead, from around which hair the colour of cheddar cheese stuck out in prongs.

'Please, madame,' he said in a foreign accent. 'Excuse me. Battersea Pleasure Gardens?'

He pointed out of the window at a railway yard.

Hazel shook her head. 'No, no. Not that. Not yet. Battersea Park's a long way yet. Five, ten minutes.'

'Ah, five ten minutes!' He sank into the seat in front of her and then turned round, pushing up the cap with the back of one of his dimpled hands. 'You will tell me? Please?'

'Yes. I'm getting off at that stop myself. But you know, the Fun Fair's no longer open.'

'Sorry?'

'They've closed the Fun Fair. Some time ago.'

'Closed? But I wished to see the Fun Fair.'

149

'Well, I'm afraid you're too late. It's closed — I think, for good.'

'Then even if I return to England, I cannot see it?'

Hazel shook her head. 'Probably not.'

She noticed that there was a yellowish rheum at the corners of the small, pale-blue, slightly protuberant eyes, and how, when he smiled, the upper lip pulled back over the teeth almost as though he were snarling. There was a pathos to his perkiness; and it was chiefly because that pathos all at once oppressed her that she went on with the conversation: 'You don't live in England?'

He shook his head and gave a babyish, gurgling laugh at the suggestion. 'No, no. I am from Poland. You know Poland?'

'I've never been there, I'm afraid.'

'You must visit Poland. It is very interesting. Very interesting.'

'So everyone always says,' she agreed, though she could not recollect having ever met anyone who had said it. 'I should like to go.'

'Yes, you must go.' He fiddled with the peak of his tartan cap, pulling it first even lower and then pushing it back again, to reveal a scarlet line, like an incision, on his forehead.

'Are you here on business?'

'No! No business!' Again he gave that gurgling laugh, a baby prodded by an affectionate finger. 'I am here for holiday, only for holiday. For sightseeing. Rest.' He was twisted round on the seat in order to face her. Now he clutched the rail between them with both podgy hands: 'I am clairvoyant,' he said in a suddenly lowered voice. He looked around him furtively, though there was no one else on the top of the bus, as though to make sure that he had not been overheard.

'*What?*'

'Clairvoyant.' Still he spoke in that lowered voice, as though confessing some shameful secret. 'You know what is clairvoyant?'

'Oh, *clairvoyant*! Yes. Yes, of course I do.'

'Famous clairvoyant. One of the most famous in Poland. Many people come to me, every day they come. I am exhausted. I must have rest.' He put his forehead on the hands that clutched the rail and left it there for several seconds, until Hazel, looking out of

150

the window, said 'Quick! We must get out here. This is the stop. If you want to see where the Fun Fair used to be.'

He jumped up and followed her as she hurried down the stairs.

'It's over there. You can't miss it.' She pointed, as they stood together on the pavement. 'Straight ahead. Just there. You'll see the Big Dipper – if it's still standing – and, oh, all kinds of other things. But they're all fenced off now.'

'You are not going that way!'

'I'm going across the Park.'

'Then we can go together?'

'All right.' She was not sure if she was pleased or not.

'Take care, madame,' he said, chivalrously guiding her by the arm across the road. Then, as they stopped on to the opposite pavement, he peered at her: 'You are worried,' he said, a statement not a question.

She did not answer, walking on as though she had not heard him. But he pursued: 'When I touch your arm, I know. It comes to me. You are worried. Something worries you very much. I *know*.'

She laughed, even though she felt not amusement but a curious sense of outrage, as though he had peeped at her on the lavatory seat or in the bath. 'Are you practising your clairvoyance on me? Please don't. I don't want to be a subject.'

'Why are you afraid? I am not *practising*, madame. I am too experienced to need practice.' She was hurrying now and he was hurrying a few inches behind her, his long arms swinging. 'Something worries you. I see it. I feel it. Here and here.' He held up the podgy hands in turn. 'I *know*. Someone is causing you trouble. Big trouble. Not an enemy, a friend. Or' – he gave the gurgling babyish laugh – 'better, a friend who is an enemy. Am I right? Am I, madame?' He had now hastened ahead of her to peer up into her face.

Suddenly the sense of outrage vanished. Curiosity began to throb and then hum in her, like the physical sensation of some machine that had jerked into movement.

'Yes. Yes, you could be right. I *am* worried.'

'Take care, madame.' Again he took her arm, guiding her out into the oncoming traffic so that for one moment she thought that his intention was to have them both killed. 'So this is Battersea Park?' he said, pausing at the gate.

'This is Battersea Park.'

'It is beautiful.' But he hardly glanced around him. 'But in England all parks are beautiful. More beautiful than in Poland.'

'I love these spring flowers.'

'You have a decision,' he said. 'Very difficult decision . . . *Please*.' For some reason not apparent to her he suddenly whipped round so that he was now walking on her left instead of her right. 'Am I correct?' He peered up into her face again, so near to her that the peak of his cap almost brushed her nose.

There was something laughable and yet sinister in the whole encounter.

'Everyone always has a decision of some kind or another. It's pretty safe to say that!'

'Then let me say more.' He stared out ahead of him now, seemingly at three muddy youths in shorts and running vests, one of them with a football under his arm, who were ambling diagonally towards them across the grass. 'You must decide whether – whether' – his voice seemed to wobble and groan on the repeated 'whethers' as though it were difficult to get them out – 'whether you will fight or surrender . . . A lawsuit.' His tongue seemed too large for his mouth. It looked oddly swollen and red as he struggled to articulate the words. 'That is your decision. If you fight the lawsuit, it will cost you money, much money. But if you do not fight it – also much money. . . . I am right?'

'You could be.'

'I am right.' Now it was a statement, calm and assured.

Hazel was suddenly overwhelmed by panic, she could not have said why. She must get away.

'You go *that* way from here. I have to go out through that little gate over there.'

'Yes.'

He seemed to be totally unsurprised and totally unresentful at her sudden desertion of him.

'Just walk straight up that path. You can see the Fun Fair – behind those trees.'

'Yes, I can see it. Thank you.'

With his left hand he was taking off his cap. She did not know why it should astonish her so much to discover that he was bald except for the thick cheddar-coloured hair that had stuck out from around it. He extended his right hand.

She took the proffered hand and was embarrassed when he held her fingers for several seconds on end, his eyes closed. Then he said, again in that effortful, groaning voice: 'You must not worry. You are worried but you must not worry. In a year this friend-enemy – enemy-friend – will be dead. I promise you. *Dead*.' He opened his eyes, the rheum still yellow in their corners. 'Goodbye, madame,' he whispered.

'Goodbye.'

As he began to walk jauntily away, the gorilla-arms swinging and the heavily-padded shoulders rising and falling, she suddenly, on an impulse, ran after him: 'Tell me – tell me – your – your name . . .'

'Is that important? It is not important.' He smiled, again removed the cap, gave another little bow, and then hurried on once more.

On the Albert Bridge, trembling insubstantially each time the wind blew, she paused and looked back; but he had vanished from sight. Had he ever existed? Or had she – a throb of an oncoming headache had started between her eyes – had she conjured him out of the dark turbulence of her own mind? A hallucination! No, he must, of course, have been real. He must. It was odd that such an experience should have come to her when she was on her way back from a visit to Arnold, who was a member of the Society for Psychical Research, who had been a friend of Harry Price ('wonderful old fraud') and who, though an atheist, believed firmly in ESP and precognition. She would have to tell him about it. He would be fascinated.

Hazel began to walk on; and now her mind kept returning to that single sentence: 'In a year this friend-enemy – enemy-friend – will be dead.' She gave a little shudder; yes, he had probed her inmost thoughts.

The night before, waking in a torment of indecision, the wish had formulated itself, insidious and shameful: if only Martha could die, if only Martha could die. She had forgotten it by the morning because she had wanted to forget it. The Pole had remembered it for her.

41

Nigel stepped over the brochures that littered the sitting-room floor, towards the wicker chair, a bird's nest afflicted with elephantiasis, on which he liked to brood on the ideas he had laid on the bus journey home from the Museum Reading Room or the London Library. The book tucked under his arm pinched his forefinger.

'Does this room always have to be in this mess?' he demanded fretfully.

'Careful! *Careful*, Nigel!' Martha, ample and exultant, was kneeling on a young couple in bathing-suits who were drinking ouzo before the Parthenon. 'I've put these in special order.'

'I can see no order at all. Anyway, what *is* all this?'

'I've had an idea. We're going to go away. For a week. Or two weeks.'

'But why?'

'A little celebration. Now that we've brought her to heel. After the strain of all these awful days.'

'But I don't *want* to go away.'

'You always say that before a holiday. And you always enjoy it in the end. I'm going to pay, you know. It's on me.'

'It's not the money that worries me. I just *don't want to go*.'

'Don't be silly.' Martha held up a brochure, shifting her knees from the ouzo-drinking couple outside the Parthenon to a sherry-drinking couple at a table beside a bull-fight. 'This seems incredibly good value. Only forty-six pounds each for five days in Paris. If we share a room. Do you mind sharing a room with me?'

'I hate to share rooms. With anyone. You know that.'

'Well, we could pay the supplement. Though three pounds per day does seem terribly excessive. Still . . . in for a penny, in for a pound,' she announced gaily, leaping to her feet. 'Or would you prefer a cruise?'

'What about Soula?'

'What about her? She can look after herself. Why not?'

'In her present state –'

'She's seldom here anyway. I don't know what's happened to that girl. I've rarely seen anyone go downhill quite so fast.' Suddenly Martha had thrown her arms round Nigel from behind. 'Oh, I'm so excited at the thought of a holiday!'

'Martha – for God's sake!'

'It's just what I need. A change, a rest. When I'm going to be so taken up in the weeks ahead. Yes, I think a cruise would be the thing!'

'Taken up? Taken up with what?'

'With the *book*, silly. All these alterations will have to be gone through with a toothcomb, one by one. I'll need your help for that.'

'I don't want to have a thing to do with it. Not a thing.'

'I'm glad she saw sense. But she's a sly one. I'll have to keep a careful eye on her. If she can get away with anything, you can be sure she'll do so.' She went to the French windows, threw them open and took deep breath on breath of air, her shoulders and her breasts rising and falling and her eyelids fluttering.

'M'm! Spring! One can smell the spring!'

The wind rustled the leaves of Nigel's book and then fluttered them over, despite a restraining hand.

'Oh, hell. Now I've lost that reference. For God's sake – shut that window. *Shut it*!'

'What *is* the matter with you? I offer to give you a free holiday and all I get in return is tantrums and bad temper. Really!' But as she stopped to pick up the pamphlets, she executed a little dipping waltz, such was her euphoria.

'You've no idea how silly you look. Idiotic!'

'I'm a damned sight less silly than you are!'

Laughing gaily, Martha waltzed out of the sitting-room, the brochures pressed against her bosom.

155

'Soula!' she called. 'Coo-ee! Soula!'

But Soula was not in.

Drat the girl! It looked as if she were going to be late for another meal.

Martha climbed the stairs. She could not be angry with Nigel, she could not be angry with Soula. The world was far too beautiful and wonderful a place.

She knocked on Soula's door and then, when there was no answer, walked in with that old quickening of the heart-beat and sudden dryness of the mouth. Beady eyes glittered at her from the cage under the forever unopen window. Bedclothes lay tangled across the bed.

Hastily she pulled open first the cupboard and then, at random, a drawer here and there. She resisted the impulse to examine the soiled underclothes in one of them or the packet of letters (in Greek? from Koula?), tied with string, in another. But the box she found in the drawer of the bedside table, among hair-curlers, the dry knot of a used handkerchief and a scattering of cake-crumbs, held her fascinated. A hand hovered over it, withdrew, returned.

She had never seen such a thing in her life but of course she had known at once what it was, what it must be. Oh, what had happened to that sweet, innocent Soula who had first come to stay with them? Why should she need a filthy thing like that? And what was to become of the girl?

Martha sank on to the bed, among the soiled bedclothes and the nightdress of pink chiffon that was tinged with grey from use. Suddenly she felt heavy and sick, as though sated from an indigestible meal.

42

'Nigel!'

'Oh, hello, Hazel.'

They had not seen each other since the withdrawal of the book. Looking ailing and furtive, shoulders sagging as though from the weight of the carrier-bag that dangled from both hands, he was skulking in a doorway of the supermarket. His nose was red, his voice husky; he must have a cold.

'What are you doing here?'

'*She's* inside. I went to pick up something she'd left at the cleaners and then came on here to meet her . . . Hazel, I'm – I'm glad that you did what you did.'

'I'm not sure that I am. But it was a case of *force majeure*, wasn't it?'

'I'm sorry if I seemed . . . I didn't want to let you down, you know. But I *was* in this terribly difficult position.' Balancing the carrier-bag between his legs, knees turned inwards, he tugged a handkerchief out of a pocket of his worn, belted raincoat and blew his nose into it with a snort and rattle of catarrh.

'Oh, I knew all that, Nigel. Of course I know all that. I have no – no hard feelings. None at all. Your first loyalty was to Martha. How could it be otherwise?'

'But you know that –'

'Don't let's talk about it any longer. It's not such a terrible disaster. We reckon there are only about eight pages to be altered. That should deal with all her objections.'

'Eight pages?'

He gulped on phlegm; his eyes skittered sideways. But she failed to notice his doubt.

'About that. That's what our lawyer thinks.'

'He's been in touch with Roddie?'

'I imagine so. Of course, yes, he must have been. And no doubt each telephone call is costing me five pounds – and each letter ten!'

157

'Oh, Hazel ... It really is *disastrous*.'

'Well, worse things have happened ... With only eight pages to reprint, we should be able to get away without a whole rebinding job. That should save me something.'

'But *you* won't have to pay for all that, surely?'

'That's what my contract seems to say.'

Again he drew out the sodden handkerchief, turning it over and over to find a dry area on which to blow his nose. 'But I'd no idea ... I'm sure Martha had no idea ...'

'Yes, it's all going to cost a pretty packet, I can tell you. And I can't be any too popular with the reviewers and the editors − or with the girls at Barlow's.'

'What do you mean?'

'Well, one can't just withdraw a book less than a week before publication date without causing an enormous amount of inconvenience to an enormous amount of people.' For the first time her tone sharpened to exasperation. 'Use your sense. And there are the booksellers, too − they can't be any too pleased either.'

'Yes, I see. I do see.'

'The only ray of light is that a film man is interested. My agent rang me to tell me yesterday afternoon.'

'Oh, Hazel, how *marvellous*. Oh, I *am* pleased.' Suddenly his raw, congested face was irradiated.

'It's not in the bag. Far from it. But he's read an advance copy and he thinks it would make a terrific film − if he can persuade the right people to appear in it.'

'Who is he?'

'Milo Seidensticker. You wouldn't have heard of him.' Nigel shook his head. 'But he's come to the fore in the last year or two. Very young, *very* ambitious. But I've had so many disappointments over films in the past. I expect *nothing* ...' This was not strictly true; all that day she had been expecting something, if only the purchase of an option.

'That would be the most wonderful silver lining. Oh, I'll keep my fingers crossed.'

'Well, I'd better get on with my shopping.'

'You're not going in *there*, are you?'

'Yes. Why on earth not?'

'But *she*'s in there. She's doing her shopping in there.'

'So what?'

'You might bump into each other.'

'If I bump into her, I'll make sure that it's a really hard bump.'

Hazel entered.

In her novel she had described how her Major Charles used to do the household shopping himself, since he could not trust his cowed and spiritless wife not to be extravagant. There had been a scene of his ransacking a supermarket (when she had written it, it had been precisely this supermarket, in High Street Kensington, that she had envisaged) in order to find outsize tins of baked beans, the staple diet fed to the lodgers.

Now, as she saw Martha ahead of her (so far from avoiding her, Hazel felt an extraordinary compulsion to play Grandmother's Footsteps and to approach as near as possible without being glimpsed), the older woman launched herself on to tiptoe, arm straining upwards and blouse straining away from skirt, to take down, yes, a gigantic tin of baked beans. But then, as the predatory fingers were about to close on their booty, some sixth sense told Martha that her enemy was close. She peeked round, hastily let go of the tin as though caught in the act of shop-lifting and, instead, pretended to be absorbed in contemplation of a mound of packets of dried apricots displayed on special offer.

Not for the first time Hazel had prophetically described in one of her novels something that lay not behind in the past but ahead in the future.

43

That morning had started well; it did not end so.

With a sudden resurgence of the exhilaration that had vanished ever since the troubles over the book, Hazel had jumped out of bed long before her alarm-clock had trilled seven o'clock, had hurried through her bath and dressing and breakfast, and had then settled herself at the desk beneath her study window, to continue for yet another day the labour of rewriting. Erwin had impressed on her that it was essential, if she wished to keep down costs, to ensure that each substitute paragraph contained exactly the same number of words as the paragraph it replaced. 'After all,' he added, 'you don't want to let yourself in for a penny more of expense than is absolutely unavoidable'; and Jerry, who was in the room, nodded his head approvingly at this tactful reminder that it was she and not they who would eventually foot the printer's bill.

At first the imposition had paralysed her. Every paragraph she drafted was either twice as long or half as short as it should have been. But then, slowly, forgetting that she was tinkering with a work of creative imagination, however faulty and inadequate, she had become absorbed in exactly the same way that she often became absorbed in the Ximenes crossword puzzle. It was her ingenuity and intelligence, not her imagination, that were being challenged. Soon she was taking a pride in constructing paragraphs that were not merely composed of exactly the same number of words but also of exactly the same number of letters. Each time that she made the final count and yes, it was precisely right, she seemed to be triumphing over both the recalcitrant material before her and, more important, over Martha.

She even began to persuade herself that this new Major Charles — benign and wise and generous — was a more effective character than the old Major Charles, who was none of these things. Strangely, he even seemed more real now to her than either his predecessor and namesake or even Martha herself. Hazel could like him as she had never liked either of them.

So absorbed was she in the act of careful re-creation that she almost did not answer the telephone as it shrilled on and on through the house. But finally she rose from her desk:

'Yes?'

'Hazel?'

'Yes.'

'Ernie here. Ernie. Remember me? Your agent, your ever-

160

efficient agent.' There was no mistaking the accent, half stage-American and half stage-Cockney, affected by this Old Rugbeian. 'How are things?'

'Pretty hellish.' She hunted for somewhere to dump the cigarette she had lit and eventually placed it across the inkwell.

'I bet! And I've had this sore throat. Thought it must be a quinsy. Real agony it was last night, I hardly slept a wink. I saw the doctor first thing this morning and he gave me this gargle. Bloody lot of good that's going to do for me. Still – I mustn't go on about my own little troubles, when yours are so much worse.' There was a sound of his clearing his throat at the other end, followed by a muttered 'Christ!' Then: 'Sorry, Hazel. Are you still there?'

'Yes. I'm still here.'

'You can hear the sort of shape I'm in. Chronic. Well, never mind. We'll all be dead in the end . . . What I really rang about – are you there, Hazel? – is this film deal.' Briefly optimism flared in her. 'I've had Milo Seidensticker on the blower to me a number of times' – in fact, it was Ernie who had done the ringing – 'and as you know, he's just crazy about your book. He'd like Glenda Jackson for the woman – the *you* character – or, failing her, Vanessa Redgrave. But the trouble is – the whole fucking trouble is – well, this libel caper.'

'Does that affect it? Why should it? In another week or two all that will be ironed out.'

'That's what I told him. But for the moment he's nervous, mighty nervous. And any backer will be nervous. I mean, the position he's got himself into now, he could get backing even if he decided to make a movie of the London Telephone Directory. But not – definitely not – if all the subscribers were planning to issue simultaneous writs and injunctions.'

'There's *been* no writ. There's only been the *threat* of an injunction. One injunction.'

'Yeah, I know, baby, I know. But if all that money has to be committed to a project, you're going to make bloody sure that no hitch, no possible hitch, can happen. Aren't you? Stands to reason.'

'So the deal is off?'

161

'I didn't say that. Don't let's jump to conclusions. But it *could* be off. Let's put it like that.'

'It's off.'

After that conversation she screwed the cap back on her pen, placed the scribbled alterations, sheet on sheet of them, far back in a drawer, and went out into the garden to continue work on the rank herbaceous border. The abandoned cigarette-end eventually dropped off the inkwell and burned a hole in the sheet of paper on which she had been totting up her sums. Fortunately it did not ignite the blotter or the desk-top underneath it.

44

'It's just not good enough. One has to watch her every moment like a lynx. I always said she was sly.'

Martha was examining a photostat copy, forwarded to her by Roddie, of the latest of Hazel's emendations, her small eyes screwed up until they were no more than holes in her round face as she peered through the spectacles that she held up in front of them.

'Why don't you ever put those things *on*?'

'She no sooner removes one dig than she puts in another. Any fool can see the sarcasm.'

'Why not get yourself a proper lorgnette and be done with it?'

'This bit about the Major being " a remarkable cook" – ;'

'He no longer *is* the Major.'

'Well, however it is. That's sarcasm. Of course it is. That's why she chose that word "remarkable".' She bunched her lips, an ominous sign. 'It'll have to come out.' She put down the spectacles and reached across the table for a thick red pencil.

'If you so dislike wearing glasses, you could have contact lenses. It's ridiculous, this squinting through – '

'My God! Oh, my God! She's now had the cheek to imply that I'm – I'm a lesbian.'

'Don't be idiotic.'

'Read for yourself!' She thrust the photostat at him, but he did not take it from her. 'It's obvious. Look at all that about his kindness to the *au pair* girl. A whole paragraph of it.'

Nigel lowered his detective-story to his knees. 'It seems to me that whatever poor Hazel does, she just can't win.'

'So it's "poor Hazel" now, is it?'

'If she says that her character is a bad cook, then it's libellous because of course' – his voice suddenly became vicious in its sarcasm – 'we all know what a wonderful cook you are. On the other hand, if she says what a good cook he is, then of course the character *must* be you, for the same reason. If he shows an avuncular interest in a female lodger, then that's an innuendo that you're a lesbian. But if, on the other hand, he were to show an avuncular interest in a male lodger, then that equally . . .' He broke off. 'Oh, it's hopeless to argue with you. You've never been capable of rational thought, never, never.'

She stared at him. 'Whose side *are* you on?'

'I don't know,' he muttered. 'I wish to God I did. I wish there *weren't* any sides. I wish I could just be left out of this whole business.'

'Oh, you're feeble. Feeble! Spineless! Well, I'm not. And I'm going to get my rights if it's the last thing I get.' She picked up the photostat in a trembling hand and with the other hand again raised the spectacles to the small screwed-up eyes.

'For God's sake put those glasses *on*!'

She paid no attention.

Minutes passed, in a silence broken only by the rustle that Nigel made by turning a page or an 'Oh', 'Really!' or 'Tsk!' from Martha when she came across something that seemed to her particularly offensive in Hazel's emendations.

Suddenly she paused. 'I'm determined that every copy gets called in. Every single one.'

Nigel turned another page, head lowered.

'Roddie's making that clear to them. I've told him he must do so.'

Nigel shifted and sighed; he did not look up.

'Beryl says a friend of hers, a librarian, saw an ad for it in something called *The Bookseller*. I told Roddie that he must write at once to them to say that it's been banned. They can't publish ads for banned books.'

Nigel said in a slow, patient voice, isolating each word as though he were dictating to a foreigner: 'The book has not, repeat not, been *banned*.'

'Oh, withdrawn then! Must we quibble over every blessed word?' She looked down for a second and then looked up again. 'And what about that *New Statesman* list of forthcoming books?'

He pretended to go on with his reading.

'Well, what about it?' she pursued. 'You can't tell me that that was "just a mischance" — as that lawyer of hers called it. A mischance! Of course it was deliberate.'

'That list was probably put together ages ago.' Again he answered her in an exaggeratedly slow, careful voice. 'It was put together from publishers' catalogues. Probably no one at the *New Statesman* knew anything about the withdrawal. Why should they?'

'But how did the book get there in the first place?'

'Because it deserved to.'

'I bet Hazel knows him.'

'Knows who?'

'The editor. Or the literary editor. They all know each other. They're all members of the same gang, they always hang together. She put them up to it. You bet she did. Well, Roddie's going to write a letter about that too. A *stiff* letter, I can tell you. Madam's not going to get away with that kind of thing, not by a long chalk.'

Nigel got slowly to his feet. He noted the number of the page he had been reading and then closed the book and put it under his arm.

'You're a dreadful woman,' he said in a quiet, thoughtful voice.

She stared at him.

'Dreadful,' he repeated. 'Haven't you an ounce of magnanimity or pity in you?'

'What are you talking about?'

'Two things you don't understand for all your silly flirtations

164

with every nonsensical religion that comes your way. Magnanimity. Pity.'

'What magnanimity did *she* show? What pity?'

'You *smashed* her book, smashed it, just as a half-wit — a Caliban — might smash the mirror that showed him his own reflection. Perhaps you smashed her too. And then, when she tried to put the pieces together again, you won't even let her do that?'

'Whose side are you on? Whose — side — are — you — *on*?' She took a deep breath that thrust her bosom out ahead of her and then blundered to her feet, to confront him.

'I've told you. I'm on no one's side. But I — I just hate to see you kicking her when she's in the dust.'

'You've always been an idiot where she's concerned. For you she can do no wrong. Never. She could get away with murder as far as you're concerned. You'd even cover up for her, you would. And when your own sister is insulted and defamed and held up to ridicule and made a laughing-stock and called a lesbian and a bore and snob and bad cook, all you can think of is the precious book in which all that filth, filth, filth is propagated.'

'No,' he said wearily. 'You can't understand. You'll never understand.'

He went slowly out of the room, the book under his arm, and even more slowly began to mount the stairs.

45

One of Hazel's saddest tasks had been to write, on the instruction of Alec Forbes, to all the people to whom she had already sent advance copies of the novel, to ask them to return them. The answers surprised her. Some people wrote to say that they had mislaid their copies; some that they had never received them;

some that they had lent them to friends who had still to give them back; some that they had destroyed them themselves, to spare her the melancholy duty of having to do so.

Then one letter, from a middle-aged actor friend, delicately made the whole situation clear to her. 'I wish,' he wrote, 'that I could comply with your request, but I am afraid that I left the book on the Circle Line two nights ago, when I must have been even more absent-mindedly convivial than usual. I am particularly sorry about this, because one day I imagine that every surviving copy will have become a collector's item and be worth a pretty packet....'

46

Soula stared out of the window at the rain, a plump hand lifting the net curtain and cheek against the glass. Ali's father, who owned a number of hotels and brothels in Cairo, Alexandria and Beirut and who had briefly been a Minister, until some squabble (not a scandal, Ali would insist) had tumbled him from office, was on a visit to London to have a tooth capped and half-a-dozen suits made for him. But for some obscure reason – did he think that she was not good enough? – Ali had adroitly sidestepped any suggestion of a meeting. 'My father is very old,' he said in explanation, no doubt forgetting that only a few minutes before he had told her how the two of them had spent most of the previous night making a round of the Soho strip-clubs. 'He is tired and not at all well.'

When, the next day, she returned to the subject, Ali confided to her that his father – 'not a good man' – had always tried to take away from his sons any girls with whom they might fall in love. To this Soula had at once protested that no one would ever succeed in taking her away from her Ali; but in reply Ali had merely muttered sulkily and ungraciously: 'You do not know my father.'

Now for three days she had not seen him. He had telephoned once from a call-box, slipping in a coin at a time, so that the flow of their conversation was repeatedly checked by a maddening peep-peep-peep, and once from the Dorchester, where his father was staying. On neither occasion had he been explicit about their next meeting. Everything was very difficult and she must be patient and meantime he was thinking of her every minute of the day and night.

There had been a single letter from Koula, full of unrestrained protestations of undying friendship for Soula and rebellion against the noose of family obligations and duties that had tightened around her. Soula had answered it that same day, covering sheet after sheet of notepaper with an absorption so profound that she had forgotten that she was long since due at the hospital; but since then there had been a total silence. Again and again and yet again Soula had written, each letter an anguished yelp of pain and loss. Yet the silence had continued.

Standing at the window, with the rain trickling down it, she now felt her desertion and loneliness as though they were symptoms of a mortal sickness. They would get harder and harder to bear; she would never recover from them. All she could do was to resort yet again to the only anodyne that provided a temporary relief.

She raised the lid of the box that contained the vibrator, as Martha had raised it; and then, as Martha had not thought to do, she raised the vibrator itself and scrabbled beneath. She unwrapped the silver-paper, her hands trembling with a disagreeable excitement, took out the squashed joint, inexpertly rolled for her by Ali (it was the last of three) and then reached for the box of matches on the mantelpiece.

She inhaled and inhaled again, standing on tiptoe, her back arched. Then she lay on the bed, shoes still on and bedspread rumpled (Martha would have been even more indignant about that than about the joint, had she seen her) and continued to smoke, her eyes on the ceiling. Around her, her dark hair, loosed from the constriction of the ribbon in which she had taken to

167

wearing it in a pony-tail, spread like a stain, darkening as the room itself darkened in the failing light of evening; until she had the sensation that the smoke escaping from her lips and nostrils was a part of that stain, something fluid that seeped out of her and congealed, leaving her light-headed and weak and yet without that terrible throb, throb, throb of desolation deep within her being. It would be like this, she thought, if one lay in a warm bath and severed the veins in one's wrists, as that wretched patient, a boy of seventeen or eighteen, dying of cancer of the bladder, had done − all to no effect, since another patient had blundered in on him and raised the alarm.

Suddenly from far away, perhaps from deep within herself or perhaps from Cyprus, she heard a muffled keening, that reminded her of Koula as the bus had approached the airport and, in a past far more remote than that, of the mourners at the funeral of her grandmother. Dreamily she listened; and instead of its filling her with any of the expected sorrow or anguish, its effect was oddly tranquillizing. On and on it went; and (the joint long since finished) on and on she listened.

But of course! Suddenly she sat up, with a jerk of giddiness that sent the room revolving briefly round her. It must be Miss Kingsley, the sound must be coming from her room. But what could possibly have upset her? Had someone died?

Soula got off the bed and wavered towards the door. Then she gave a little shrug, hitched at a stocking and returned once more to the nest her body had made for itself.

The keening continued.

47

Was she really so contemptible? Was she really so vile? No, she was *not*! (Hurrying down the hill to catch the bus, her eyes still raw with weeping and her nose inflamed, Martha felt in the

pocket of her coat for a glacier mint and popped it in her mouth.)
It was all very well to talk of magnanimity and pity and turning
the other cheek, but what sort of place would the world be if the
worst kind of people were allowed to get away with the worst
kind of things? The trouble with Nigel was that he had never had
any guts, any guts at all. He had a rare talent for endurance,
bearing with insults and injuries and atrocious toothache or
stomach ache or headache with uncomplaining fortitude; but the
thought of a row or even 'words' made him scuttle down into his
burrow. If one cared about things, one had to be prepared to fight
for them; but Nigel had never fought for anything in his whole
life – even in the war he had managed to get himself a funk-hole
in the Ministry of Information.

But how cruel he could be! He was cruel, paradoxically,
because he did not have the courage to do anything that did not
seem to him kind. Anyone else would have told that bitch from
the start that she could not get away with that sort of defamation,
even if it had meant a row with her. Anyone else would now have
been as determined as herself to see the whole thing through in a
proper and decent fashion . . .

'If you are in such a hurry to get on this bus, madam, then do
by all means board it ahead of me.' The voice was cuttingly
precise; its owner middle-aged, shabby, scholarly-looking.

Martha knew that she had indulged in her old habit of queue-
jumping; but she replied boldly, as Nigel never would have done,
'I *think* that I was here before you. Do let us have some manners!'

Somehow, just when she had been getting over all those horrible accusations, this little incident unnerved her all over again.
She blew her nose, cleared her throat and clutched her fifty-pence
piece tighter in her gloved hand. She hoped she was not going to
break down again.

Was she really so contemptible? Was she really so vile?

This time she could not answer with that vehement No, she
was *not*! Instead, she reminded herself of all she had done and still
did for her 'girls', of the scrupulousness of her honesty, of the
help she had given Hazel with the child, of the help she had given
to so many other people, of her care for her dying mother (months
and months of it, Nigel had funked that too), of the way in which

169

she had never done anything 'immoral' (which meant, of course, sexually sinful). . . . No one could say that she was a hard or unforgiving woman, no, they could not. But it was no virtue to be spineless and to invite people to walk over one . . .

By the time she was descending the steps, slippery as though someone had spilled grease on them, down and down into the murky area outside the cracked and peeling front door that led into the headquarters of the Sanctum Regnum of the Grand Orient, Martha had again, if precariously, recovered her self-belief. She even wondered, as the bell buzzed deep within the basement flat, if she really needed the confirmation of Bronislaw Mozoomdar. She was sure that he would agree with her. What was it that he had once given them as their weekly subject for meditation? 'Better the serpent beneath the heel than the serpent within the heart.' Was that it? Yes, surely, it was. And Hazel was a kind of serpent.

At that point her meditation was cut short by a belated opening of the door by a child – male or female it was not clear from the trousers on the one hand and the long dishevelled hair on the other – who came up little higher than Martha's knee.

Pale blue eyes, beneath one of which was a violet bruise, stared at her. Then, with a wail, the pigmy fled.

'Now what *is* it?' Martha recognized the voice as that of the Master's wife; but she had never heard her speak either so loudly (usually she whispered, like a little girl asking to be excused) or so disagreeably. 'Open the door, silly! Can't you be of some bloody use?'

The door was jerked back; and there was the etiolated girl, her reddish hair dangling to her bony shoulders, with a child seated, unwinking and motionless, on the crook of one arm, and another child, the pigmy who had first opened the door or one just like it, clinging to her flowered apron. 'Yes?' she said rudely, as though she did not recognize Martha despite at least half-a-dozen visits at each of which she had made a more than generous donation.

'I came to see the Master. I couldn't telephone first because you don't seem to have a telephone.'

'It's not Thursday.'

'I know it's not. But I wanted to ask him something – wanted

170

his advice – help . . .' Martha was both surprised and annoyed to find that this frail, sniffling and seemingly feeble-minded woman had the mysterious power to fluster her.

'He can't see you now . . . Give over, do!' she shouted over her shoulder as a wail echoed down the labyrinthine corridor.

'Oh, he's out?'

'No, he's not out. But he's sick.'

'Sick?'

'He keeps bringing up this blood.' She shoved at the child at her skirt with a hand so pale that it looked as if it could not possibly have any blood in it. 'At least a pint this morning.'

'Oh, no!' Martha was horrified. 'But shouldn't he see the doctor?'

'He doesn't believe in doctors. Never has. He's daft on that subject, it's no use arguing with him.' Someone in the street above peered down through the railings at the murky area in which the two women confronted each other and then hurried on with a clack of high heels. 'It takes it out of him, that's the trouble. It's too great a strain on him.'

Martha looked puzzled.

'These meetings!' the woman almost shouted at her, her pale face suddenly beginning to turn magenta and her eyes flashing. 'All these people! People like you! Each time it's like as though he was giving a number of blood transfusions, that's what he says. It's killing him. It's going to finish him off.' Suddenly she turned, though Martha had heard nothing. Her voice again became a little-girl whisper. 'What d'you get out of bed for then?'

'What is it?'

'There's a lady wants to see you. Says she has to consult you about something. Urgent. Can't wait until Thursday, she says.'

In a faded blue towelling dressing-gown, ripped beneath a sleeve, his thin grey legs bare above woollen slippers trodden down at the heels, Bronislaw Mozoomdar, Grand Master and Convener-in-Chief of the Sanctum Regnum of the Orient, peered out at her over the shoulder of his wife.

His eyes were like knives, yes, just like knives, glittering and amazingly sharp, as they pointed at her.

171

'I can't . . . Not now,' he said. 'Ill.' There was something crusted and black along his lower lip. Blood? 'I got up because I had to go along to . . .' Long fingers retied the cord of his robe.

'Couldn't I do something? Anything, anything at all?' Martha suggested, her whole being gushing out to him in a thunderous flood of compassion and worship and love.

He shook his head and his wife in front of him pursed her lips and also shook her head faintly, as though to say 'I've got your number, all right, my lady. I've met your sort before.'

'If you need food – money. . . . Anything.'

'You must go,' he said. 'Thank you.'

Obediently Martha turned; her foot sought the first of the greasy iron stairs. Then he said behind her, in a voice strangely velvety and caressing:

'What is it, daughter? What is the matter?'

Martha faced him again. How could she put it all into words for him – Hazel's beastly book and the threat of an injunction and a writ and Nigel's attack on her and her sudden loss of faith in herself and everything she had ever done – here, out on this doorstep, with the woman and the two children staring at her with such contemptuous hostility and he so obviously ill? But then she realized that the question was merely a rhetorical one. She did not need to tell him. Of course he knew.

'You know,' she said, in calm, simple faith.

He coughed, his whole narrow frame shaking like a dead tree in a gale.

'I have one thing to say. I have one thing for you to ponder.'

'Yes! Yes!'

'THE FUTURE IS ALSO IN THE PRESENT, IT IS NOT WHOLLY CONTAINED IN THE PAST.'

He stared at her, with a strange look of surprise as if it were she, not he, who had said it. Martha stared back.

'But I know that. You've told us that before.'

'You do not *know* it. You have heard it.'

'But –'

'You have *heard* it. You do not know it.'

'But –'

172

He came between his wife and the half-open door and then the door was half-open no longer.

She stood alone and waited. From within she could hear the sound of coughing, like some engine that racketed on and on and could not be switched off.

Then she hurried up the stairs. She felt an amazing jubilance. Yes, his wife had been right. It was as though he had given her some kind of spiritual blood transfusion.

THE FUTURE IS ALSO IN THE PRESENT, IT IS NOT WHOLLY CONTAINED IN THE PAST.

She said it to herself a number of times as she floated down the street, hands slightly upturned at the wrists to assist her in the flight on which, an aerodart launched by the propulsion of his spirit, she was now dizzily spinning away at an angle to the world.

No, she could not grasp the words, not so as to explain them. But she knew that they were his way of telling her that she was right and Nigel was wrong. The good was only good if one were prepared to stand up for it and fight for it. The bad was omnipotent if one grew weary or relented in the battle. Yes, that was it, of course that was it. How well he understood her. They were at one.

48

Martha and her three cronies — two Baltimore widows and a German spinster — had just been brought their Martinis by their favourite steward, a pert, pink-faced youth from Newcastle, who always addressed them as 'girls'.

Nigel read, dozed, read. Had one of the American women really talked of the thrill of seeing the Changing of the Beefburgers and the other of the beauty of the Aga Khan viewed by

moonlight? Had the German woman really addressed Martha as
'*Püpchen*'? Or had he dreamed these things?

'Nigel!'

'Yes?'

'You've been asleep again. How about a little drinkie before we
go down?'

'Nothing for me, thank you.'

'He finds he gets liverish on board ship.'

Nigel, dozed, read, dozed.

Then he heard Martha's voice clacking: ' . . . Can you imagine
it? This woman – this so-called friend of ours – more than a friend
– Nigel, believe it or not, once nearly married her – this woman,
this creature, put me in this book of hers. Well, that's not a
novel, is it? I mean, a novel must be imagined, the characters
must be imagined. Yet she has quite a reputation, some people
think quite highly of her. But she can't invent, she just *cannot*
invent. . . . Well, I had to take drastic action. At once. Nigel is
hopeless in that kind of situation. He can't bear to do anything
decisive. But I'm just the reverse. I wasn't going to stand for it.
So I went to this lawyer, a young man, son of one of my oldest
and dearest friends. Even he rather dragged his feet at first. But
with me behind him . . .'

The Changing of the Beefburgers? The Aga Khan by moonlight? *Püpchen*?

Nigel's head nodded forward, as though some weight inside it
had suddenly dislodged itself.

49

'I was worried about you.' Evidently Miklos felt that he had to
explain his sudden, unannounced presence on her doorstep that
afternoon. 'All today I have been saying to myself "I am worried
about little Hazel", and so as soon as the boss takes himself off, I

say to Muriel – no, you do not know Muriel, she is at least sixty and ugly, ugly, ugly – I say to Muriel "Look after things for me, won't you, duckie?" and here I am.'

'Here you are. Well, come in.'

'I am disturbing your work, perhaps?'

'What work?' She gave a little laugh. 'That woman, God knows how, has made it impossible for me to do any work at all. It was all going so fluently and now it won't go at all.'

Miklos put an arm round her shoulder. 'So what have you decided?' he asked, propelling her into the sitting-room. 'You are going to fight her?'

'But I told you – surely I told you ... The last time we met ... I'm sure I did.'

'You must not give in, Hazel. You must fight her, fight, fight, fight. You must show her that you are not frightened of her. She is that kind of woman. A bully.'

'It's too late.' Hazel went over to the window and stared out into the overgrown garden. 'Too late, I'm afraid.'

'What do you mean?' He was behind her. She felt his breath on the back of her neck and then his hand again on her shoulder. He turned her round towards him: 'What do you mean?'

'The book has been withdrawn.'

'What does that mean?'

'Withdrawn. It's not going to appear. It has to be rewritten. That's how I spend all my bloody time now – rewriting and rewriting. Like a rat on a treadmill. I've become her prisoner and my sentence is hard labour. Nothing satisfies her. The number of the pages she wants altered grows and grows.'

'But you must tell her to go to hell.'

'It's too late. That's what I ought to have done – that's what I would have done if those wretched publishers had backed me up at all. But now ... it's too late.'

'You can't give in without a fight!'

'It was all a question of money. Like most things in life. I just couldn't afford it. Justice in a libel action is a luxury – a luxury way beyond my means. Or so the leading libel lawyers have assured me.'

'But, Hazel' – grabbing her by both arms, just above the

175

elbows, he turned her to face him once again – 'if it is question of money, you know that I will help you. I have my savings. You can use those!'

'You need those for your shop. What's it to be called?' She laughed because otherwise she would have wept. 'Shabitat?'

'My shop can wait. Your book cannot. It is a wonderful book, Hazel. You *must* publish it.'

She slowly put out a hand and rested its palm gently, even tentatively along his cheek, as though afraid of doing so. 'Too late, Miklos,' she said. 'Too late.' Her eyes became shiny and then filled with tears. 'But it's good of you – wonderful – to offer.'

'What is wonderful? You have been kind to me, always, many times. We are old friends.'

'Oh, yes, we're that all right!'

'And besides' – he smiled – 'I have always hated that woman.'

'But even if I accepted your money, my dear – which I wouldn't, couldn't – it's too late, it's far too late.'

It took her a long time to persuade him of that. He kept urging her to telephone to Jerry and Erwin, to the lawyers, even to Martha to say that she had changed her mind, she would put out the book as it stood, not a word in it altered; and patiently she then tried to explain to him about the copies that had been withdrawn and would soon be pulped, about the reviews written, and even set up in proof and then at the last moment spiked, about the difficulty of resuming any battle once one had allowed one's opponent to confiscate one's arms.

At the end, outstretched now full-length on the sofa, he was still sighing and shaking his head and muttering.

'I don't know what has happened to you, Hazel. You were always a fighter.'

'And I wanted to fight! I've told you. But that bloody couple – and those bloody lawyers – and that bloody little Nigel ...'

'You fought Jan for Peter, we fought him together. Didn't we?'

'Yes, yes.'

'Well then?'

She was silent.

'Is this so different?'

She looked down at her clasped hands, her lower lip between her teeth.

'How different?' he demanded.

'Until now ...' She faltered and again her teeth savaged her lower lip.

'Yes?'

'I felt so *alone*.'

'But you know that you had only to call me –'

'No, I didn't. I didn't! You had, well, you'd vanished from my life. Hadn't you?'

He was silent, still outstretched on the sofa, with his large hands crossed over his stomach and his eyes staring up at the ceiling.

'It's odd,' she said. 'I think you only really like me when I'm down. Perhaps you only really like people, any people, when they're down. Like Lydia. When she was in all that mess, then you wanted her. But once she was out of it ...'

'You are talking nonsense.'

'No, I'm not, I'm not. Jan loved me less and less because of all my misery over Peter and in the end it was that that really finished things between us. But you loved me precisely *because* ...' She got up from her chair and went over to him, again making that tentative, almost fearful gesture of laying a hand slowly along his cheek. 'Perhaps you have to pity people in order to love them. Is that it?'

His own hand covered hers. 'I don't know,' he said, as though now, for the first time, he were considering it. 'I just don't know.'

'We are close now because you feel sorry for me about the book.' He was drawing her down on to the sofa beside him. 'But if the book had appeared and if it had been a great success, then you'd have been totally indifferent to me.'

He was undoing her blouse.

'Wouldn't you? Miklos? Wouldn't you?'

He was struggling with her brassière.

'The death of Peter – which everyone thought was such a blessing – was, in fact, the worst thing that could possibly have

177

happened for me. Not only because I loved him, not only because of that. But because once he was no longer there as my perpetual cross, there was no reason for you to be there either to carry it for me.'

His fingers had touched her nipple.

'No reason at all. You must always have someone's cross to carry.'

Her voice died away. She gave a little groan and at last turned herself to him.

50

The door squeaked open, Molly careful not to be seen behind it. Previously crouched, a famished cat, behind the privet, Maggie flashed through.

'Okay?' she asked.

Molly's hand, a piece of grubby sticking-plaster over the place where small, loving teeth had met the previous night, went up to the light switch. 'You don't have to whisper, love. We've got the whole bloody place to ourselves.'

Maggie sighed and adjusted a glove with a finicky, ladylike gesture.

'What's the use of these elaborate jobs on the door if they're so fucking careless that they forget to double-lock?' Molly went on, lifting up and examining a small bronze copy of the Dancing Faun on the hall table.

'Put that down for a start. It's not worth its weight in bronze – let alone gold.'

Maggie began expertly to appraise objects, rejecting some – often by just dropping them to the floor – and putting others, a minority, on the Nigel's armchair in the sitting-room, prior to packing them into the suitcases already brought down by Molly.

'How about this?' Molly upturned a sauce-boat to the light. 'It's Meissen, isn't it?'

'Japanese.'

'Japanese! It's got the bloody crossed swords, hasn't it?'

'If the Japanese can copy a flower-design, they can copy a couple of blurred crossed swords. . . . Well, look at it. Look at it carefully.'

'Can't see all that wrong with it.'

Maggie shrugged.

'Well, you're the expert. We'll take your word for it.'

'Not a bad little carriage clock. Pity it's got this inscription engraved on it. . . . Look, why don't you go upstairs and see if there are any furs or jewellery? The old cow's not the kind of person who'd have much of either but you never know your luck. . . . And try and find another suitcase.'

'At your bidding, my lady.'

The whole house trembled as Molly mounted. Maggie drew in her lips primly and shook her head.

Ten minutes later, Molly thumped down. 'Not much there,' she announced. 'Some odds and ends of his – cuff-links, tie-pin, a Rolleiflex just about ready to pack it in. Her fur-coat's rabbit – or cat. No bloody use to anyone who hasn't got a stall in Petticoat Lane. A few stones – nothing valuable. Well, look for yourself.' She scooped out of the suitcase a handful of coral and amber.

'What's that?'

'What?'

Maggie pointed. 'That box.'

'That was in that foreign girl's room – the lodger's.' Molly retrieved the box, made of dull Jannina silver, and eased off the lid. Inside, there were a few pathetic trinkets and among them a large ruby in a setting of white gold, a present from Ali to make up for the period of neglect.

'Oh, take that back!'

'Are you out of your bleeding mind?'

'We don't want to take that from the girl. Go on – put it back.'

'That ring's worth something. I'll put the rest back and – '

'Put it all back. *All*.'

179

'Very well, my lady. But I sometimes think you're fucking daft.'

At last, their meagre loot stored away in the suitcases, they were ready to go. Maggie gave a last scrutiny to the sitting-room, her feet from time to time crunching on broken china. Then she smiled with pleasure. 'Well, that's it,' she said. She opened her legs wide.

'Christ!' In the recesses of Molly's punchdrunk brain there came together a blurred picture of her father's mare — Tricky, Trixie? — standing in the cool gloom of its Blue Mountains stable while a little girl, her hair cropped like a boy's and her large hands deep in the pockets of her slacks, watched her. 'What do you want to do that for then?'

'The relief. The exquisite relief.'

'I'm surprised you didn't do the other job too — while you're about it.'

'I might at that.'

51

'It looks like an inside job to me. What d'you say, Frank?'

'Yep. Definitely, Bill. An inside job.'

Martha, who had just noticed that part of a smashed Doulton vase had rolled under a chair, was down on her elbows and knees to fish for it, her rump far higher than her head. 'Do you really think so? . . . Drat this thing!'

'Leave it,' Nigel said. 'It's broken. Leave it.'

'You might give me a hand.'

Nigel moved to help her and stumbled over one of their suitcases. They had just come home from their cruise. 'You could move the chair for a start,' she snarled. He shoved it with his thigh.

Mind my head!'

'There.' Nigel handed her the fragment.

Martha turned round but remained on the floor, her face glistening and flushed and one stocking twisted around a leg. 'A put-up job?' she asked.

'An *inside* job, madam. Wouldn't you say, Frank?'

'Yep. That's right, Bill. Well, I mean to say – '

'Those locks – you can't just come along and pick them.'

'They certainly cost a fortune,' Martha said. 'Didn't they?'

Nigel nodded, remembering that Martha had still not paid her promised share of the expense.

'And there's no sign of a break-in. Not a window, not a door.'

Martha heaved herself up, one hand pressing deep into the chair beneath which she had been scrabbling for the Doulton vase. 'Where *is* that girl?' she suddenly demanded.

'What girl, madam?'

'Our lodger. A Greek girl – a Greek girl from Cyprus. She must have been out all night and not come home. If she'd been here and seen all this, she'd have been the one to telephone you.'

'She might have been too frightened,' Nigel said.

'Don't be idiotic. Why on earth should she be frightened of calling the police?'

It was as soon as she had said that that a suspicion began to spread like a stain in Martha's mind.

'And you think that a great deal is missing?'

'Yes, yes.' Martha looked about her at the ruin of the sitting-room and then began to gabble distractedly. 'Yes, many things, many, many things. Things of value. Of sentimental value *and* of financial value. There was this dear little miniature, of a boy in an Eton suit, Victorian, it was our great-grandfather, he later became a Governor of the United Provinces or Bengal or somewhere like that in India. Oh, and where, *where* is my glass paperweight, I once took it to the V. and A. and a young man there, *the* expert, told me that it was worth, oh, I can't remember the sum but a lot, *lot* of money ... And, Nigel, the Atkinson Grimshaw picture' – her voice became shrill – 'the canal picture, Nigel, it's vanished!' She continued to move around the room, finding one theft after another that had gone unnoticed during their first horrified inspection, until, totally overcome, she col-

181

lapsed into a chair, sobbing loudly: 'It's the *vandalism* that I just *cannot* bear. I can understand people stealing things – we all might steal things if circumstances forced us to it – but to smash things, to smash things in this totally irresponsible and *evil* way . . .' She gulped, put a handkerchief plucked from a sleeve to her eyes, gulped again and at last managed to swallow the indignant tears welling up from her throat. 'When you say a put-up job, what exactly do you mean?'

'An *inside* job, madam? Well, by that we mean that someone living in the house – or having access to the house . . .'

'A key might have changed hands . . .'

'Or a door might have been left unlatched . . .'

'Ali!'

'I'm sorry, madam?'

'What did you say, madam?'

'The girl's friend. That Egyptian. Where does his money come from? How does he run that enormous car of his? He took her to the Café Royal – and to a box at Drury Lane – and on a day-trip to Dieppe. And he gave her a ring and a fur stole and some Bentinck's Bitter-mints and an enormous bunch of winter roses – '

'Martha, do be careful what you're saying. You know that Soula is absolutely trustworthy and honest.' Nigel put a warning hand on her shoulder. One of the detectives was examining a late Victorian watercolour of a woman in pince-nez with huge coils of hair concealing her ears. The other was scratching with a fingernail at the dry earth in a pot in which an azalea (Soula had been told to water it) had shrivelled up and died.

'I am not speaking of Soula. I am speaking of that revolting Egyptian boy-friend of hers. You know you yourself said he looked thoroughly shifty and dishonest. Those were your very words! And you know the effect he's had on Soula.'

'We shall have to interview this girl – this Soula – of course.'

'Of course,' Martha agreed. 'But it's this man, this Egyptian lounge-lizard, this Ali that you ought really to see.'

'Yes, we may also have to do that in due course.'

'With your experienced eyes' – Martha looked dubiously first at one of them and then at the other – 'you will be able to sum up at once the kind of character he is. I should doubt if he had a

182

residence permit. My guess would be that he's on drugs. For all we know, he may have even persuaded that wretched girl to – '

'Martha!'

'We'll never catch the culprit – or culprits – if we're not absolutely frank with the police. Aren't I right, Inspector?'

The two detectives nodded.

'I am not saying that that Ali necessarily had anything to do with all this – much less that Soula had. But what I am saying is that there's a real possibility – which must be investigated – '

Nigel was staring at the carpet between his legs. He stopped, peered closer, then ran the back of one hand along the pile. He raised his hand to his nostrils, sniffed, wrinkled his nose in amazement. The detectives turned their attention from Martha to him.

'What *are* you doing now, Nigel?'

'Do you think that these burglars could have come in with a dog?'

'A *dog*?'

Nigel extended the back of his hand to Martha.

The detectives both lowered themselves, on their hunkers, to the carpet. They too peered, then sniffed.

One of them cleared his throat.

'It is a common phenomenon – '

'One often observes – '

'Some psychiatrists think that it may be a result of the nervous strain – '

'Though there are criminals who claim that an act of this nature ensures them luck – '

'What do you mean? What *are* you trying to say? What *is* it?'

'It could have been worse, madam,' one of the policemen pronounced, rising and dusting off the knees of his trousers.

'It could have been much worse,' the other agreed.

52

'Arnold! You're up!'

'Yes, for the moment all that borrowed blood seems to have done the trick. Unless it's Mrs Toomey's bracelet.' He raised his hand and shook it. 'She's convinced that it is. But as I told you before, I've never believed in miracles.'

'But this *is* a miracle.'

'No. Only what they call a remission. But still – it's a pleasant surprise.'

He walked briskly down the corridor ahead of her, head erect and shoulders braced. His hair was glossy again and below it the nape of his neck had a healthy glow.

'Oh, Arnold, I *am* pleased.'

'Mrs Toomey's left us these cold cuts and a salad. The claret should be good. I have *the* most enormous appetite. I seem to be eating for two – myself and death.' He went over to the tray of drinks. 'The usual?'

'Have you got a brandy?'

'Yes, of course.'

'I felt giddy and rather faint on the bus.'

'Poor thing. You've been overdoing things, I expect.'

'Well, it's more that things have been overdoing me. Thanks.' She took the glass and gulped.

'Better?'

She nodded.

'Sit.'

'When did this improvement begin?' She sank into the sofa.

'Well, it was really that evening when you visited me. Remember?'

'Yes. I feel so bad that I never visited you again.'

'No need to feel bad. I know what you've been going through with that wretched woman ... Yes, after you'd gone, I went into some kind of coma, it seems – for several hours. I had the strangest dreams. About you.' He wrinkled his forehead in the effort of remembering: 'Yes, you were in them. And her — Martha. Quite precisely *what* I dreamed. . . . But she died. Yes, she died — or was dead. I remember that. Because when I came to, it was with this extraordinary feeling of exhilaration, joy. I said to myself "The old brute's dead. Hazel doesn't have to worry any more." '

Hazel stared at him, her eyes large and startled in a face that had thinned and paled terribly in the last few weeks. Anyone seeing them would have assumed that it was she who was mortally ill, not he. She was remembering that curious encounter with the Polish clairvoyant — had it ever really taken place or had her distracted mind produced an hallucination? — and his valedictory assurance to her that she had nothing of which to worry, that her persecutor would die. Had that 'vision' in Battersea Park, whether hers or a Polish stranger's, been connected in some inexplicable way with Arnold's dream of the same time?

. . . Arnold was still talking. She forced her attention back. '. . . and the specialist was astounded. They'd really thought, you see, that that was the end. The sister even told me that they'd made arrangements for that Boston queen to move into the room the next day — as you know, he'd been coveting my view of the gas-works. Poor devil! Well, he never got it. It's he who's dead now . . . Here! Help yourself to something to eat!'

Hazel felt sick; she had no appetite. But she forced herself to take a slice of cold fillet, beaded with blood, and a leaf or two of chicory.

'I'm even writing,' Arnold went on. 'Some of the best poems I've ever written — I like to think. And after all these years! You know, something similar happened to Bartok. He was also dying of leucaemia and then suddenly the gods allowed him this marvellous Indian summer and he wrote the work that seems to me the greatest of them all, the Concerto for Orchestra. Did you know that?'

Hazel shook her head.

'But he died, of course. It got him in the end. As it's going to get me. But it's nice while it lasts,' he added cheerfully. He helped himself to three slices of beef, three of tongue, a mound of salad. 'Not, of course, that my rather feeble little poems are on a level with the Concerto for Orchestra. But you must look at them for me.'

'I'd like to do that.'

He crunched and gobbled for a while, gulped at his claret, wiped his mouth fastidiously on a white damask napkin. Then he leant forward: 'Here am I talking about myself, as usual, and not a word about you. How's the book?'

'Still rewriting. Nothing satisfies her.' She forced herself to swallow another raw hunk of meat. 'It's very odd, you know. It's no longer just the passages in which the Major appears that now concern her, it's the whole book.'

'Well, that's none of her business – '

'Of course not. But she now thinks it is. It's fantastic. It's as if – as if *she* had become the author and the book was *hers*. She writes – through Roddie, her solicitor, of course – that she thinks that this should be "clarified" and that that could be shortened or expanded and that something else "doesn't ring true".'

'It looks as if she were a novel-reviewer *manqué*.'

'It's fantastic. And fascinating, too, in a rather sinister way. There's a scene – you may remember – in which the me-character and the Miklos-character have a row in the waiting-room at the Great Ormond Street Hospital and forget all about the child. Well, her last lot of demands contained a little paragraph to the effect that on page so-and-so, wouldn't it be far more effective if they actually began a physical tug-of-war with the child? Now how on earth could a woman like that have come up with a suggestion like that? Because, as I thought about it, my fury that she should dare to interfere in something that had nothing to do with her whatsoever, suddenly turned into amazement. It's a *good* suggestion, I might even act on it.'

Arnold shook his head 'How odd. Life *is* odd – as dear Mrs Toomey never ceases to tell me.'

'Another thing – I never felt really close to her in the past, it was poor old Nigel who was really close to me. But now, don't ask me why, she seems much nearer to me, whereas he has somehow faded bit by bit into the background. I never *think* about him now. I often think about her.'

'Having an enemy *is* rather like having a lover. There's an

186

astonishing intimacy. .... I suppose all this is costing you a pretty penny?'

'I can't bear to think about it. The lawyers have already asked me for an advance of five hundred pounds.'

'*What?*'

She nodded. 'Doctors don't yet ask for an advance before agreeing to remove an appendix – though they'll probably come to it soon. And we writers don't as a rule ask for an advance before we put pen to a novel. But that apparently is how the lawyers work.'

'Five hundred!'

'That's only a beginning. There'll also be all the reprint costs.'

'Surely those publishers of yours are going to make *some* contribution?'

'They haven't offered to do so.'

'Well, *ask* them. For God's sake ask them.'

She shook her head, obstinate. 'It's in the contract. I'm the person who's financially responsible. It's a bloody unfair clause but like every other boob of an author I signed it and there it is.'

'To hell with the contract! You tell them you can't find the money, you're stony broke, and they'll damn well have to give you some help.'

Again she shook her head. 'I can't do that.'

'Why not?'

'Because it's the kind of thing I've never been able to do.'

'Well, you're an idiot! Honestly, Hazel. Any writer in your situation – '

'Yes, I know, I know. But I can't do it. I have this thing – this thing about not owing anything to anyone and not being beholden to anyone.'

'It's such stupid pride!'

She stared miserably at the one slice of beef still on her plate. The small beads of blood glittered hypnotically.

'At least let *me* help you!' he cried out.

Again she shook her head.

He knew then that he would never persuade her. An infinitely generous giver, she had never learned to receive.

She sliced the piece of beef and then sliced it again. 'My only hope is that the book – when at last it appears – makes me some money. A lot of it.'

'Oh, it will, it will. I feel sure of that. I think it'll be a bestseller, you know. All this publicity must have been helpful.'

'There's not been much publicity. There couldn't be. That's the damnable part. One or two newspapers rang me up when the book was first withdrawn but the lawyer said that I was not to say anything, anything at all. It would only make things worse, he said.'

'Nonsense.'

'One has to listen to them. They're the experts . . .' She sighed, still toying with the meat. 'There was this film offer that came to nothing – I think I told you. Well, I suppose that another *might* come along.' Suddenly, as she spoke the words, she felt certain that one would. A weight of despair and frustration slipped away from her.

'It's going to make your fortune. You'll see. It's so good, Hazel. A wonderful book. I know it's going to be a tremendous success. And not just a success with reviewers and other writers. It's got a kind of universal quality. Every woman's going to identify herself with your heroine and every man with your Miklos-character.'

'Oh, if only, if only,' she said.

She knew that her sudden optimism after weeks of pessimism was totally unreasonable. But she felt buoyed up, light-headed, in total command of a situation that had previously filled her with exasperation and despair.

53

Martha stared out of the window (oh, really, Nigel had still not pruned that privet, it was too bad) and scratched at her scalp with the end of her biro.

Swivelling round in her chair, she asked: 'Is it different from or different to?'

'Is what different from or different to?'

'I mean — what is correct?'

'Well, I myself would always use "different from". But I believe that Fowler — if my memory serves me right — says that objections to "different to" are mere pedantries. Or words to that effect. ... Why?'

'Hazel uses "different from" in this passage and I was wondering whether — '

'What business is it of yours *what* form she uses?'

'One may as well get it right.'

Nigel rose and wandered out through the French windows into the garden, the *Daily Telegraph* tucked under one arm. He preferred the *Guardian* or even *The Times* but Martha said that it was extravagant to have more than one daily paper in a household so small and it was the *Telegraph* that she liked.

'The privet!' Martha called after him.

Nigel heard but affected not to do so. It would have been impossible not to hear when the voice was so shrill and the garden so tiny. He sat himself down on a rusty iron bench, shielded from Martha's gaze by the privet in question, and stared into the sunlight reflected off the surface of the small stagnant pond.

Suddenly, as though a spear had transfixed him through the breastbone, he experienced a piercing, distracted longing to see Hazel once again. The newspaper fell from his fingers; he squirmed and bit his lower lip.

Martha returned to the xerox of the latest emendations submitted by Hazel through the intermediary first of Alec Forbes and then of Roddie. She scratched ferociously in the margin 'NO!' and then further down 'Certainly NOT' and then 'This simply *will not* do!' As though to recover from some uncontrollable nervous spasm, she followed this activity with a long period of motionlessness. Then, in a writing the neatness and smallness of which contrasted with the scrawl in which her other comments had been incised, she deliberately wrote in: 'I fail to see why the author should maintain that it is difficult to change the locale.' (Did 'locale' have an 'e' on the end? Yes, it must do, to differentiate it from a pub.) 'What the book purports to describe could as well take place anywhere else in the British Isles or indeed abroad. Campden Hill is in *no way* essential. I myself – again she looked out of the window at Nigel's shadow and again her biro dug deep into her scalp – 'would suggest either Cambridge, Oxford or Bath. All three have something of the same atmosphere as Campden Hill and all are retreats of so-called "intellectuals".' (She smiled to herself; she liked that last phrase.) 'I urge on the author to consider one of these three possibilities. At all events, Campden Hill is OUT.' She paused again, to re-read the comment, and finally underlined: 'OUT'.

The front door grunted open (something was catching beneath the jamb, she had spoken about it to Nigel time and time again) and then there was a knock, an aggressive rat-tat-tat, on the door of the sitting-room.

'Yes?'

Soula, her face crimson and the skin beneath her eyes as green and shiny as the olives for which her native village was famous, strode towards the desk. One hand clutched a still unopened letter from Koula, which she had snatched from the hall table. 'For why do you tell such stories to the police?' she demanded in an English that, Martha was alarmed to notice, seemed all at once to have regressed to the condition it had been in months and months ago, when the girl had first come to stay with her.

'What *is* the matter? What are you talking about? Calm yourself.'

'Why do you think that Ali is thief? Why? Why?'

(Could the girl have been drinking? Martha thought she detected a distinct whiff of alcohol as the girl's face, with its strange boiled look except about the eyes, approached nearer and nearer.)

'*Control yourself*, Soula.' She spoke very slowly, very distinctly, very patiently, isolating each syllable as though otherwise the girl would not understand her. 'I never said that Ali was a thief. I don't know what all this is in aid of.'

'You tell police that Ali has stolen this house. You tell them. You bad woman, bad, bad.'

190

'I said nothing of the kind to the police. Naturally they questioned both me and my brother and naturally we had to tell them everything we know. That's the custom in England whatever it may be back in your country. If the police ask us a question, we try to do everything in our power to answer it. The police seemed to think — whether rightly or wrongly I just am not in a position to pronounce — that this was a *put-up job*.'

'Put-up job?'

Martha nodded. 'Someone had somehow got hold of a key. Or had somehow been let in. Well, as you know, my brother and I were away at the time on our cruise and you were the only person in residence. If, indeed, you were in residence. Well' — Martha sighed, pushing back damp hair from damp forehead — 'naturally the police wished to know who you might have entertained during our absence. And no less naturally we had to tell them. We mentioned Ali, yes, certainly we mentioned him. But — *but* — we made no accusation of any kind whatever.'

Soula shook her head; tears were forming in the corners of eyes already bloodshot from weeping. 'You bad woman. Police come to Ali's flat, question, question, question. "What you do here in England, where you get money, residence permit, work permit, what bar you go, what club you go, what friends you have, maybe you have grass?" '

'My dear, what questions the police in their wisdom decide to put to your boy-friend is no concern — or responsibility — of mine. Or my brother's. If they put such questions, they probably had excellent reasons for doing so.'

'They search Ali's flat! You understand? They search Ali's flat!'

'I understand perfectly. And as I said. . . . Look, my dear, it's quite pointless to work yourself into this hysterical state just because the police in the course of their duties . . . Now sit down, there's a good girl, and let's discuss this calmly.'

'Do not touch, do not touch!' Soula whipped away from Martha, her teeth bared like a starved bitch's defending her young.

'I'm sorry — of course I'm sorry — that Ali should have been put to all this embarrassment and inconvenience. But I must say — with the best will in the world — that he does not strike me as the

191

kind of person one would automatically dismiss from any inquiry of this nature.'

Soula scowled, unable to follow this complex sentence. 'What you mean?'

'What I say my dear, what I say. I think it a great pity you ever met that boy. His influence on you has been only for the bad.'

'Ali is my friend! You do not say such things! He is my friend!'

'Yes, I know he's your friend, Soula my dear' – Martha remained dignified and calm – 'though I must say that I have often wished that he wasn't. You're really, basically, a very good, sweet, nice, homely kind of girl. But you're impressionable, like many girls of your age. And, being a foreigner, you don't always find it easy to see what people are really like ... Now' – she looked at her watch – 'lunch will be ready in about twenty minutes. I'm going to start frying the fish fingers almost straight away and I've got some of that nice pickle of which you're so fond. I suggest you go and have a good wash and that we forget all about this – '

'Fish fingers! Pickle! I do not wish fish fingers! I do not wish pickle! The police take away Muhammed!'

'Muhammed? And who is Muhammed?'

'He live in the same apartment as Ali. Police take him away. Because of what *you* say, bad woman!'

'Are you out of your mind? I know no Muhammed. I have never heard of this Muhammed. And I certainly never mentioned to the police anything remotely connected with any Muhammed – '

'Police also search his room. Police find pipe, pipe from Morocco.'

Martha shook her head, bewildered. 'I know nothing – nothing *whatsoever* – about Muhammed and his pipe from Morocco, nothing at all. That is strictly a matter between him and the police. ... Now get along, dear. I want to finish this work – this extremely important work – before I start on the lunch.' Martha swivelled the chair away from Soula and picked up the biro.

But the girl loomed over her: 'For why you tell police that thief steal nothing from me?'

'Because it happened to be true. They asked me what was missing and whether anything was missing from your room . . . I told the truth, because in this country we usually try to tell the truth to the police. What would be the point of lying about it?'

'I think you think that maybe Ali and I steal this house?'

'I think nothing of the kind. Now do be sensible, Soula, and let's drop this whole silly matter. The loss of so many things – so many valuable things, so many things that cannot, simply cannot be valued because of all the memories they hold for me – has been upsetting enough without a scene of this kind. I don't know what has happened to you these last weeks, really I don't, my dear. Ever since Koula went.'

'You do not speak of Koula! Koula my friend! Koula good girl!'

'I am saying nothing *whatsoever* against Koula. I am as fond of her as you are. Now that's enough, Soula. I refuse to wrangle any further with you.'

Martha began to pretend to read, holding the carbon sheets close to her eyes with one hand while the other poised her glasses over the bridge of her shiny nose. She could not do more than pretend because all at once she was in such a turmoil of rage and hurt feelings and indignation and shock that she could not decipher a single letter.

Malevolently Soula stared at her, her teeth again drawn back in that canine expression of hostility and threat and her hands extended before her, fists tight, as though preparatory to laying into Martha. She no longer looked young or attractive or carefree. She might have been some peasant mother, worn down by work, procreation and bereavement, in her native village.

'Run along, dear,' Martha said at last, without looking round. Suddenly she felt terrified of what the girl might do to her and had to control herself from throwing wide the window and screaming to Nigel to come and save her from she knew not what.

Soula continued to stare.

'Now run along. I have a lot else on my mind.'

At last Soula went; and only then Martha realized that she was shaking with tremors as of fever.

193

Soula mounted the stairs, Koula's letter clutched in the fist that had never for a moment relaxed its grip, and then threw herself on her unmade bed as the sobs tore through her. Ali had blamed it all on her, she had now blamed it all on Martha. Would he consent to see her again? Or had he meant it when he told her to get out, to go to hell, and never to show her face in the flat again?

Snivelling, her mascara running down her cheeks, she eventually sat up on the bed and slit open Koula's envelope with a long scarlet fingernail. She began to read, deciphering with difficulty the squiggling Greek characters:

'Kouklaki mou (my little doll),

Of course it is to you that I write first to tell you my news. I am engaged! He is called Sotos Evangelides and he comes from Morphou and he is the greengrocer who is the partner of my cousin in Levcosia. He is a widower and he is forty-seven and he has five children. But he does not wish for a large dowry and he has a pleasant house *tout confort*' – she had inscribed the French phrase phonetically in Greek script – 'and I think that he is kind and generous ...'

Soula flung the letter from her. She turned over on the bed, leaning on her elbows so that her hair dangled over her arms and hands and her face was a few inches above the pillow. She might have been, from her writhing and moaning, at the approach to an orgasm with some invisible lover pinned beneath her. 'Ah – ah – *ah* – AH!'

Martha looked up to the ceiling, shook her head and then put down her biro.

Well, she'd better see to those fish fingers. One thing was certain: however much that girl bawled and bellowed, she could always be relied on to make a good knife and fork.

54

Erwin was leafing through agents' prospectuses. Sonia would not care for 'a former olive-press in Corfu', transformed into 'an attractive country residence', he himself would not care for 'a unique Arab-style dwelling in the heart of the casbah in Marrakesh', and neither of them would care for 'a most desirable modern development fronting the sea eleven miles from Torremolinos'. She wanted the exotically exciting, he wanted comfort and quiet; neither of them wanted the commonplace.

Since the sale of Barlow and Braintree, in which his had been the majority holding, he had decided to retire and embark on the novel, long meditated but never begun, that his friends had been urging him to write ever since, quarter of a century before, he had won, just down from Cambridge, a short-story competition organized by a now defunct weekly in a fruitless attempt to revive its dying circulation. Jerry, who had less capital, no literary ambition and three children to support, had decided to stay on with the firm in the capacity of managing director.

'Hazel will soon be here.' Jerry's face appeared round the door.

'Oh lord! Couldn't you deal with her yourself? I think I could do without Hazel at this precise moment.'

'Do I *always* have to deal with her?'

'Well, from the end of the month she's going to be exclusively your headache.'

'Is that any reason why she should be exclusively my headache now? I should have thought the opposite.'

There was a knock at the door. 'She's here,' Eileen said.

'Well, show her in.'

'Hazel love!' Jerry held out both hands, his head on one side and his teeth bared. It was the sham behind this kind of effusiveness to women that had made a vinegary authoress describe him as 'a closet heterosexual'.

Erwin shuffled the prospectuses together and covered them with the latest copy of *The Times Literary Supplement*. He rose. 'It's awfully good of you to come, Hazel dear. We thought it better if we had a little natter, all of us together, rather than a telephone conversation or an exchange of letters.'

'You've some more bad news,' she said, drawing off a glove.

'Not at all . . . Do sit down.' Erwin pointed to a chair.

'Quite the contrary . . . Do sit, Hazel love.'

'In fact' — Erwin returned to his seat behind his desk — 'we had a long session with Alec yesterday afternoon and he agreed with us, with all of us, that the time had come to call a halt.'

Hazel nodded. 'Good.'

'That preposterous woman can't go on and on making more and more preposterous demands. We've given in to her for far longer than we should have done —'

'That's precisely what I've been telling you for weeks and weeks.'

Ignoring this, Jerry took up: 'Alec thinks the time has now come to tell her firmly "Thus far and no further". We've long since met any sensible objections she may have had. If she doesn't like it — if she decides to bring an action or an injunction — then the time has now come for us to fight. Alec thinks we could not possibly lose.'

'After all' — Erwin adjusted the *Literary Supplement* so that the words 'distinctive paved patio' could no longer be read on the mimeographed sheet that had been peeping out beneath it — 'we *could* not have been more accommodating. We withdrew the book at once, we made sure that not a single review appeared — annoying some literary editors — and we have provided one rewrite after another in endless succession.'

'I thought it was I who had provided all the rewrites.'

Again ignoring her intervention, Jerry took up once more: 'Alec thinks that any judge who reads the correspondence — which is, you must admit, pretty bizarre — will see at once that we have been dealing with a maniac.'

'So at last we're to go ahead?' She still could not believe it.

'Ye-es.' Erwin's voice dipped uncertainly and she felt her whole being dipping with it. 'With one proviso.'

'One proviso?'

'She's not only mad, she's also dangerous. And as you know,

the only thing that would really satisfy her would be to see the book suppressed once and for all.'

'I sometimes think that's the only thing that would satisfy the pair of you too.'

'Now, Hazel – that's not at all fair!'

'You must be joking, love! We're dead keen to see the book out. You know what we feel about it. We both think it's – well – terrific. Absolutely super.'

'As good as Muriel any day.'

'Or Maggie.'

'Or even Iris.'

'Well, what is this proviso?'

Erwin cleared his throat primly, the tips of the fingers of one hand to his lips. 'The old bitch – I don't have to tell you this – has been desperate to stir it up. Those two homosexuals – you remember how you told us that she had been to see them?'

Hazel nodded.

'And that doctor friend of yours,' Jerry took up. 'The one who first diagnosed that, well, that something was wrong with Peter. Didn't she write to him?'

'Yes.'

'Well, we've still got to be careful, jolly careful, love, with people like that. I mean, if she managed to get them to –'

'None of those people is going to take out an injunction or brandish a writ. I can promise you that. I've talked to them, all of them.'

Again Erwin cleared his throat but this time it was an unused, still folded handkerchief, not his fingertips, that he pressed to his lips. 'No, we realize all that. We realize we're – um – safe there. It's . . .' His voice trailed off. He looked at Jerry.

'It's . . .' Jerry looked back at him.

'Well, we're worried about this Lydia – Laura character.'

Hazel felt as if she were being sucked down into a whirlpool of liquid mud. She opened her mouth, gasped, shook her head, almost got to her feet in panic.

'There's no cause for worry there.' The words were almost impossible to get out with the mud over her mouth.

'Are you sure? If that old cow gets at her . . .'

197

'Gets round her,' Erwin took up.

'If she persuaded her that there was money in it . . .'

'Or that she could get the book suppressed.'

Hazel now struggled up out of the chair. She put both hands on Erwin's desk as though to lever herself out of the quagmire sucking at her. 'It's absurd,' she said. She began to explain: the last thing that Lydia would want would be a scandal, she wasn't that vindictive, besides she'd always hated Martha . . .

But as she spoke, Erwin and Jerry kept sighing and shifting in their seats and shaking their heads and muttering.

'That may indeed be the case,' Erwin at last cut in. 'But we can't risk it.'

'No, we just can't risk it.'

'We're not our own masters now, as you know, and our new bosses have decided in their infinite wisdom that, as we say, we just can't risk it.'

In fact, the new bosses had never been consulted.

'So?'

'So . . .' Erwin looked at Jerry.

'Well . . .' Jerry looked at Erwin.

Both men spoke at once:

'It's essential . . .'

'We have to insist . . .'

'Well, love, what it boils down to is that we can go ahead if — and only if — this Lydia character will give us a release.'

'*What?*'

'We've already got releases from the Romanian character and from your once-beloved husband. We'll now have to have one from her too.'

'But if one goes to ask her — that, that just means that one's needlessly creating trouble.' Hazel knew that she could never bring herself to go, book in hand, to Lydia to beg such a favour.

'It'll be more trouble if, once a new edition has been printed, we have to go through this same caper all over again.'

'I don't see why she should object.'

'No reason at all.'

Hazel stared at them. 'Don't you? Don't you really?'

'Well, there it is . . .'

198

'That's the little proviso ...'

'Once we have that release we can go straight ahead ...'

'Alec's in agreement with us about this ...'

'Absolutely ...'

'It's — it's impossible.' Hazel again felt that mud sucking her down.

'Nonsense. You go and have an all-girls-together chat with this Lydia — Laura. You can handle a little thing like that with no trouble at all.

'Of course you can, love. You could charm the birds off the trees.'

Erwin looked at his watch. 'And now how about some lunch?' he said. 'We had been thinking of taking you to the Café Royal. But as we both have appointments at two — how about the pub round the corner?'

'They have first-class sandwiches.'

'And the Stilton's not at all bad.'

'A sandwich and a pint,' Erwin said, reaching for his coat with its fur-lined collar.

'And some Stilton,' Jerry added, holding open the door for her with a little mock bow.

55

Nigel awoke soon after four that morning with pins-and-needles in his left hand and a line of Tennyson's on his tongue like the taste of a hangover. *Oh death in life, the days that are no more* ... Half sitting up in bed, he massaged the hand while he shifted the quotation, sour-tasting and heavy, round and round his mouth. Then he sank back again, feet together, hands straight to sides and jaws clenched, as though awaiting the discomfort and indignity of some intimate medical examination. *Oh death in life* ... With lugubrious stoicism he saw all the past years with their trivial accumulation of events as a prolonged process of dying which had now, at last, culminated in this. I could be dead, he thought. I *am* dead. A shrivelled leaf that was whirled hither and thither on the gale of Martha's rages, indignations and enthusiasms; that was crunched under the feet of her obstinacy and pride. He had long since ceased to remonstrate or reason with her. She was impervious and inflexible. 'Oh, do drop it, do drop it,' he whimpered now aloud. But 'Do drop her' was what he really meant, seeing Hazel as a lacerated body in the slavering jaws of this juggernaut. Not that he ever said such things to Martha herself, since he knew the fury with which she would then round on him: 'I will drop the matter – as you put it – just as soon as I am satisfied, fully satisfied, that every trace of poison has been removed from those pages.' The small pricks that Hazel had inflicted on Martha's self-esteem had become suppurating wounds. They had (yes, literally) driven her mad.

For hours on end now his desire to see Hazel once again and to have everything be as it had been in a prelapsarian past of daily visits and shared holidays and books lent and Martha's vagaries laughed over, would become like the actual physical ache of some long-standing, deep-seated illness. The ache would go underground, as he wrestled with the Spenserian stanzas into which he was attempting to parcel up Homer's loose hexameters, or sat with a child's unblinking gaze fixed on some scene of smashed bones, pulpy flesh and trickling blood at the back of an empty cinema in the early afternoon, or listened (Martha not there to shout 'Do we have to have this ear-splitting din?') to music on a portable transistor radio bought off a previous lodger, a Japanese whose funds, carefully hoarded, had nonetheless run out. But then with the spring of a sleeping beast aroused from the dankness and darkness of its lair, the ache would all once fasten its teeth into him yet again.

As now.

It was odd, he mused, shaken by the pain of it, that things so everyday and muted should in recollection now flash by with the brilliant plumage of birds from a long-lost Eden. How often had he returned from the Museum or from the Library or from a shopping expedition to Barkers or Safeways, and halfway up the hill, books heavy under his arm or the strings of the two shopping-bags biting deep into his palms, had then decided to mount the four cracked steps between the garden-urns and ring at her bell. Often Hazel had not seemed particularly pleased to see him and he had wondered why he had bothered to call at all. But he had gone in and followed her down the stairs to the kitchen or up the stairs into the little drawing-room where she did most of her work; and then, while she had continued with her tasks – making up a parcel of books or slicing beans or dusting the mantelpiece – he had sat and talked to her. 'Would you like a cup of coffee? It'll have to be Nes. You don't mind, do you?' She had asked that so often and always he had said No, he didn't mind. He had never minded anything – the dust that she raised around him or the smells in the kitchen or her inattention to so much that 'he told her – provided that they were together. Sometimes he would wonder if she really liked him at all or merely bore with him out of her kindness and tolerance. She was a person of habit, like himself. Perhaps he had merely achieved the status of being a habit for her, like the careful reading of weeklies that, she often declared, had become so unutterably boring, or the patronizing of this or that shop despite changes of staff and rudeness and inefficiency. It was easier to keep to the grooves; and perhaps for her their intimacy had been just another groove.

But he wanted, oh how much he wanted, to return to that trivial routine! He saw now that his whole life of service to Martha in this house had only been supportable because for a brief time, almost every day, he could escape to that other smaller, more elegant house so near to it. To others it might not seem much to spend half-an-hour or so sipping Nescafé and eating a shortbread biscuit while Hazel half-listened to him. But to him it had been everything: the patch of blue sky to the prisoner in gaol, the brazier to the night-watchman through the long, cold hours.

He did not know what impelled him suddenly to get out of bed and go to the window. He had, consciously at least, heard no sound. But suddenly he was there, narrow bare feet on narrow chill boards and a hand supporting the curtain in a loop.

Below, the front door clicked. And then he saw, her body foreshortened by the angle at which he peered down, Soula in her

201

electric blue coat, a scarf round her head and two huge suitcases and at least four carrier-bags suspended from her arms. She staggered to the gate, hardly able to walk, and attempted to open it with a raised knee. Then, defeated by the latch, she had to put down all her burdens, one of the carrier-bags tipping over to spill out a pair of shoes, a jumper rolled into a ball, a lipstick, a comb. . . . Silently, cautiously she retrieved them. Then, lips nipped between teeth, she eased her way through the wicket.

The light at that hour was an icy grey; and her face was grey and the hand with which she had adjusted the headscarf before raising the larger of the two large suitcases. What was she doing? Where was she going? Surely she could not have loaded the suitcases with things from the house?

Since that outburst of the previous week, when she had been so insulting to Martha and even, later when he had climbed up to her room to urge her to come and eat, to himself, she had then become oddly docile, nerveless and limp, like a patient convalescing after a bout of influenza. She had eaten little and she had talked hardly at all. When she had eaten, it had been in tiny, laboured mouthfuls; and when she had talked it had been in a voice so low that it had had the effect of making Martha, straining to hear it, boom yet louder. The girl had not gone out to work. 'Aren't you on duty today?' Martha had asked, and Soula had then shaken her head. 'Not on duty?' the voice more penetrating. Again the little shake. 'Are you on sick-leave?' The little shake again. 'Then oughtn't you to be reporting for work?' 'Perhaps tomorrow,' had come the whisper. But tomorrow and the day after and the day after that, Soula had stayed up in her room. Martha, at her most solicitous, had gone up from time to time to try, as she put it, to get some sense out of the girl. 'If something's worrying you, dear – or if you're not feeling well – you would tell me, wouldn't you, dear? . . . Because my brother and I, we just want to help you, that's all. We're both very fond of you, we both think you're a very, very exceptional kind of girl, and we want only what's best for you, that's all.'

From such expeditions to the bedroom under the eaves Martha had returned with brows knitted and mouth bunched. She would shake her head and make a chk-chk-chk noise. 'I can't, I simply

202

can't make it out. What's the matter with the child? I can get nothing, absolutely nothing out of her. It's so disturbing.' Did Nigel think that she was perhaps, well, in trouble? Pregnant? Or had she got herself hooked – that was the word they used, wasn't it? – on some drug that that Egyptian might have sneaked to her? Or could the hospital have given her the sack? – though God knows these days they so badly needed help that one had to do something pretty disastrous or desperate for that to happen. 'It's as though she's lost all interest in life. I gave her a letter from home this morning and instead of reading it at once – you remember how thrilled she used to be whenever she heard from anyone in Cyprus? – she just chucked it on to the dressing-table, just chucked it like that.' Martha had demonstrated with a flick of the wrist. 'Frankly, Nigel, I'm worried.'

Last evening Martha had spoken of another, less altruistic source of worry. 'I don't like to remind the poor child when she's in this run-down state but, you know, it's more than two weeks since we had a penny of rent.'

'Really?'

Martha had nodded, 'Of course if she doesn't go to the hospital, then she's not drawing any pay. And I don't suppose that she's put anything by – or that her family can send her anything. We can't support her forever, can we?'

Give her some more time, Nigel had urged. There was no hurry, it was not as though they themselves were short. Probably in a day or two she would come out of this fit of depression or whatever it was and go back to work and that would be an end of the matter.

Watching her now, Nigel had no impulse to race down the stairs and into the street, after her. Nor did he have any impulse to throw up the window and shout. Later this apathy puzzled and frightened him; and because he thought that Martha certainly would not understand – 'You actually *saw* her going and yet did nothing, nothing at all!' he could hear her saying – he never mentioned the incident to her in all their subsequent discussions, endless in their ramifications and futile in their final result, as to why the girl should have vanished so mysteriously, without either warning or goodbye.

Down the winding street, under blossoming lilac trees that in that early light seemed clouded in puffs of mist, Soula tottered. She was strong, there was no doubt about it, she had that enduring, clumsy, patient strength of a peasant. Suddenly there came back to Nigel a memory of a Sunday evening when, the cold supper of sardines, watercress salad and thick slices of bread and butter on the table, Martha had urged Nigel to be a dear and go up and see what had happened to that girl. She had shouted herself hoarse. 'Perhaps she's gone out?' No, no, she would have heard, she always heard that front door even when she was in a deep sleep. (She had not heard it now.) Nigel had knocked on Soula's door and then had called out 'Soula! Are you there, Soula?' But there had been no reply. Sometimes, recollecting what had followed, he persuaded himself that he had then decided, despite Martha's brusque dismissal of that possibility, that the girl must have slipped out, but at other times he admitted to himself that something – an odour, the faintest of rustles, some emanation – had told him that she was there. At all events, he had then opened the door – so clumsily that his right foot kicked against it as he entered.

'Oops! Sorry!'

Soula lay on the crumpled bed in nothing but a brassière and pants, one leg cocked and the other balanced on it. He could only have looked at her for a second, perhaps not even that, as his eyes alighted on her flesh and then darted away for safety, but in that brief time he had taken in a number of things: the ribbed texture of the skin at her waist (something must have constricted it, he had decided): the yellow-grey of the unwashed sole of the foot dangling in the air; the way that, her head tucked in above the support of an arm (a tuft of dark hair sprouting like some algae from the armpit), she seemed to have a double chin; and the incredibly bright eyes, pin-points of light in the frowsty semi-darkness created by the curtains, transfixing him from the valley, deep and fertile, between her breasts.

'I'd no idea . . . I thought you must have . . .'

The jerbil leapt off her, tail erect, feet scrabbling over the bare flesh of a thigh. Then it had vanished, who knew where.

'You frightened him, Mr Kingsley,' she said in the voice,

fretful yet dopey, of someone aroused needlessly from the deep sleep of exhaustion.

'Yes, I'm sorry.' He was backing. 'Sorry. I just come to say ... Supper ... Do come down, there's a good girl. We've been waiting for you.'

When he returned to the dining-room, Martha was already munching watercress. 'What on earth were you up to?'

'Up to?'

'You were away so long.'

He shook his head, did not answer. Sat. Drew his napkin from the silver ring that since their childhoods had exactly matched his sister's but for the first initial. Pulled the dish of sardines towards him. (He did not like sardines in tomato sauce, he preferred them in oil; but that was how Martha liked them and that was how they had them.)

'I think she's coming,' he said.

And now she was going, had almost gone, tottering past the pillar-box, the launderette, the little newsagent's where he had heard a day or two ago (he could not have been mistaken) that young university lecturer say to his wife of him, 'Isn't that the Major's sister?' Soon she would reach the corner where the white Triumph, with the smoked glass windows and the imitation leopardskin upholstery, had always waited for her. But it was not there now.

Nigel felt the desolation that comes to one when one sees a ship vanishing below the horizon with one's friends aboard; or gazes down at the gleaming rails on which a train has just glided out into the night, rocking a loved one away from one. He was left; she had gone on. With her high heels wobbling under the weight of her burdens, the shopping bags flopping around her calves and her breath coming in effortful gasps, she was still alive, still struggling in the net. Whereas he ...

Again he tasted the hangover bitterness and heaviness of the Tennyson line on his tongue. *Oh death in life, the days that are no more* ...

56

Ever since, three days before, Erwin and Jerry had told her that republication of the book depended on Lydia signing a release, Hazel had been in a state of depressed inertia. But today, she decided as she groped her way, head throbbing, out of bed and to the bathroom, must be a day of action.

First she would see her bank manager; and if he continued to be unhelpful, she would see one of the house agents in the district about putting the house up for sale. After that she would have to get in touch with Miklos. Even if he refused to intercede with Lydia on her behalf, it would be necessary to get the girl's address from him.

Her bank manager was no longer the plump old grizzly bear in a rumpled suit, huffing and wheezing and admonishing her in a benevolent fashion before giving in to any request, however extravagant, that she might make of him, but instead a youngish, immensely tall, immensely thin figure with sandy hair brushed across a thinning crown, who proved polite, sympathetic but obdurate. No, he was afraid he really couldn't see his way. . . . Yes, he fully understood . . . The sad truth was that, in his profession, writers, like actors, were regarded – whether justly or unjustly – as a bad financial risk . . . (A brief rustle of laughter, first somewhere behind his immaculate white-and-black striped shirt-front and then behind his no less immaculate teeth, to indicate a joke.) Yes, he appreciated that the book might eventually make a lot of money and he shared her hopes that it would . . . But. Well. Yes. Well. These things were all rather chancy, weren't they?

The young man at the house agents was so excited at the prospect of selling her lease ('Campden Hill is *very* much in demand these days') that his voice shivered with emotion, as did his bouffant hair-do and huge cravat. But when she mentioned that she would, once her lease was sold, then require a flat, preferably also on Campden Hill, the tremulous reed became a bulrush, ramrod still.

'And how many rooms would you be requiring?'

'It would have to be a minimum of four.'

'And what is the highest figure to which you would be prepared to go?'

Hazel told him.

'*Two* rooms might be possible. Not, of course, in a purpose-built block, you understand.'

'It must be at least four.'

'Had you perhaps thought of *south* of the river?'

Bearing the weight of her defeat and depression, Hazel trudged back home up the hill. Her tenants, no longer Persian students but Turkish ones, were cooking something that smelled in the hall as though it were glue. She nervously puffed at a cigarette, walking up and down the small sitting-room – the cigarette, too, seemed to taste of glue – and then picked up the telephone.

When Mrs Boreham, the retired actress from whom Miklos had rented the top floor of her house in Notting Hill Gate, at last answered and Hazel announced who she was, there was none of the usual effusiveness.

'I'm afraid he's not here. Moved on. To pastures new.'

'Moved on?'

Hazel had not seen Miklos since the occasion when, so touchingly, he had offered to lend her his savings to help her fight Martha. She had decided that her point-blank refusal, with no hesitations or evasions, must have caused him offence. He did not care for such assertions of independence from his women.

'About ten days ago. Lock, stock and barrel. I hope eventually to recover the bath-towel that – no doubt by mistake – he managed to pack.'

'Have you got his new number?'

'Number? Oh, no, he hasn't got a phone.'

'Then perhaps you could let me have his address?'

'Yes. If I can find it. Let me see . . . Yes, here it is . . . In Turnham Green. If you've any idea where that is. I haven't.'

When Hazel had scribbled down the address, she made one more attempt to be friendly:

'And how have things been going with you?' she asked.

'Oh, fine, fine.'

'And the children?'

'Fine.'

When she had put down the telephone, Hazel wondered yet again, as she had often wondered in the past, whether Miklos and Mrs Boreham (she had never learned her Christian name or, if she had, had at once forgotten it) might not have been sleeping not merely under the same roof but also, from time to time, in the same bed, despite that horde of ubiquitous children.

It was a long journey to Turnham Green, made even longer by her mistake in getting on to a train that rasped and rattled its way through the station and on to Acton Town. The block – when she found it, having been misdirected by one woman with a shopping-basket and redirected by another, identical-looking woman with a shopping-basket – must, she decided, be a Council one, as it reared up, a vast upended matchbox supported by concrete matchsticks, on the moth-eaten green baize of an inexpertly landscaped garden that was rapidly being reduced to wasteland once again by the children and dogs who played on it.

Up and up she went in the lift, faced by graffiti that someone had made a half-hearted attempt to erase with a black felt-tipped pen.

A girl – sixteen, seventeen? – with a slight cast in her right eye but otherwise beautiful in the serene regularity of her features and the freshness of her complexion and the luxuriance of her ash-blonde shoulder-length hair, suddenly let a wedge of light thud downwards on to Hazel as she stood in a long, eerily silent, eerily shadowy corridor and waited, waited on and on, after ringing the bell.

'Oh, hello.' The girl spoke, in a nasal Cockney, almost as if she had been expecting her.

'Hello. I called round –'

'Have you been standing there long?'

Hazel tried to smile. 'Well, in fact, I did ring twice.'

'I thought you might have done. I was washing my hair. And Mike was using his shaver.'

Mike. Miklos? So he did live here, there had been no mistake.

208

And presumably he and this girl, with the bare feet and the small hands, nails bitten, clasping the edges of a Japanese kimono, a dragon embroidered over her small left breast, in front of her, were living here together.

'It was Mike – Miklos – I wanted to see. Just for a moment.' (Why the hell should she sound so apologetic?) 'Business. It's rather urgent.'

'Well, come in then. Everything's in one hell of a mess. But we've both only just come back from work and we're going to a party. My brother's. His birthday.'

'I'm sorry,' Hazel mumbled, stepping round a bicycle –which of them rode it? – and thrusting her umbrella into an elephant's-foot stand. 'But as you have no telephone ... His former land-lady gave me the address.'

'That bitch? If she's rung up his office once about a towel he's supposed to have nicked she's rung up a hundred times. I suppose she didn't give you a message about it for him?'

Hazel pretended not to have heard the question.

'Miklos!'

The tiny sitting-room, with its prematurely drawn curtains and its two lamps, one with a scarf thrown over the shade, managed in some curious way to be claustrophobic despite the absence in it of anything but a few basic pieces of white-wood furniture.

'Yes! What is it?'

'Visitor for you.'

'Visitor?'

'It's me. Hazel.'

'Hazel!' He came into the room wearing only a singlet and trousers low on his narrow hips, a towel – perhaps the missing one? – far from clean, over a shoulder. 'How wonderful! Hazel!' He held out both hands.

The gesture, hands outstretched to take hers and head on one side, was curiously similar to that with which Jerry had greeted her. But whereas Jerry's had immediately struck her as false, she now felt no less immediately, with a tranquil, happy conviction: 'He's genuinely glad to see me.'

'I've come at the wrong time. I gather you're going out to a birthday party any moment now. But there was something I had to see you about. Urgent. To do with the book.'

'Well, sit down, sit down.'

He drew a straight-backed chair out from under the dining-table and sat on it in his old position, back to front, his legs wide.

'I'm in a fix about it. I need your help.'

'I knew that in the end you would come to me.'

The girl looked first at Miklos and then at Hazel. 'I'd better get on with my dressing,' she said, with no suspicion or resentment or hostility. 'Would you like me to get you a cup of tea or coffee first?'

Hazel refused.

'Hazel will have some sherry,' Miklos said, leaping up. 'That is the drink she likes best at six o'clock.'

'No, really, Miklos. Really.'

But he insisted on getting the sherry for her, brown and sweet, splashing it out into a tumbler until it was almost half-full, because he could not find a glass of any other kind.

'Now what's the trouble?' he said, resuming his place back-to-front on the chair. A hand massaged his crotch, making it all at once the focal point for her as she gazed across at him.

She began to explain, ending: 'I know it's an awful thing to ask of you. But she wouldn't do it for me, not in a hundred years. If she thought she had me at her mercy, well, she'd take advantage of it, to the full.'

'Lydia's not like that, Hazel.'

'Not like that to you, of course not. But to me ... Well, it stands to reason.'

He shook his head. 'She's a good girl.'

'Even good girls have enemies – and would like to see them punished.'

'So you want me to see her?'

'Please.'

He deliberated, the large hand still gently massaging the crotch and his lips drawn in. Then he said: 'But we don't see each other any more. It's – well – at least two months. More, much more. It's – it's difficult, Hazel. Don't you see? It's bloody difficult.'

210

'*Please*, Miklos! . . . Everything depends on this. If she won't sign, then these two little shits will wriggle out of reissuing the book. And all this agony and effort and expense will have been for precisely nothing.'

'She may have another man by now.'

'Would that matter so much?'

'She doesn't know about Irene.'

'Irene?'

He indicated the room next door with his head. Hazel realized that this was the first time she had been told the girl's name.

'I have the book here.' She could see that he was wavering. 'It's one of the very few copies now in existence. Apparently she must read it. On the document it says something about having read it, in law she has to do that, otherwise a release has no validity.' Her hand plunged again into her bag. 'And this is the document.'

He took the document and looked down at it, as though he were about to read it through. Then he folded it up and stuffed it into a pocket of his trousers.

'Don't lose it!'

'Of course I won't lose it. But I don't like this, Hazel, I don't like it at all. It's – it's bloody difficult.' He got up. 'I had better go now.'

'*Now?*'

'No time like the present – isn't that what you say over here?'

'But you have this birthday party.'

'Do you think I can enjoy a fucking party with something like this hanging over me to be done?' he demanded in a sudden flare-up of anger. 'Use your sense!'

It was as though he had punched her in the face.

As he strode towards the door, she asked: 'Aren't you going to telephone her first?'

'No. With luck she'll be in. There isn't a telephone here and every public phone-box on the estate is smashed.'

'She might not be.'

'Then I'll have to go again.'

'But wouldn't it better – ?'

'Look, Hazel.' He strode back. He leant over her, one hand on

211

the towel over his shoulder, as though he were about to use it to whip her. 'If I ring up Lydia, she's not going to see me. I know that. *I know it*. If I take her by surprise, well, possibly, just possibly . . .'

He went out and Hazel waited, flicking over the pages of a tattered copy of *Woman's Own* that she found on one of the chairs. Then from next door she heard their voices:

'But it's gone seven already.'

'You go ahead and I'll meet you there.'

'Thanks a lot. What's so important then that it can't wait until tomorrow?'

'I can't tell you. But it's something urgent. Something I've *got* to do.'

'Everything's bloody urgent if it has to be done for other people or for yourself. But if it's me that's concerned . . .'

'Oh, for Christ's sake!'

Now they were shouting at each other.

The argument continued, increasingly abrasive and pointless. Then, knotting his tie, Miklos came in:

'Well, let's go,' he said. 'The sooner we get it over the better.'

'But you don't expect me to come too?'

He pursed his lips, still in a temper. 'No, I do not expect you to come too. But since Lydia now lives in Earl's Court, we might as well share a taxi.'

Hazel rose, glad of the opportunity to leave the flat.

In the hall, Irene met her. Unlike Miklos, the girl showed no sign of the acrimonious argument of a few moments before. Evidently, while shouting back at him, she had retained sufficient control of herself to continue to get herself ready for the party. Her feet were still bare and her dress still unzipped at the side; but her face was now made up, all its previous freshness deadened to a greenish pallor, and her hair had been first dragged back from her forehead to give her a curious straining look and then arranged in elaborate curls that tumbled about her bare, freckled shoulders.

'Don't keep him too long.' She smiled, with no animosity. 'My brother won't be at all pleased if we have to wait to eat.'

'I won't be more than twenty minutes,' Miklos said impatiently, though the journey from Turnham Green to Earl's Court would alone take that time.

'You do choose the most wonderful times to go on errands,' the girl said, but goodnaturedly and again without any trace of the annoyance that had made her usually soft, nasal voice sound so aggressive and crude through the intervening wall.

'I'm afraid it's all my fault,' Hazel said humbly. 'And I really *am* extremely sorry.'

For most of the taxi-ride the two of them sat in silence.

'Has Lydia got someone else?' Hazel asked at one point.

'I don't know. I don't think so.'

'What broke it up?'

He shrugged. 'What breaks things up as a rule. We'd had enough of each other.'

'But you didn't part on good terms?'

Again he shrugged. 'You know that we stopped living together. Then we stopped seeing each other very much. And then we stopped seeing each other at all.'

She restrained herself from saying: 'That sounds like us too.'

Later she touched his hand: 'I'm grateful, awfully grateful,' she said.

He did not answer. The back of his hand felt scaly, cold.

'I like her. Irene. That *is* her name? She's beautiful, really beautiful. The most beautiful you've ever had. How did you find her?'

'I can't remember.'

'You must remember! Don't be silly.'

He shifted impatiently and then withdrew his hand from under hers, to pull out a handkerchief from a pocket to blow his nose.

She wondered if this withdrawal was because of the argument with Irene, exasperation with her for ruining his evening or nervousness at the prospect of having to face Lydia once more.

'I'll let you out here.' He rapped on the glass.

'You've got the book?' But she could see that he had. 'And the document?'

He nodded.

'Will you telephone to tell me how it goes? I'll be on tenterhooks.'

213

He was out on the pavement.

'Will you?'

Again he nodded. Then he strode off down the Earl's Court Road.

She wondered why he had not let the taxi-driver take him to the door.

57

Hazel sat on by the telephone, although it was nearly ten o'clock and she had eaten nothing since mid-day. There was a glass of whisky beside her, her third, and the edges of her anxiety at last seemed to be fractionally blunter as she ricocheted from one of them to another. What could have happened? Perhaps he had never gone to see her at all. Perhaps she had been out. Perhaps she had said No and he had not had the courage to telephone to pass on news so disastrous. Perhaps he had rushed on to the party and had thought heedlessly 'Let her damn well wait.' Perhaps. Perhaps. Perhaps.

At last – it was by then twenty to eleven and the whisky had begun to make her feel sleepy, tearful and confused – a bell rang. But it was the front door, not the telephone.

'Miklos! What happened to you! I was so worried!'

He stumbled in, hair wild and clothes dishevelled. There was what looked like either a bruise or a bite on his upper lip and his pallor was deathly.

'There,' he said thickly. Like herself he must have been drinking.

He was holding out the release; and her eyes caught the bold signature: 'Lydia M. Carroll,' with a curlicue beneath it.

'Oh, Miklos!'

'I've done it for you.'

'But did she read it, did she read it?'

'How could she read it? In so short a time? She never reads. Perhaps she cannot read.' He pushed her aside and went into the sitting-room, where he threw himself full-length on the sofa.

'But she has to . . . Don't you see . . .?'

Now her triumph turned to a dismayed exasperation.

'She refuses. I told her about the book — the plot, everything. But she did not wish to hear and she does not wish to read. She has signed to say that she has read it and, if anyone asks her, she will say that she has read it. But she refuses to read it, ever, ever.'

Hazel sank into a chair.

'That's the best I can do,' he said.

She was thinking, extremely fast and now with a mounting sense of victory. She would not tell Erwin and Jerry exactly what had happened. Lydia had signed a document that stated that she had read the book and that was what they would have to be left to believe. In a court — if the matter ever came to a court — she would merely say that she had assumed that Lydia must have done what she had said she had done. But the matter never would come to a court. Not now.

She rushed at Miklos. Stooped over him. 'Oh, Miklos, Miklos! You've saved me. Saved me!'

But he was beginning to sit up, to push her away from him.

'Never ask me to do such a thing for you again. Never, never. If it hadn't been that you were my oldest friend, Hazel — my oldest and best . . .'

She knelt on the carpet beside him and clasped his knees. 'But what happened? What happened? How did you persuade her?'

'I do not wish to talk about it. Ever. Ever, ever. Understand?'

'But, Miklos . . .'

'No. *No!*'

She could get nothing more out of him; she was never to get more out of him. When she told Arnold of the incident, he had said that probably the poor creature had had to go to bed with the girl as the price for her signature. Arnold thought it a joke. Extravagantly he had mimed the scene, with Miklos holding out the document, like a van-man, at the crucial moment and saying 'Either you sign or else the goods don't get delivered.'

But to Hazel it was never funny, either then or later. It was excruciating. She would never be sure what had happened in those two-and-three-quarter hours; but she did know that she had imposed on Miklos the savagest of ordeals.

Muttering something about getting hell from Irene and having to dash to the party, he had soon let himself out into a night now streaked with a faint, blurring rain.

'I'll walk with you till you find a taxi.'

'No, no. It's raining. Go back. *Go back.*'

She went back.

The book rested on a coffee-table with the document on top of it. She shrank from touching them, as from the bloodstained spoils of a pyrrhic victory.

58

Martha's eyes were streaming as she chopped onions vigorously in the kitchen. She had got through more than a dozen and that was only half.

'What are you going to make for them?'

'An Irish stew.' Martha caught the tear rolling down one shiny cheek on the back of her hand.

'Oh but, Martha, isn't that what you — ?'

'So what? That was months and months ago. And they both said how delicious it was.'

'Do you really want all this bother of preparing a meal? I thought we might take them out.'

'What is the point of wasting money at expensive restaurants when I can do just as well at home? This'll only take me a jiffy. Once I've got it simmering, I'll nip round the corner and buy a treacle tart. With custard. We've got more than three pints in the fridge now, you know. I thought you said you'd leave a note for the milkman?'

Nigel gave up.

Tony and Mabel were in London, staying at Brown's Hotel for a week of shopping, theatre-going and seeing of friends. They had not told Nigel of the visit – in discussing whether to do so, they had agreed that, fond though they were of him, he was really too depressing – but when an American professor with whom they were supposed to be having lunch had slipped on the steps of the Public Record Office and had sprained an ankle, they had reluctantly decided to tie up the loose end at which they found themselves by asking 'the poor old boy' out.

When, however, Nigel had told Martha about the invitation, she had at once urged him to ring back to suggest that, instead of eating out, they should come to the house on Campden Hill.

'Oh, you don't want to be bothered with them,' Nigel had protested.

'What do you mean? I shall be *delighted* to see them. You know how much I like them both. And besides – I want to talk to them about the book.'

'The book?'

'Yes. Roddie's attitude. Tony might be able to recommend someone else. Less defeatist. And those absolutely crippling bills – I want his advice on those.'

As Nigel had been passing his sister's message on to Mabel, Martha had shouted out: 'Tell them it'll just be pot-luck! Pot-luck!'

Now the four of them sat round the pot, a huge aluminium saucepan blackened round the base, into which Martha dipped a ladle to serve them. 'Enough! Enough!' Tony cried. 'We had a very late breakfast.'

'And we seldom have anything at all for lunch except a salad and some cheese.'

But 'Nonsense,' Martha said, dredging for glutinous balls of pearl-barley and wisps of meat attached to waxen gobbets of fat.

'Though I say it myself' – Martha smoothed her check napkin over her ample thighs and raised knife and fork – 'Irish stew is one of my specialities.'

Tony and Mabel exchanged dolorous glances.

'Now where was I?' Martha chewed, raised a hand to tug at a fragment of meat pinned between two front teeth and swallowed.

'Yes. Roddie. He seems totally to have lost all interest and all guts. Each time I telephone him or go to see him, he just says all over again that we've achieved all that we're likely to achieve and had better now drop the whole matter. Drop it! Can you imagine?'

Tony put a sliver of bone on the side of his plate with fastidious distaste. 'I must say, Martha, I do find myself in agreement with him.'

'You *what*?'

'A little more of this claret?' Nigel urged, hoping to produce a distraction.

But Tony went on, having given him a brief nod: 'You've had your pound of flesh, Martha. And more. Now let the wretched woman have a break.'

Martha flushed, the colour mounting up the wattles of her neck into her cheeks and then her forehead. 'I am not' – she spoke extremely slowly and precisely, as she used often to speak to Soula and Koula – 'I am not – let me get this clear – out for a pound, or any other quantity, of flesh. I am out for my rights. Which is a totally different matter. If she chooses to make outrageously untrue and damaging charges against me, then it is my right – yes, *my* right – to see that each and all of those charges are deleted.'

Mabel, who had given up on her stew, now joined in: 'I think that Hazel has made as many changes as anyone could reasonably expect her to make.'

'Have you *seen* them?'

'Well, no. But from all you've told us . . .'

'Her latest thing is to make this awful Major character into a retired NCO. Well, of course, that's just her malicious way of suggesting that I'm not quite top-drawer.'

'But, Martha, do be reasonable,' Tony urged in a languid voice, though he knew that this was the last thing that Martha was ever capable of being. 'The character has to have *some* attributes to exist at all. And he can't be a saint, however much you'd like him to be one.'

'I do *not* want him to be a saint. The idea never entered my mind. But I have a right to insist that, if people identify him

218

with me, then he must be – a – well, honourable and right-thinking and decent and Christian and, yes, basically likeable kind of person. I don't think I'm demanding too much in demanding that.'

Tony pushed his plate of half-eaten food from him and rested his elbows on the table. 'Of course, you know, I was always against you starting this whole thing.'

Martha almost leapt to her feet. She leant across the table: 'How can you say that? How *can* you? Why, you – you encouraged me! You agreed with me!'

Tony shook his head. Mabel shook her head. Nigel looked panic-stricken at the three of them in turn, his eyes scurrying hither and thither like nocturnal animals suddenly exposed to the glare of headlights.

'What *are* you saying, Martha?' Tony asked in the same lethargic, bored voice.

'On the telephone . . . When Nigel was staying with you . . . You – you as good as told me that it was my duty to bring an action . . .'

Mabel laughed. 'Oh, I'm sure you must have misunderstood him. Tony's the least litigious person in the world. *Private Eye* once had a piece about him – it was when he was on one of these university selection committees – and though everyone told him he ought to sue, well, he just couldn't be bothered.'

'I mean, what would have been the *point?*' Tony took up. 'Within a week everyone had forgotten that they had accused me of deliberately keeping out any student, however brilliant, who seemed to me politically unsound. But if I had brought an action, I'd only have given more publicity to the silly *canard.*' He tilted his chair backwards, thumbs in waistcoat pockets. 'And it's the same in your case – over this silly novel. Far more people now knew that Hazel said beastly things about you than if you'd kept your mouth shut. Who reads her, anyway?'

'You're just a defeatist! Like Roddie!'

'A realist.'

'And what about these expenses?' Martha demanded in a hostile, accusatory voice.

'What expenses?'

219

'Well, do you realize, that *I* shall have to pay all my legal costs. *She* won't have to pay a penny.'

'Well, since there hasn't been a lawsuit – '

'But by withdrawing the book, she admitted – or as good as admitted – that she was at fault. And now that silly boy – that silly Roddie – sends me in this huge bill and says that *I* am responsible. Well, in that case, why didn't he tell me that much sooner? That's what I'd like to know.'

'You seem to have got yourself into a fine old mess,' Tony said with satisfaction.

'The law in this country is a farce, an absolute farce!'

'Yes, I'd go along with you there.'

At last the meal had ended. Preparing the Nescafé in the kitchen, Nigel was glad to hear their voices no longer raised in acrimony but discussing the mystery of Soula's disappearance.

'I just don't understand people,' Martha was saying. 'Each time I think I do, something like this happens. I was so good to that girl, you've no idea. Like a mother. And then she just walks out like that, without a word of warning or goodbye and owing us two weeks' rent. I ask you!'

Tony and Mabel left their coffee, like their food, only half-consumed and then said, tripping over each other to make a multitude of excuses, that they must be going, they had this American professor to visit at the London Clinic, Mabel must catch Harrods before it closed, they hadn't got umbrellas and it looked as if it was coming on to rain, someone was going to call them at the hotel at half-past three . . .

'Fine friends,' Martha said, as the front door closed on them.

'Your Irish stew was a great success.'

'Yes. Yes, I think it was.' Then she burst out: 'How Tony could have the face to sit there and say that he had been against my doing anything about the book, I just do not know. I suppose he was once another of Hazel's precious conquests.'

'He's never liked her,' Nigel said, unwontedly firm.

'It was he who pushed me – well, all but pushed me – into it. I was undecided, I rang you up, he spoke to me. Surely you remember?' Nigel shook his head. 'After all this time . . .'

'But something so important. You *can't* have forgotten.'

Martha made her way, limping, into the sitting-room, a look of aggrieved suffering on her face. Her feet ached, her back ached, her head ached. One slaved to produce a first-class meal and all one got was opposition and criticism in return. Well, she wouldn't be seeing that pair again in a hurry. She'd never trusted them, never liked them. They were tricky, disloyal.

'I feel done in,' she announced. 'I think I'll go and put my feet up for an hour.'

'Good idea.'

Martha began searching among the piles of unanswered and sometimes even unopened letters, the out-of-date newspapers and the pamphlets and circulars. 'I know it's somewhere here.' A stack of copies of the *Radio Times* slipped over and lurched to the floor. Nigel bent down to gather them up again.

'What have you lost?'

'*The Lady*. And I've hardly looked at it. You didn't throw it out, did you?'

'Of course not.'

'You say of course not, but can you be sure? You took out that pile of newspapers yesterday – or was it the day before? – and I told you then . . .'

'Those were back-numbers of the *Telegraph*. There was no *Lady* among them.'

'You might have made a mistake.'

Both of them were now searching.

'If you'd get out of my way, perhaps I'd find it.' Nigel backed away. But after a few seconds Martha muttered: 'He stands there, he just stands there!'

'Would you like me to go out and look in the dustbins?'

'Well, that would certainly be a little more helpful.'

Some animal must have knocked off the lid of the first of the bins – after frequent nagging from Martha, Nigel now never failed to replace them – and there was water inside it and rubbish scattered all around. With a pained, long-suffering look, he stooped, a fist in the small of his back, to scrabble up some potato peel, orange rind and eggshell chips. Then he took them all out again and placed them in another, empty bin, to which he continued to add the contents of the full one. Ugh! A-a-a-gh! The

221

Irish stew was still heavy and greasy on his stomach and his tongue. He thought that at any moment he would puke.

He was halfway through when Martha shouted behind him: 'Any luck?'

'Not yet.'

An unpleasant sweat was pricking him under his arms and his nostrils were full of the sour odour of the garbage.

'You'll be a month of Sundays like that. Tip it all out. Tip it out! Then you can take a shovel to it to get it back.'

Martha pushed him aside, grabbed the bin and heaved it up and over. Rubbish cascaded on to her shoes; a piece of greaseproof paper whirled away in the wind.

'What's that?'

A shoe, extricated from the potato peelings, pointed.

'What *on earth* is it?'

Both of them stared.

'It's the cage,' Nigel said at last. 'Of that animal.'

'But look inside it.'

Yellow teeth like orange pips. Yellow claws. A rictus of solitary, starved agony.

'She must have left it there *alive*,' Nigel said on a shuddering exhalation.

'Oh, the fiend! The beastly little fiend!'

59

'Do you think we ought to give a party for Hazel?' Jerry asked.

'Parties don't sell books.'

'No, but they keep authors happy.'

'Having cancelled that previous one at such short notice. I don't honestly feel that I can go through it all once again. Besides it'll be so costly.'

'With little hope of much return on the investment.' Jerry sighed. 'The travellers are *extremely* gloomy.'

'I know.'

'There's been that other novel on almost exactly the same theme, and now there's this play. It looks as if poor Hazel may have missed the bus.'

'The *impetus* has gone. That's the trouble. Everyone was prepared to get excited about the book a year ago. But the literary editors will say 'Oh, we've had this one before' and the reviewers will have probably lost their copy and will feel disgruntled at having to read the book again.'

'What a business!'

'What a bloody business!'

'I can truthfully say that no book – not even that Mafia disaster – has caused me quite so many sleepless nights or quite so much indigestion.'

'And at least that eventually made us money.'

'And goes on making it.'

'Poor Hazel. I must say she's behaving surprisingly well.'

'Not surprisingly. Hazel does behave well. You know, any other author might just have left us to pick up the bills and then said "Sucks to you!" '

'Hazel would never do a thing like that.'

'No, bless her heart.'

'Then we do nothing about a party?'

'Nothing . . . But what we might of course do is give her a really slap-up lunch. Yes, we could do that.'

60

'How are you feeling this morning?'

'Oh, don't keep asking me that question, breakfast after breakfast, breakfast after breakfast!'

Martha's voice was husky and fretful as she splashed tea into her cup. Her clothes hung on her and even her skin did so, sagging at the jowls, the wrists, the knees. There was a coppery sheen to her cheeks beneath the bruise-like shadows ringing eyes that seemed, in their furtive panic, to be sinking deeper and deeper back into her head.

'Paper?' He held it out, though he was in the middle of reading an article about a new discovery of treasure at Mycenae.

She shook her head. 'I had this dream. Nightmare.' She put a trembling hand over her eyes. 'About that creature. In its cage. Running round and round and not being able to find a way out. Starving. No food, not even water. How *could* she have done that to it? How could anyone? She seemed such a sweet, kind sort of girl. It's — it's beyond my comprehension.'

'It's no use thinking about it.' More than five months had passed; and during those five months Nigel had often wondered if Martha now ever thought about anything but the jerbil and the book.

Martha took a piece of toast and slowly buttered it. 'It's beyond my comprehension,' she repeated.

Nigel's pity for her, as she sat opposite him with her sagging skin and her trembling hands and her spasmodically blinking eyelids, suddenly sharpened into an intense exasperation. 'Why don't you see a doctor?' he said, his voice urgent and brutal. 'You're not well.'

'I've seen Prosser, you know that. He could find nothing wrong with me. A nervous spasm, he said.'

'Probably there *is* nothing wrong. But you're brooding on it, Martha, I know you're brooding. Why not have a proper overhaul? Go to one of the really top men. Put your mind at rest.'

'It's not this — this little physical upset that's on my mind.'

She laid down the piece of toast. He knew she could not eat it.

He leant forward and again his voice became over-loud and abrasive as he told her: 'For God's sake forget the book. Forget Hazel. Forget Soula. And, above all, forget that wretched little animal.'

She stared bleakly ahead of him. 'I can't. I wish I could.'

She picked up the paper, with a lassitude that contrasted

cruelly with the briskness with which she used once to perform this action, opened it – one hand smoothed the page as though in a caress – and then began to read.

There was a long silence.

Nigel lapsed into a state of numbness close to one of total non-being. Increasingly these days such self-induced non-being had become his bolt-hole from the pity, horror and exasperated love that she incited in him. Then suddenly she aroused him:

'There's a review here. A stinker.' Her voice, previously sagging, had now miraculously tautened and sharpened. 'This woman says that it's a "thoroughly depressing theme executed in a key so low that I had difficulty in forcing myself on to the end". There!'

'The woman's a fool!'

'I must say that for the masterpiece the work was supposed to be she hasn't exactly had rave notices, has she?'

'She's had some marvellous reviews. From the people who matter. The rest . . .'

'The people who matter are, of course, the people – the few people – who like her work.'

Nigel chewed his lower lip in silence.

'Minette says that young man who runs the bookshop at the top of Church Street told her that he had sold only two copies in a week. It's not going to make her fortune, that's certain. It wasn't even in that *Evening Standard* list of bestsellers.'

Nigel covered his ears. 'Oh, for God's sake. What *is* this obsession? It's all in the past. Let's forget about it. Why do you have to go on and on pursuing the wretched woman with this hatred? No wonder you're ill. No wonder you can't sleep and can't eat and get tired as soon as you try to do anything. No wonder!'

At that, as though he had put his hand out and turned off a tap, she ceased to bubble with malicious triumph. She raised her napkin, pressed it to her lips, pressed it again, as though to staunch a cut. Oh God, was she going to cry again?

'Perhaps I should see someone,' she said in a quiet, forlorn voice. 'Perhaps you're right. I'm not myself. I've not been myself for a long, long time.'

225

Harrowed, he jumped up and went round the table to her. He put an arm round her shoulder, a cheek to hers. 'I'll arrange it,' he said. 'The best man there is. Don't worry. I'm sure it's nothing really. But let's make certain. The best man. Let me fix it for you.'

61

'I think it would be worth your while to let this lady and gentleman see over the property.'

Hazel could visualize the bouffant hair-do, the huge cravat and the wet-look shoes with the brass buckles on them.

'What's the point?' she asked. 'I'm sick of showing people round. And the lease is as good as sold.'

'Mr Rabinowski is, I gather, a *very* rich gentleman. You've probably heard of him?'

'I can't say I have.'

'There was a piece about him on the money page of the *Express* the other day. I remember reading it. His wife says she won't live anywhere but on Campden Hill.'

'Well, I suppose if the Maitlands fell through . . . But it seems hardly likely. They've paid their deposit and my solicitor says that —'

'The Maitlands are very nice people, of course, but they're hardly in the same league . . . I mean, Mrs Saunders, Mr and Mrs Rabinowski, well, I think you could get any price you liked from them.'

'But I'm committed!'

'Committed?'

'To the Maitlands.'

There was a gay tinkling laugh at the other end of the line. 'Until the contracts are actually exchanged, you're in no way committed at all, Mrs Saunders. Not at all. I assure you of that.'

'But I gave my word.'

'Every house-owner has the right to get the best possible —'

'I gave my word.'

'Well, if you feel like that, then of course —'

'Yes, I do feel like that, I'm sorry.'

'It's a marvellous chance missed.'

'No doubt. But there it is . . . Now this flat you were telling me about . . .'

'Oh, yes. Yes.' The voice had become remote, bored, super-cilious. 'I have the details here before me. The price is just five hundred above your maximum. Four rooms — well, almost. One is a dressing-room off the bedroom. Rather wee. The building is not *exactly* in Prince of Wales Drive but it's only just the other side of it. And Prince of Wales Drive, as you probably know, has now become an *extremely* fashionable address.'

Gloom enveloped Hazel. But bravely she asked: 'When could I see it?'

'As soon as possible, would be my advice. Such a desirable property at such a low price — well, you have to be the early bird.'

'All right. Now. Today. At once. How about that?'

The voice became evasive: 'I must just make sure that it hasn't gone already.'

62

Martha sat in the towelling dressing-gown, faintly redolent of carbolic and so tight over her bosom that she had to clutch it together with a hand, and nodded and sighed and nodded. The gas fire scorched one leg, while the other felt icy.

The eminent consultant, whom Nigel had arranged for her to see privately in his Harley Street consulting rooms, had a heavy cold and was feeling tired both from it and from the effort of not sneezing or blowing his nose in front of his patients.

He could find nothing, nothing at all, amiss. She was in remarkably good health for a woman of her age. Extensive and exhaustive tests. Blood, urine, X-rays, cardiograph. Well, she knew herself how during these last two days they had left not a stone unturned. No, apart from a certain tendency to rheumatoid arthritis – nothing out of the way in a woman of her years – he could, to all intents and purposes, give her a clean bill of health.

He smiled at her, his nose red and puffy and his eyes watering as though with tears of sympathy at the pale, worried face that she still persisted in upturning to him.

'Then why do I feel so terribly ill?' she asked.

Again he smiled, reassuring and benign. 'I'm coming to that. I'm not going to tell you that you don't *feel* ill. All I am saying is that physically you are *not* ill. But, as your own doctor rightly diagnosed, you are suffering from a nervous spasm that produces these rather unpleasant attacks of vomiting and diarrhoea and so forth. *They* are a reality, of course they are. But there is no organic cause for them.'

She licked her dry lips and stooped to scratch at the skin of the leg shrivelled by the gas fire. 'Then what is to be done?'

'What is to be done? Well, in the first place' – he allowed himself to touch the dripping tip of his nose with a handkerchief, though not to blow it – 'I am not going to tell you that it's all just nerves and then send you about your business. No. I am going to prescribe two sets of bills – er – pills for you.' His face, already flushed from the cold, darkened further at his embarrassing slip of the tongue. 'One set will, I hope, control the spasms. And the other should act on your – er – general well-being. If – *if* – these distressing symptoms still continue after, say, two weeks, then I think we'll have to think again.'

'Think again? How?'

'Well . . .' He paused, sniffing and then swallowing the catarrh. 'It might, for example, be a good idea for you to see a psychiatrist.'

'A psychiatrist! But there's nothing wrong with me mentally!'

He laughed to reassure her. 'These days a lot of perfectly sane people consult psychiatrists about such minor difficulties.' He wanted to get the interview over as soon as possible and retire to bed – she was the last patient of the day – but something about her attitude, unnaturally rigid and intent, made him decide that he must expatiate a little further. 'Would I be right in thinking that you've been through a rather troubling time just recently?'

Martha nodded. There were few patients who did not nod when he put this question to them.

'I thought so. I should say that anxiety of some kind – strain – tension – are the root causes of this physical upset from which you've been suffering. It's the mind taking its revenge on the body. Psychosomatic – to use the fashionable jargon.'

'Yes, I *have* been through the *most* worrying period.' She was mastered by a longing to pour out everything – Hazel's horrible book, Nigel's failure to stand by her as a brother should, Roddie's ineffectiveness and lack of guts, Tony's and Mabel's withdrawal of support, Soula's departure and that revolting business of the jerbil – everything, everything in a single uninterrupted stream to this kind, sweet, tired-looking man before her. 'It all began about a year ago when this woman, this woman I had thought was one of my closest friends, suddenly, out of the blue . . .'

But he was not listening. He had drawn a pad towards him, was scribbling on one sheet, then scribbling on another.

He rose, a small pear-shaped man of indeterminate years with a large mole on his pointed chin: 'You must try not to worry. A counsel of perfection, yes, I know. Which of us doesn't worry? I do, we all do. But at least try to worry less.' He was holding out the prescriptions and nervelessly she took them with her right hand while the left still held the folds of the ill-fitting dressing-gown together over her breasts. He opened the door, he gave a little bow.

'I can find my own way to the dressing-room,' she said in a remote, desolate voice.

'Nonsense. I'll take you there.'

Again he opened the door, again he gave the little bow.

'When you're ready, just give this bell' – he waved a small soft hand – 'a push, would you? Then my secretary can show you out. You'll excuse me if I say goodbye now but I have a lot of things to tie up before I go home.'

As she dressed, Martha said over to herself all the things that

229

she had been about to say to him, fumbling clumsily with straps, buttons and hooks and getting herself entangled with sleeves.

She rang the bell.

A fresh-faced girl, pert and trim, arrived, an envelope in her hand.

'Ready, Miss Kingsley? Now don't forget your umbrella! It's started to spit.' She thrust out the envelope. 'Would you like to give me your cheque before you go?'

63

Having paid out so much, Martha denied herself the taxi that she had promised Nigel to take, and instead scrambled on board a bus, pushing aside two elderly Swedish women tourists who had tried to jump the queue. The nerve of it! She battled on to the top of the bus and then, between raincoats and protruding umbrellas, thrust to the front, where she found a seat next to a dark-skinned man with pockmarks on his cheeks (was there anyone in London who wasn't foreign?) about half her size.

Staring out through a window lashed with rain but seeing nothing, she thought: He as good as said that I was bonkers. Or heading for a breakdown. Well, of course, I've not been myself, not for a long time, he's right about that. People always used to say that I was such fun, even when I was a schoolgirl they said it. You always cheer us up, that's what Minette used to say on those days when Roddie had been beastly or she had gone and paid far too much for something that turned out not to be what it was supposed to be. You're always the life and soul of any party, that's what Beryl used to say. But somehow, since that horrible business about the book, she could no longer *enjoy* herself and she could no longer give out enjoyment. It was as if something within her – some channel – had got blocked. Nothing *flowed* any longer. Food these days passed through her, almost as soon as she had swallowed it, but that was different. Nothing else did. The joy was bottled up, clogged. It grew stagnant. Soured. Septic.

Suddenly it came to her: today was Thursday and the Sanctum Regnum of the Grand Orient would be in weekly session. Since that rebuff (because it had been a rebuff, though it had taken her some time to realize it), with the Master ill and that shrewish wife of his more or less putting her out of the door, Martha had not been back. But if anyone could solve this problem of hers – if anyone could make things flow again as once they used to do – surely it was Bronislaw Mozoomdar? Perhaps this long, debilitating illness of hers had really been a kind of punishment for her pride in not returning . . .

'Please stop! Please stop here!'

She came clattering down the stairs.

'Wasn't that a stop?'

The conductor, a woman, nodded indifferently as she counted some small change in a mittened hand.

'Well, then, why didn't we stop?'

'Request.' The woman went on turning over the coins.

The iron steps down to the basement – Martha was soaked from the rain that seemed to have scimitared in at her from every direction simultaneously and her low-heeled shoes were squelching – still felt as though they had been smeared with grease. She stepped with extreme caution, ungloved hand on icy rail. But though she was aware of the dampness of her shoulders and around her ankles, of the threat of the steps, of the metal on her palm, of the sounds of water running into gutters and buses swishing by, yet it was only with some small part of her being and the rest of it was tingling with an all-absorbing expectation. High, high, high an invisible bow was drawing out of her a note of piercing sweetness and vibrancy, as it moved slowly across strings on which the dust had long lain thick.

The door was not on the latch as on previous Thursdays; and when she pressed the bell it was not the Master's wife who opened the door but a squat girl with a flat nose and fringe, in trousers and a poncho. 'Hi,' she said in a not unfriendly American accent.

'Have I made a mistake? I thought . . . I came to see Mr Mozoomdar . . .'

231

'Yeah. He's in.'

'But isn't this ...? I thought that on Thursday ...'

'It used to be Thursday. Now we've made it Tuesday ... On account of my pottery classes. I like to be here if I can. To lend a hand.'

'Then isn't ...?' Martha wanted to ask about the Master's wife and his children; but she stopped herself from doing so, instead shaking out her umbrella before entering.

Inside, all had been transformed. Martha gazed about her. The grey walls, that once in the dim light had seemed to be covered with the finest of cobwebs, now blazed out with every colour of the spectrum. In an alcove – had it been there before? she could not remember that alcove at all – stood a statue, daubed with gold and vermilion, of some god, yes, it must be a god, with innumerable arms and legs waving in a dance. A spotlight shone on it, affixed to the top of one of the bookshelves. Shaggy white rugs stretched down the long passage, making it look much shorter than she had remembered it from her previous visits.

'It's – it's all different.'

'Yeah.' The girl gazed at her intently as she in turn gazed intently at the statue. 'Well, we wanted to make it all a little less depressing. It's bad enough to live in a basement but one doesn't have to live in a *cellar* ...' Martha was looking around her, dripping macintosh in hand. 'I'll put that in the bathroom, shall I? Then I'll tell Bronnie that you're here. What name is it?'

'Miss Kingsley. Miss Martha Kingsley ... But I – I don't want to disturb him if he's busy. I thought, you see, that as it was Thursday –'

'He's only sewing.'

Could she have said that? *Sewing? Sewing?* Why and what should he be sewing? Martha waited under the statue in a state of mingled bewilderment, excitement and dread.

'Miss Kingsley.'

He came towards her in some kind of long, off-white robe, rough in texture, with a square neck, picked out with embroidery, that revealed his prominent adam's apple and his no less prominent collar-bones. His feet, long and narrow, were bare and he now had hair reaching to his shoulders and a small goatee

232

beard. There was a circle of red – wasn't that called a caste-mark? – on his forehead and a huge Maltese cross of beaten silver dangling from a silver chain on his breast.

'Master.' She took his hand and then, on a mad impulse, bowed over it and kissed it, all but bruising her lips, in her wild eagerness, on a huge opal clasped in writhing silver.

He looked down at her, as though she had done nothing surprising.

'I came . . . I thought . . . It used to be on Thursday . . .'

'It doesn't matter, daughter.' (Last time, hadn't he called her 'sister'? What *did* the change mean?) 'Come. Come into the Sanctum.'

He walked slowly down the corridor, followed first by Martha and then by the girl.

'Are you better?' Martha asked in a high, nervous voice that ricocheted back and forth from brilliant wall to wall.

'Better?' He half turned his head.

'You were ill the last time I called.'

He did not answer.

The Sanctum, too, had changed, its walls hung now with some kind of black material – velvet probably, she could not be sure in a light so dim – with an altar at the far end, on a dais draped in a cloth of purple and gold, and behind the altar a huge lamp made of slivers of different-coloured glass set in a metal that looked like putty.

He pointed to a banquette that ran down one side of the room, covered with the same kind of white fleecy rugs as the floors.

'Sit.'

She sat. One of her eyelids was twitching uncontrollably and she suddenly had a terrible desire to make water.

He sat opposite her, on another similar banquette with the whole width of the room between them. The girl stood, a shadowy presence, arms crossed under breasts, against the door, like a guard.

'Something is troubling you.'

She nodded. 'Yes, yes, you're right. That's why I came to see you, *had* to come to see you. I feel that only you can help me.'

'I can help you.'

'You gave me that advice the last time I came.' Now the words were gushing out of her after the initial hesitancy of her dread and bewilderment. 'THE FUTURE IS ALSO IN THE PAST, IT IS NOT WHOLLY CONTAINED IN THE PRESENT. Or was it' – suddenly she was transfixed with panic – 'was it the other way around?' She tried it, on an interrogative note: 'THE FUTURE IS ALSO IN THE PRESENT, IT IS NOT WHOLLY CONTAINED IN THE PAST?'

But he did not enlighten her. Instead, he stroked the pointed beard and said slowly: 'I gave you advice but you did not understand it.'

'At first I seemed to. Yes, I did, I did! But then – slowly – oh, I don't know ... I got discouraged. I felt so confused ... Perhaps I – I lost the key.'

He nodded. 'You lost the key.'

'Give it back to me! Please give it back to me!' He stared at her with his passionless, milky-brown eyes. He smiled. 'Oh please! These last months – they've been such, oh such hell! I don't know why. I can't *enjoy* anything any more. The *taste* seems to have gone out of things.' Still the eyes stared; still the long fingers with the long, far from clean nails stroked the beard. By the doorway the girl shifted and then became motionless once more. 'Well, yes, I do know why I do. You see, there was this woman, this woman I thought was a friend of mine, and this woman, this woman I thought was a friend –'

The hand came away from the beard. Then slowly he raised it. 'You are full of hate,' he said.

Martha hung her head. She knew it was true.

'You do not have to tell me. You are full of hate. You cannot pour it out. The chalice is clogged with it. How can joy stream in when the chalice is clogged?'

Martha writhed, her hands twisting together in her lap and her legs entangled, damp stocking on damp stocking. Then she looked up, her gaunt face rapt and beseeching: 'Help me! Help me, Master!'

He nodded, rose. Went over to a cupboard that stood low against the furthest wall. It, too, blazed with the same brilliant colours in smears and slashes as the corridors and walls outside. He opened it.

Martha stared. He had taken from it what looked like an extremely sharp bodkin – the blade glittered in the variegated light from the lamp – with a handle of twisted silver.

He came towards her. She was not afraid.

He pointed to the altar steps, and at once she knew what was expected of her. She got up, walked slowly over to them and then lay herself down on them, her head at the top of them and her feet at the bottom. Sprawled like that, with the middle step digging into her buttocks, she nonetheless felt no discomfort.

The girl glided forward and lit the single candle in a silver candlestick on the altar. Then she backed away, her hands behind her back and her eyes half-shut.

The Master passed the bodkin back and forth through the flame of the candle, back and forth, back and forth, a number of times. His lips trembled slightly, as did his cheeks, in the shuddering light.

He stooped over Martha; he took her right hand in his. He murmured 'The gate of darkness is the gate through which the sun shall ride.' She felt a sharp prick; drew in a breath; almost screamed. An overmastering drowsiness began to creep up and up and over her.

. . . The field shimmers silver in the first light of day. It exhales puffs of mist here and there, as though the sun, an orange ludo-disc balanced on the crown of the hill, were already warm enough to suck up its moisture, as from a lake. The two children's zigzag trails, separating, converging, overprinting each other, then separating again, look deep and dark as Martha glances back over her shoulder. In the field that they have already left there is a herd of cows, their udders heavy, their eyes blurred as though with sleep. When they saw the brother and sister, they lowered their heads and moaned. Nigel, terrified, first quickened his pace and then broke into a jolting run, an ankle from time to time buckling from what appeared to be the weight of the basket over his skinny arm. His red jersey! – bulls hated red, he had heard that often. He ducked under the barbed wire and felt the wool catch on one of its iron thorns, as if it were his own pink flesh impaled upon it. Then he pulled free, with a ripping sound. The basket tipped, the mushrooms scattered. Oh, he cried, oh,

oh! Martha approached him slowly, her own full basket clasped
before her in both her hands. Silly. They're only cows. They can't
hurt you. And now you've dropped almost all your mushrooms.
He made no attempt to pick them up. It was she who did so,
rejecting some that had fallen into a cowpat shining, crusty and
yellow-green, beside a tussock of grass.

You'll have to pick those ones up yourself.

Still he didn't move.

Coward, she told him.

Now, in the other field, he peers into her basket. You've many
more than me. She nods. Many more. Their mother, who sent
them out, will say the same thing, with triumphant satisfaction.
Trust you to pick only a tenth of Martha's lot. She uses one child
to humiliate the other, with complete impartiality. This morning
it will be Nigel's turn to be humiliated, because mushroom-
picking is a practical business and Martha is the practical one.
This afternoon Nigel will outshine Martha at three-handed whist
or Lexicon or Monopoly and their mother will remark that Nigel
has all the brains. Again Nigel peers. His hands and bare knees
have a bluish tinge to them; the tip of his nose too. Their mother
will not only be contemptuous about his load of mushrooms; she
will also be angry about the ripped sleeve of his jersey. Your new
jersey! Really! I knew it was a mistake to let you wear it! But he
has no other for a chill, damp autumn morning like this.

You've many more than me. He is almost whimpering.

Well, you don't *look*. Do you? *Do you?*

His face gathers into little puckers. Is he really going to cry?

For a moment Martha wants him to cry. She is proud of the
mushrooms, still wet with dew, that glisten up at her from her
basket; and she is disdainful of his own meagre gatherings, their
cups often chipped or their stalks broken because of his clumsi-
ness. But then, as the rising ludo-disc of the sun suddenly flashes
fire in all directions, pride and disdain both simultaneously flame
up and then shrivel into ashes.

Oh – what is one to do with you?

The still rising sun seems to have pierced through her overcoat
(a cast-off from an older, boy cousin, the buttons the wrong side)
and her blouse and her liberty-bodice. It is against her soft,

236

virginal skin and then, somehow, it slips within her skin to make
a solid, throbbing core of warmth. Here. She tips her basket and
the mushrooms shower out from it into his.

Oh. Oh, Martha.

Don't tell her. She means: Don't tell their mother.

As if I would.

Oh, Nigel, what are we going to do with you? What on earth
are we going to do with you? She cries it out, not in exasperation
as so often before, but with a wild, protective passion.

   ... Martha's eyes fluttered open. Where was she? She hardly
knew for a moment but she felt no panic at not knowing. The
Master was now taking her other, her left, hand in his. He
repeated those same words: 'The gate of darkness is the gate
through which the sun shall ride.' Once more a blanket of
drowsiness, thick and furry, was drawn up and up and over her.

   ... The Serpentine shimmers silver in the waning light of
evening. It exhales puffs of mist here and there, as though, deep
beneath its tranquil surface, hidden geysers were seething. Their
zigzag wake crosses and recrosses the wakes of other boats. Five
khaki-clad youths, in a boat so small that their combined weight
has sunk it almost to its gunwale, bawl out ribald comments
across the darkening waters. She can't make out what the comments are, not exactly, as she tugs, tugs, tugs, manfully at the
oars, but from an expression, furtive, ashamed and fearful on the
countenance opposite to her, she knows that Frank has made
them out. She also knows that he feels that he ought to say
something or do something but that, so sleek and meek and
peaky, he will deliberately ignore the whole scene.

Suddenly she realizes what those shouts are all about. She feels
a profound shame and humiliation as she releases one of the oars
and gives a downward tug to her skirt. The soldiers have glimpsed a suspender, a flash of pink flesh, perhaps even a lace-edge of
knickers. She glares in their direction, because Frank will never
glare, and the five ruddy-faced, larky youths fall silent. They are
not really interested in her. Plump, plain, dowdy. Nor are they
interested in her army chaplain, with that long, smooth face that
looks as if a razor had never been over it and that soft, pale hair,
the colour of condensed milk. Over there, under the bridge, two

ATS girls are trying to change places, one standing up in their rocking boat and squealing while the other, hands over heavily lipsticked mouth, attempts to stifle her own squeals. Their once crisp khaki blouses have darkened under armpits and between shoulder-blades from the exertion of rowing.

Dreadful people, Frank says. Most people are dreadful for him, in the literal meaning of the word.

For a moment she too thinks: Dreadful people. But then: No, they're not, they're not. Not that she contradicts him. She never contradicts him because, though so feeble and yielding with others, with her he does not care for contradiction. Instead, she leans on the oars, the boat gently rocking up and down and up and down, as the last light seems to flow away from the centre of the lake and withdraw to its edges. Soon the one-legged gypsy-like man in charge of the boats will begin to whistle and then to shout.

Oh, Frank, she says. Frank.

He smiles uncertainly.

She puts out a hand but she cannot quite reach the hands, thin and pale, that dangle between knees that she has never seen except in trousers. He makes no move to approach her. She shifts forward on the seat, stretches, stretches, stretches. It is all so beautiful: the trees darkening around the lake; the laughter and shouts, far-off now, of the five soldiers and the squeals, no longer frightened but provocative, of the two girls in the boat that they pretend that they cannot manage. Now the tips of his fingers, strangely cold and strangely nerveless, rest on her palms. The position is an uncomfortable one but she is aware of no discomfort. Only this sense of untroubled contentment and peace and love.

What have I done to deserve you?

He does not answer. He only smiles uncertainly, his fingers cold and nerveless on her hot, throbbing palms.

I'll never love anyone as I love you.

She knows that to be the truth. That truth, so bitter in after years, makes her supremely happy.

. . . Martha wriggled and moaned; a thread of saliva glistened on her chin. What was the girl doing? She felt her jerking off first

238

one of her shoes and then the other; next, she was fumbling under her skirt for her suspenders. Now those deft, soft hands were drawing off her stockings, peeling them, sodden, off the flesh as though to expose a fruit.

The Master raised her right foot. Martha knew that it was he who had done that and not the girl, seconds before she had focused her eyes on his looming presence. 'The gate of darkness is the gate through which the sun shall ride.' Had he pricked her again with that bodkin? She was not certain as once more that irresistible, soporific tide flowed up and up and over her.

. . . The doctor, who was once in the Indian Medical Service and who, with his stiff carriage, bristly white moustache and close-cropped white hair, might easily pass for a retired naval officer, sips dubiously at his glass of sherry. He can see motes of dust on its surface as he holds it in a shaft of sunlight; he knows that it will be tacky and sweet, the sort of sherry that his second wife, French and many years younger than himself, would use only for cooking. Nigel is opposite to him, leaning forward in his chair, with his hands under his thighs, his tie askew and an ink-stain on his right cheek, like a bruise. He might be a school-boy facing his headmaster.

So that's your advice.

The doctor nods, sips, nods. It's too much of a strain for Martha here. Martha is standing silent by the window, a hand clutching the curtain as though for support. And for you too, of course.

But a home, Nigel protests. *This* is her home.

The doctor shrugs, sips, sighs. She won't know the difference. She's past all that. She doesn't know you, she doesn't know Martha. Does she?

Martha is sometimes not sure about that. Sometimes she thinks that her mother, lying motionless there with the right side of her face all twisted upwards as though, in a moment of exasperation, a sculptor had given a blow to the putty on which he was working, *does* know her. She has sometimes come into the sickroom and a light has seemed briefly to flare in those dull, dead eyes under their drooping lids, like a match flaring behind some cobwebbed window.

239

There's the expense of course, the doctor goes on. I know that. Because I'm sure you wouldn't want her to go into an institution.

Oh, no, not that, not an institution, Nigel cries out, writhing on the hands on which he is still sitting. Oh no.

The home I have in mind is in Brighton. An easy journey from here. The matron is a really splendid woman. Old people are her vocation. And she has such a splendid staff. All as dedicated as she is.

Nigel withdraws his hands from under him, locks the fingers together and then pushes them outwards, so that Martha can hear the joints click. She has always hated it when he does that, it sets her teeth on edge. Now she finds the sound almost intolerable. She steps forward, out of the shadow of the curtain into the sunlight.

We couldn't do that, Nigel, she says. Ever. You know we couldn't. Nigel looks helplessly from her to the doctor and then back at her again. His mouth opens, he seems to be gasping for air.

It's best for everyone, the doctor says lugubriously. He has known them for many years. Best for you both and, more important, best for her.

Nigel nods now.

Martha says nothing. Instead, she turns on her heel and goes out of the room, down the long passage and to the door of what was once their dead father's study and has now been converted into a sickroom for their dying mother. She turns the handle and goes in, her nostrils twitching and her stomach churning at that stench that no sprays or disinfectants can ever wholly eliminate. The dying woman might already be dead, so motionless is she, so rigid, so grey. Martha stares at her and, as she stares, she is suddenly overcome with fury and loathing. You mucked up my life. You ruined it. He'd have married me on his own terms and I was prepared to accept those terms. I didn't care about all those horrid things you hinted at. But you weren't having that and I listened to you, I was a fool and listened to you. And then, when someone else might have come along, Daddy died — because you'd worn him out — and I had to take his place as your errand-boy and whipping-boy. After that, I never had a chance. You

240

never gave me a chance. So why should I give you a chance now? Why shouldn't you go into a home? Why should I waste any more of my life on you? Why?

Suddenly that match seems to flare behind the cobwebbed pane. Or has she imagined it? The match flares again briefly.

Martha kneels beside the bed and takes the limp, cold hand in hers. There is no wedding-ring on the third finger now, because it kept slipping off, so they put it away in a drawer. All there is now is what looks like a scar where the ring used once to be. Mother, she says. Mother. She puts the hand to her lips. It doesn't matter. I don't mean all that. I'm overwrought, tired. Probably it wasn't you. Probably it was me – silly, hopeless me. Who knows? Who *can* know? She feels the tears on her cheeks and then tastes one, salt and bitter, as it trickles into the tuck at the left corner of her mouth. You did your best. You wanted the best for me. It doesn't matter. It honestly doesn't matter.

The woman on the bed doesn't stir; the match does not flare again.

Resolute now, Martha rises to her feet, leaves the room, goes back down the corridor and once more enters the sitting-room, where the shaft of autumn sunlight, eddying with motes of dust, still illuminates the doctor and his half-drunk glass of sherry. He looks up at her inquiringly from under bushy eyebrows. He is thinking of the luncheon that his French wife has prepared for him and that is now overdue, and no longer of the problems of this sad, silly, vacillating pair, brother and sister.

Martha surprises him. She'll stay there to the end, she says, in a voice that has suddenly become authoritative. To the end. I want that. She'd want that.

Well, of course, my dear.

Martha, whom he has always thought so totally insignificant, has suddenly acquired a strange kind of majesty. He finds it hard to gaze back at her through the whirling motes of dust between them. It is as though she had become even brighter than that shaft of sunlight.

. . . Martha opened her eyes and smiled dreamily at the Master as he raised her left foot as he had previously raised her right. The same words pattered down on her like a cooling rain: 'The

241

gate of darkness is the gate through which the sun shall ride.'
Was that a prick of the bodkin that made it feel as though some
small insect, a midge or mosquito, had stung her on the instep?
Once again a wave of somnolence rippled up and up and over her
outstretched body.

. . . Hazel is staring at her, unweeping, from the day-bed, the
baby, oh so beautiful, roseate and cuddlesome, held in a crook of
her arm.

He'll never be like other children. Never.

But he's much more beautiful than any other child. Much
more.

Oh, Martha, please! Please! You do manage to say such idiotic
things.

Martha stiffens and takes a step back, affronted.

I didn't mean that. But. Hazel's eyes now fill with tears.
Hopeless. It's so utterly, utterly hopeless. She jerks an arm and
the child tumbles away from her, as though it were no more than
a bundle of expensive baby-clothes.

Take care! Martha puts out a hand.

What a sentence, Hazel says. Martha does not understand what
she means until she adds: A life sentence.

Don't you love him at all? You *must* love him! Of course you
do!

Martha stoops, picks up the boy and begins to rock him in her
arms. There's always hope. It's not the last word. Other special-
ists. If it's money. My little legacy. New drugs are being disco-
vered every day. New treatments.

Hazel groans. She can't bear to listen to this drivel.

Martha goes on rocking the child and then begins to croon to
him. It must be his heart and not her own that she can feel
beating stronger and stronger, thud, thud, thud within her. He's
beautiful, she's never seen so beautiful a child. She meant that
when she said it to Hazel. Can't Hazel see his beauty for herself?
And then, suddenly, Martha realizes that Hazel — at this moment
so unhappy, so distraught, so consumed with hatred for herself,
for life, even for her baby — is also beautiful. Martha sits down on
the bed, a squat figure in a skirt too long and a blouse too short to
be fashionable. Still she holds the baby very close; and still, still,

there is that strange thud, thud, thud somewhere at the core of her being. She stoops. The child in the crook of her right arm, she is now half squatting and half lying beside Hazel on the bed. She has always secretly hated this woman for all that she has done to Nigel but now, abruptly and surprisingly, she loves her with a profound, selfless, sexless love, that seeks for no reciprocation and accepts that no reciprocation is possible. She puts her lips to Hazel's forehead and, when Hazel gives a small, involuntary shudder of recoil, she accepts that too. The child's heart against her own thuds on and on and on.

. . . Martha opened her eyes. 'Don't move until you feel you want to move.' It was the voice of the Master, far away and faint. She went on lying there, she did not know for how long, looking up at the multi-coloured web of light thrown by the lamp on the ceiling. There was a faint singing in her ears, almost a tune, though its precise shape perpetually eluded her. She gave a yawn that stretched her jaws wide and then another, smaller one. She sighed.

At last, ungainly and aware of her ungainliness, she began to get off the steps. The girl extended a hand, gave her her stockings, pointed to the banquette. Martha felt giddy, slightly sick, parched. But all the time, as though some cistern were filling after months of drought, she still felt joy pouring into her.

She sat on the banquette, put her head between her hands. Then she shook herself.

'I feel better.'

'I knew you would,' the girl said.

Martha looked around her. The Master had vanished. She did not think to ask what had happened to him or if she would see him again before she left. Everything that happened had to happen in precisely that way.

The girl was now kneeling, one of Martha's clumsy low-heeled brogues in her hands.

'Oh, no, dear! I can manage by myself!'

But the girl insisted on easing first one shoe and then another on to Martha's swollen feet.

Martha put out a hand. 'You have lovely hair,' she said. In fact the girl's hair, greasy and lacklustre, badly needed washing; but at that moment it seemed lovely to Martha.

'Thank you.'

The cistern went on filling, filling and filling, from some endless source high up among mountains she had never seen.

She got to her feet, picked up her bag and opened it. Her hand took out all the money that it contained in notes.

'For him,' she said, placing the notes on top of the cupboard.

The girl nodded, saying nothing.

Martha did not see the Master again, as the girl let her out into the teeming rain.

64

The rain felt soft and slithery on her face as she upturned it to the pewter sky. The splashes were splashes from that torrent that was now pouring down into her being, thundering above the thunder of the traffic and racing through her as the rain raced down the gutter by her feet, bearing on its tide the filthy detritus of the city. He had unclogged that channel deep within her, he had provided the four secret egresses – a clotted head of blood marked each – for all that was evil and destructive, he had made the waters of love and forgiveness pour down through her.

She pushed a sodden hank of hair away from her cheek and again, umbrella furled in one hand, gazed up into the sky out of which the rain descended. It was on her eyelashes and on her lips and had even entered her nostrils. She would go to Hazel – she gave herself a little shake like a dog – now, at once, and say to her 'I forgive you. I have no more hatred within me. I will never talk of the book or even think of the book again.'

She braced her body in its bandages of sodden clothes on the edge of the pavement by Barkers, preparatory to taking off on this mission.

It was then that she saw the 73 bus on the other side of the road, water swishing from either side of it as from the cleaving prow of a boat. She saw the shoulder-length brown hair, streaked with grey, at one of the two facing seats at the entrance, that beige raincoat, that slightly aquiline profile. It was as though her resolve had at that very moment summoned Hazel.

She launched herself. 'Hazel!'

An old dilapidated Austin Princess, turning from Church Street into High Street Kensington, screeched and skidded, two terrified children's faces beside the no less terrified face of the woman at the wheel as she attempted to swerve and brake. But the car was too near to Martha; and besides she made no attempt to evade it.

She flew like a huge bird, up, up, up towards the pewter sky and then landed in a puddle at the feet of a group of dumb-struck women shoppers.

One stooped, shopping basket over arm and a plastic hood dripping water down on to the battered, blood-seamed face. 'Are you all right, dear?'

'Don't move her,' another said. 'Wait for the ambulance.'

A third cried: 'Ring for an ambulance! Ring for an ambulance!'

A young man leapt from a car, holding the lapels of his coat together as a protection from the rain. 'I'm a doctor,' he said. 'Please stand back.'

He knelt beside her.

She opened her eyes, opened her mouth.

Click. 'Haz.' Click. 'Forg.'

Her lower jaw drifted sideways. Jammed.

'What did she say?' the woman shopper in the hood whispered to the doctor.

He either did not hear or ignored the question, as he told the body of Martha: 'It's all right. It's quite all right. The ambulance will be here in a moment or two.'

'What did she say?' another white-faced woman shopper whispered to her companion.

Her companion shrugged, huddling closer to her.

'No idea.'

In the stationary 73 bus the woman with the shoulder-length

brown hair streaked with grey, the beige overcoat and the slightly aquiline profile, licked her lips and tried to swallow down her rising nausea. She was older, plumper and dowdier than Hazel, though she did, indeed, bear a slight resemblance to her.

That afternoon Hazel was out at Putney Vale Crematorium, watching Arnold's coffin glide away into the consuming furnace.

65

'It's quite like old times again,' Nigel said, gripping his hands, palms together, between his knees.

'Is it?'

He looked plumper, sleeker, trimmer. He had started to grow a tuft of a gingery moustache, his tie had a jazz-age pattern on it, and he was now at last, he had just told Hazel, within sight of completing his translation.

'You miss the house.'

'I miss Campden Hill even more. It's so horribly *depressing* in this area. Still' – she got up and poured some more coffee into his cup – 'I suppose if I can't have a view of Battersea Park, it's some consolation to have a view of *that*.'

She pointed to Arnold's Dufy.

Nigel screwed up his eyes. He did not care for modern painting but 'Yes, it's lovely,' he said.

'It's ironic, you know. If Arnold hadn't had that Indian summer of his, well, I'd probably still be in the house.'

'How do you mean?'

'Oh, I'd have found a place for that picture on a wall in Sotheby's or Christie's and the money would have bridged the yawning chasm to the satisfaction of my bank manager.' She sighed: 'But I'm glad to have it there. And I'm glad that poor old Arnold had those extra few months and wrote those poems.'

'It's really rather a nice flat,' Nigel said, sensing her desolation.

'No, it isn't. It's horrid. You know it's horrid. If Martha were alive, she would appreciate that I'd got my deserts by having to live here ... I still often think of her – of Martha – you know.'

'Do you?' He, too, often thought of her, with a mingling of loss that that other clamouring identity no longer pressed on his own and guilt for the fact that he was, yes, happier on sum for her absence.

Hazel nodded. 'I wonder why she killed herself.'

Nigel started, as though she had pricked him with one of the knitting needles in her hands. 'Oh, we don't *know* that she killed herself, Hazel. It might have been an accident. The coroner –'

Hazel shook her head. 'Those women said that the lights were against her and she just walked out – or flung herself out – in the path of that wretched woman's car. With two children looking on! People become so totally self-absorbed when it comes to taking their lives. With two children – I ask you!'

'Perhaps she didn't see them.' He pondered, the coffee-cup to his lips and his eyes gazing at the bright, bobbing boats of the Dufy on the wall beyond her head. Hazel turned a row. Then: 'I think she was frightened,' he murmured.

'Frightened?'

'About her health. The doctor and then the specialist – she'd been seeing a specialist that morning – both told her that there was nothing physically wrong with her at all. It was a spasm, they said, one of these nervous spasms. But I think that secretly – she never put it into so many words – I think she thought she'd got – It.'

'Oh, poor Martha!' Hazel's cry was one of genuine pity.

'She was not herself, not herself for several weeks before the end. I think all that ghastly business of the book – going on and on and on – put more strain on her than any of us realized. She became obsessed with it. She could talk of little else, think of little else. It was her whole life in the end.'

Hazel put down the knitting. 'I still feel guilty about all that.'

He jerked his head down from his continuing contemplation of the boats. 'Guilty? After all she did to you?'

'Well, I see now' – she spoke haltingly, with none of her usual fluent command of words – 'that in a sense I – I – well, kind of

247

infected her.' He opened his mouth to say something and then snapped it shut again, when she went on: 'Arnold said something of that kind – he always saw things so clearly. All that terrible, unreasoning hatred of hers – it was so unlike her, really, wasn't it? – well, she caught it from me, from the book. You see, I *did* hate her. I see it now. I hated her long before the book made her hate me back. Oh, she never greatly liked me or approved of me, I know all that. But she didn't *hate* me. It wasn't in her to hate.'

Nigel ran a finger down the braiding on the arm of the chair on which he was perched. 'But why, Hazel – why should you have felt this hatred?'

'Oh, I think for a number of reasons. Firstly there was you. I hated what she had done to you – and what she was doing to you. And she was always there, we could never do anything together without her butting in. And then there was her consuming curiosity – always questions, questions, questions – and, oh yes, her nastiness to Miklos. But more important than everything was – well, Peter.'

'Peter?'

She nodded. 'He preferred her to me.'

'Oh nonsense!'

'Yes. He preferred her to me. Don't ask me why but he did. Perhaps the poor creature thought in his confused mind that it was she, not I, who was his mother. I just don't know. But he preferred her. I'm certain of that.'

'You're wrong, Hazel. I'm sure you're wrong.'

'The book – I see it now – was my act of revenge on her chiefly for that. Because I fudged the mother-son relationship, you know. I made it in the book that the son really adored one person, his mother, and in the book there's this extraordinary wordless communication between the two of them. That kind of communication really existed not between us but between him and Martha.' She nodded as again he opened his mouth: 'Yes, Nigel. That's the truth.'

'It may be, it may not be. I just don't know.' But he knew perfectly well; he had known all along. He got up, went to the window and stared down into a paved courtyard where two little boys were bouncing a tennis-ball between them. He turned: 'But

248

the book also has its truth. And the book is always there.'

'Not an awfully good book, let's face it. We deluded ourselves about that.'

'Of course it's good. *Very* good. What *are* you saying?'

'The reviews were pretty dismissive. And I don't think it's yet passed the three thousand mark – or ever will. All that fuss and bother and expense for so little!'

'The reviewers who count – that man in *Encounter* – and that piece by – you know – by that woman novelist –'

'Oh, that was just for services rendered. I once helped to give her a prize.'

'Don't be so cynical. I hate it when you speak like that.'

She sighed: 'Anyway, I suppose the book *had* to be written.'

'And that's what makes it so good – that it *had* to be written. One feels this tremendous pressure. You had to get it all out of your system.'

She nodded. 'All those feelings about Peter and Miklos and Lydia and Martha – they were somehow all clogged up inside me, festering on and on. By writing the book, I somehow unblocked the four channels that they represented. All the hatred and – and frustration – and guilt – well, they could all flow away. Until that had happened, I'd never have been able to write anything else.'

'*Are* you writing something else?'

'Oh, yes. Yes. I'm – tinkering.'

Soon after that Nigel remembered that he was due at the dentist – for months he had been putting off the visit – and got up to leave.

At the door he hesitated, hand on latch, and then turned:

'You know, Hazel – if you can't bear it here – you could always . . . The house seems so large without either lodgers or Martha and you'd be very welcome . . . I've been thinking of making two flats of it . . . But I'd much rather . . .'

Pierced by the appeal of his desolation, she put an arm round his shoulder and hugged him briefly to her. 'Nigel – how sweet of you! But honestly – honestly, my dear – I don't think it would work.'

'Why not?'

'Well ...' It would be needlessly cruel to enumerate the reasons. 'Let me think about it. May I?'

He smiled his relief. 'Please.' He took three of the steps, then turned: 'There's nothing I'd like more, you know.'

When she had closed the door on him it was with a sense, shaming and exhilarating, of relief. It was with positive happiness that she went into the little cubby-hole off her bedroom, seated herself at the portable typewriter and stared out at the blank wall, some eight feet away from her, that was the only view.

Then, like some maestro preparing to whirl off into the first arpeggios of a piano concerto, she adjusted the chair, wiped her hands on the handkerchief beside her on the table, bent slowly forward.

Her hands struck the keys.